Thomas Talbot

The Granvilles

an Irish tale - Vol. 3

Thomas Talbot

The Granvilles
an Irish tale - Vol. 3

ISBN/EAN: 9783744739160

Printed in Europe, USA, Canada, Australia, Japan

Cover: Foto ©Andreas Hilbeck / pixelio.de

More available books at **www.hansebooks.com**

THE GRANVILLES.

An Irish Tale.

BY

THE HON. THOMAS TALBOT.

IN THREE VOLUMES.

VOL. III.

London :

SAMPSON LOW, MARSTON, SEARLE, & RIVINGTON,

CROWN BUILDINGS, 188, FLEET STREET.

1882.

CONTENTS.

CHAPTER XVII.

An Evening Walk and a Declaration of Love   PAGE 1

CHAPTER XVIII.

Denny Mullins, the Piper, pays a Visit to
the Glazement—Nelly Corcoran and Himself hold high Discourse 30

CHAPTER XIX.

The Art of Roguery—Piety assists it   . 68

CHAPTER XX.

The Captain has his Eye to Windward—The
Plot discovered 103

CHAPTER XXI.

Herbert Granville prepares to join his Uncle
in Canada—Various Councils held, and
various Opinions offered in consequence 129

CHAPTER XXII.

PAGE

GENERAL DOHERTY IS PUT IN MOTION—A PLAN OF ATTACK IN TWO DIVISIONS . . . 153

CHAPTER XXIII.

THE ATTACK—ITS CONSEQUENCES . . 184

CHAPTER XXIV.

AN UNEXPECTED ARRIVAL—GREAT REJOICING AT ASH GROVE HOUSE 208

CHAPTER XXV.

CONCLUSION 233

THE GRANVILLES.

CHAPTER XVII.

AN EVENING WALK AND A DECLARATION OF LOVE.

AFTER dinner, on the day above mentioned, Fanny called her brother aside in the drawing-room, and intimated that she had something of importance to communicate to him. It is scarcely necessary for us to apprise the reader that Joe Whitmore formed one of the dinner party on this occasion. We have already hinted that he had arranged to spend a week at Mooloch House, under pretence of enjoying the sport of shooting in its vicinity ; and we have now to add that his arrangement in this respect was made by express invitation from Mrs. Credan in furtherance of her views with reference to the alliance between himself and her niece, on

B

which she had so much set her heart. That on this point, however, she had been undeceived by the decisive declaration of Fanny during the walk in the garden, we have already seen; and yet, it must be owned that a lingering hope still remained with her that, notwithstanding such declaration, things might be brought about in conformity with her wishes by the accidents of time and the force of circumstances. She was one of those who never give up any design they have formed until every inch of ground is cut from under their feet, and no possible chance remains on which to build a hope. She thought that, after all, Fanny might change her opinions, or that she did not perhaps exactly know her own mind. She loved, it may be, or she fancied she loved Herbert; but did Herbert love her? or did he love her to such a degree as to sacrifice his pride, or his prospects, if he had any, in order to make her his own? It was hard to decide with regard to these matters: and so long as a clear decision could not be arrived at on these points, it was well not to give up any hope she had of gaining the wished-for end. So Mrs. Credan reasoned; and she was not a woman to surrender her views, as long as she had any ground at all on which to raise a superstructure of reasoning, no matter how shifting and untenable that ground appeared to be. Joe Whitmore, therefore, occupied a firm footing still in her mind; and at dinner she neglected nothing that was calculated to convey this idea to all present. She expressed herself as delighted with his success on the hills and at the coverts, and declared she was so happy that he enjoyed himself; and hoped that during the week he intended to remain he should be equally successful and equally well pleased with the sport. She was exceedingly attentive to all his requirements, and was sincerely interested in his appetite, trusting that his exertions had not over-fatigued him, and thereby diminished his desire for food. Nothing indeed could be more gracious than the anxiety she manifested for his health and comfort.

And so Joe felt, and indeed expressed himself, very, very happy. But after dinner, as we have said, Fanny took her brother aside in the drawing-room, to intimate to him that she had something of importance to communicate to him. They both left the drawing-room together, and stepping out upon the terrace, they walked along for

some minutes in silence. At length Fanny
said,—

"Harry, what I wished to tell you is, that
Whitmore is invited to stay here for a week
—at least he has accepted the general invitation given to him by Aunt Credan, and has
declared his intention to remain a week for
the purpose of shooting. I cannot, therefore,
stay here longer than to-day; to-morrow I
shall return home. You know how detestable
that man is to me; and you know also how
Aunt Credan has been planning about him,
with the idea that I should get married to
him. You see then, Harry, how impossible
it is for me to content myself here. Of
course, I don't desire to deprive you of your
shooting; but perhaps you might, without
inconvenience to you in that way, accompany
me a part of the way home at an early hour
to-morrow morning. If I were a mile or
so away from this place I shouldn't feel lonely
for the remainder of the way home.",

"Yes, I see," answered Harry; "that will
suit admirably. Would you wish to know
how I feel? I shall tell you. Just like a
fellow convicted of high treason, and sent to
prison where he has to herd with thieves and
cut-throats. You understand me. Since I

saw that brute, Whitmore, at the covert
to-day I have made up my mind to decamp
from here. And that is a pity, for I had
intended to have two or three days' enjoyable
sport about here with my cousin ; but that confounded fellow has spoiled my contemplated
enjoyment. I don't wonder that you feel
dissatisfied to remain under the same roof
with him; for I, who ought to be better able
to endure anything in the shape of impudent
vulgarism and presumptuous ignorance, feel
myself quite inadequate to the endurance of
this fellow's bestial manners. So I shall
have our horse and gig ordered out at five
o'clock to-morrow morning; and we shall
be ready to start immediately after that.
Besides, i' faith, I feel otherwise a longing to
get back, short as it is since I left."

Here he looked with a twinkling eye into
his sister's face, and added, " Absence makes
the heart grow fonder."

Fanny smiled, and lifted her hand, as if to
slap him on the cheek, but then, dropping it
immediately and resting it on his breast,
where it played with his vest buttons, she
said, " I am so glad, dear brother, that you
like Julia. I am so fond of her. She is such
a nice lovable creature. Don't you think

that she is a real Granville—I mean in feature as well as in manner. I heard my cousins say that she rather resembled the Browns, her mother's family."

" I think," replied Harry, " that she partakes of the leading characteristics of both. She has the noble bearing and graceful manners of the Granvilles, with something of the complexion and features of the Browns. But why do you say you are glad I like her? Like her, Fanny? I idolize her. She occupies every corner and crevice of my heart. She is my idol, my angel, my heaven!"

"Oh, stop!" interrupted Fanny, "for goodness' sake, do stop, or I shall imagine that you are *daft*, as the Scotch say. I know you like her; and I am so glad of it. But, Harry dear, have you asked her to marry you?"

Harry hesitated, and coloured a little, as if something wrong or dishonourable had occurred to his mind. But it was not so. Harry Moore was one of the most upright and honourable young men that ever existed. An ignoble thought never stained his mind. He was incapable of contemplating anything that was tinged with shame or dishonour; and yet, strange as it might appear, he manifested those symptoms which are usually attributed to guilt and shame, as soon as his sister referred to that which struck him as a point of honour. He *hesitated* and *coloured.*

How often do we find popular ideas and maxims destitute of any foundation in truth or in nature. So far from the hesitation and change of colour exhibited by Harry when the question about marriage was put to him by his sister being an indication of any wrong he either did or contemplated to do, it was the strongest manifestation of the extreme purity of his mind, and of the un-sullied honour by which he was swayed. A low, unprincipled, and hardened ruffian would have never shown any feeling on such a question as that put to Harry by his sister, or indeed, on any question involving delicacy of feeling or moral principle. It was only the warm-hearted, high-souled, pure-minded Harry Moore, that could feel his blood agitated at the mere fancy of anything low, base, or in the slightest degree discreditable. And yet, looking at the matter calmly, as Harry himself did look at it, after a few seconds, there was nothing in the question that ought to disturb the finest sensibility, the most refined sense of honour.

"Did I ask her to marry me?" he repeated, after a few seconds; "why, no, Fanny; I did not think it at all necessary to do so under all the circumstances. In the first place, you know, the family are in mourning since the death of old Mr. Granville; and to talk of marriage with Julia, in the presence of such an event, would not, it strikes me, be exactly proper or delicate. Besides that, it would look on my part as if I were endeavouring to take advantage of her misfortunes with the view of promoting my own happiness. I could not think of winning her love through her sorrows. I must have it wholly or not at all, through the medium of her free and unembarrassed will, and in the best sunshine of her fortunes. I believe she loves me, and that she does so from no motive on earth other than the voluntary impulse of her pure and noble heart; but while I believe this, I feel, and have felt ever since I thought she loved me, the more solicitous to guard my conduct against any act or expression that might possibly be calculated to wound her tenderest susceptibility. As I have told you, I love her with all my heart and soul; and there is nothing in this world that could satisfy my heart and mind but to be

united in marriage with her, yet I have re-
frained from any allusion to that subject
on the sole ground of delicacy and honour.
I feared she might not like it in the circumstances surrounding her; and I feared she
might attribute it to a want of consideration,
on my part, for her peculiar situation. I may
have been wrong in all that; perhaps I have
been; but I am now explaining to you the
motives which have ruled my conduct."

" I understand you," observed Fanny;
" but, still, I don't think that you did right;
for do you know, Harry, if I were in her
place, I think I would rather be asked. It
is so nice, you know, to hear the person you
love telling you everything that he thought.
Stop now, Harry; don't tease me:—ah, do
stop, now."

Harry had taken her by the shoulder, and
was shaking her, and tapping her on the
cheek with one hand, while his eyes were
twinkling with fun. He understood that her
mind was wandering to the presence of
another, while seeming to respond to the
observations which he had addressed to her.
He then said, " Never mind, dear sis., we
shall be off early in the morning, and leave
dear Aunt Credan to the luxury of the bril-

liant Joe Whitmore's conversation. By Jove,
I was amused at dinner with our cousin's
exquisite ridicule of him. How she did sting
him with her arrows ; but the fellow scarcely
seemed conscious of the ridicule she showered
upon him. Come ; let us go in : they may
miss us—at least aunt will ; and so will the
gallant *amoroso* of my sweet sister."

He laughed, and stepped on before Fanny,
who followed him at a little distance. When
they entered the drawing-room, the younger
Miss Credan was seated at the piano ; and
Whitmore standing by her side, watching
her performance, and turning over her music.
The moment the latter saw Fanny enter, he
abruptly left the piano, and walked across
the room to meet her.

" Miss Moore, I was wishing to have you
come in," he said, with a vulgar affectation
of flattery, " for your touch on the piano
exceeds anything I know."

" I feel quite complimented, I assure you,"
was the reply, while the least perceptible curl
rose upon the corner of her mouth ; and she
passed on towards her Uncle Credan.

Mr. Credan was a fine jolly man, fond of
his claret and his joke ; and who cared for
little else than the enjoyment of the passing

hour. He followed the fox-hounds, always keeping along the roads and open fields, and soothing his hunter with voice and touch whenever he came to a small hedge over which he wished him to jump gently. He shouldered his double-barrel, too, in the shooting season, and tumbled over partridge, and plover, and woodcock with as ready an eye, and as unerring aim as in the days ere he won the hand, if not the heart, of his dear Fanny. In short, he was a good-natured, kind, cheerful, and ease-loving man, who took the world at the sunny side, and shut his eyes to the clouds and the mists. He liked Fanny Moore very much, almost as much as his own daughters ; for her name being Fanny, which was also his wife's name, he could not but feel a very remarkable leaning towards her. This, at least, was his own account of his own feelings ; and no one can doubt that he knew best what it was that afforded him comfort and satisfaction.

"Ha, ha ! you little loiterer," he exclaimed, as she approached him, "where have you been all this time?" Your most estimable gallant, Whitmore, has been like a plover in distress during your absence, rolling himself from one spot to another and striving to shun observation. Why are you so heartless as to permit discomfort to darken over his gizzard. He is a tender chick—eh? Ha, ha, ha!"

"Why do you say he is a gallant of mine, uncle?" asked Fanny, looking into his face, with a smile, compounded of drollery and derision; "I didn't think that you would treat your niece to such a high compliment as to insinuate that she was the object of admiration to so exquisite and immaculate a Lothario as the proprietor of Castle Whitmore."

"Ha, ha, ha!" exclaimed the uncle, "you are a funny little rogue! you are a funny little rogue! By the piper of Moses, you always put me in mind of my own Fanny, your aunt; when I was tracking her through the *moors*—ha, ha, ha! eh?—through the *moors?* Well, when I was pursuing her, gun in hand, and trying to get her within range, I met with many disappointments. She was very wary—sensitive to the lightest tread; and so before I came within the required distance she was up and off. She led me many a weary tramp before I winged her— ha, ha, ha! Well, I took her at the rise, at last; and brought her down. And a good day's sport it was. By the piper of Moses, she has made my days cheerful and happy. But, you see, she is a practical woman, Fanny; and knows the difference between an oyster-shell and a plum-pudding. She eschewed poetry; she cared nothing for painted fribbles—not that I dislike poetry either—that is, I am fond of it when it is twisted into the shape of a good merry song—

> Tally-ho ! tally-ho ! ish a vugga, ish a voun !
> We'll rouse up reynard in the morning.

That's what I call poetry, Fanny. There is life and merriment in it ; and poetry is no poetry without that. Why, those people over there think I am mad ; see how Whitmore gapes at me. Ha, ha, ha! what a genius he is, to be sure! Come over to the piano, now : I want you to give me Tommy Moore's song; what do you call it ? it is the air of ' Reynard,'—oh, ay—' On Lough Neagh's Banks.' "

Fanny was greatly amused with her uncle's rambling observations; and her spirits began to play in gay and sprightly ripples. In answer to his request she replied that she would be most happy to play him the song he desired, but requested, at the same time, that he would do her the favour of standing by her side, and turning over her music. She said this in order to draw his attention to Whitmore's position, who was then performing a similar office for Miss Credan.

" By the piper of Moses, Fanny, I shall not deprive your Lothario, as you call him, of that extreme felicity. When I was like him, I would shoot the fellow who interfered with my privilege in that way. At the twelve paces, though—at the twelve paces. No, I never could take a man at a disadvantage. We should stand on equal ground. Then let fortune rule the day. Come, then, I shall be your Lothario, as you like it ; though I feel for your love-sick swain—ha, ha, ha ! Come along."

Miss Credan had just concluded a lively and rattling air ; and, as she paused to receive the incoherent compliments of Whitmore, her father requested her to make way for Miss Moore.

Fanny took her seat, ran her fingers along the keys, and looking up to her uncle, said, " Now, uncle, commence."

" Allow me, Miss Moore," interposed Whitmore, arranging the music in the stand ; " I shall be so happy to stand by your side."

"I feel complimented, very much indeed," replied Fanny, smiling, with the slight curl on her lip : "but you will oblige me by standing *aside*—not *by my side.*"

Whitmore coloured, and laughed : and then stepping away, made room for Mr. Credan, who whispered in her ear, "By the piper of Moses, you have stunned him."

Fanny played the air in accompaniment with the song of "Lough Neagh's Banks," to which her uncle did the most ample justice : but he always took care to conclude each stanza with—

Tally-ho ! tally-ho ! ish a vugga, ish a voun !
We'll rouse up reynard in the morning.

Shortly after the conclusion of the song the party retired for the night. Joe Whitmore, after reaching his room, threw himself into an armchair, and devoted at least an hour to a review of the different scenes which had occurred in the drawing-room, and in which he felt his interest concerned. The prevailing feeling of his breast, while thus occupied, was disappointment, and its attendant vexation. He looked at each scene again and again, and grew more and more dissatisfied and angry as he performed the operation. The conclusion of his review was a fixed determination to be revenged in some way or other, but he was unable to determine the mode or manner of the accomplishment of his resolution. Troubled with this uncertainty he undressed and threw himself into bed, where he slept a restless sleep, dreaming of dark glens, and silent nooks, and lightning, and thunder, and screaming women, and wild beasts, until morning.

Early next morning Harry Moore was astir. He looked into the stables, ordered his horse to be put to, and, returning to the parlour, found his sister and cousins arranging the materials for an early breakfast. His cousin, Harry Credan, soon joined them, and the four young people sat down to a most cheerful and appetizing meal. Buttered rolls, newly-laid eggs, fried ham, cold mutton, tea, coffee, and rich cream, with oaten cakes, and a decanter of whisky on a side-table, constituted the chief elements of this meal.

Fanny and her brother had on the preceding night apprised Mr. and Mrs. Credan of their intention to return home early the next morning; and although Mrs. Credan expressed

her astonisment and disappointment in words
and looks fully equal to the intensity with
which those feelings operated upon her; and
although Mr. Credan protested by the piper
of Moses that he wouldn't wish it—that is,
their going away—for the best day's sport
he had ever had, or expected to have hereafter, yet the thing was arranged, and all
objections and regrets were obliged to suc-
cumb before the decree of fate, and Mr. and
Mrs. Credan therefore wished their niece and
nephew a warm-hearted adieu ere they had
retired to rest. But the breakfast had been
scarcely commenced when Mr. Credan was
heard thundering along the hall, ordering the
servants hither and thither, and desiring to
be informed of the prognostics of the weather.
He fumbled into the parlour, and had scarcely
seated himself at the table, when Mrs. Credan
glided softly in, and the whole family, with
the exception of the younger children, were
thus assembled at breakfast between the
hours of five and six o'clock on that bright
September morning. ,

In about half an hour after this Harry
Moore and his sister were rolling along on
the broad smooth road leading to Ballydine,
amid the bright-tinted scenery that spread

itself out on either hand in long diversified sweeps, over which the early sunbeams played and twinkled like beaded diamonds on a lady's breast. The landscape, as they drove along, was here and there enlivened by the laugh and song of the peasantry as they moved about near their homesteads, and drove the cattle afield, or whistled to their teams in soft and winding melody, and eyed the even sod rolling from the ploughshare.

It was a sweet and lovely morning, and Fanny and her brother drank in all its delicious influence, for their hearts were light, and their minds free from disturbing cares. They made brief observations now and then upon the scenes around them, and then fell into silence, during which each luxuriated in the bright field of imagination, and indulged in that gentle and delightful occupation of erecting *Châteaux d'Espagne*, or castles in the air.

In less than two hours they were passing up the avenue to Brookfield Hall, where they were welcomed with no less astonishment by their father and mother for their unexpected arrival than they had been parted with by their uncle, and aunt, and cousins, for their unexpected departure. Such may be regarded, however, as a miniature of life. We come, and we go, when it is least expected; and regret and surprise are our constant companions through this journey here below.

On the afternoon of this day Harry Moore strolled into the lawn, and along the grounds of Brookfield Hall, meditating on the events connected with his visit to Mooloch House, and speculating in a sort of reverie on coming years. His imaginings were vague and indefinite, and if they fell into any shape at all of a determinate character, it was when the idea of his becoming, at some time or other, the owner of the lands on which he was treading, and of a lovely woman whom he could call his wife walking by his side, stood out in relief amid the mental chaos. That wife too assumed in his thoughts the figure and complexion of his beloved Julia. This current of thought was but the natural result of the conversation which he and his sister had held on the terrace at Mooloch House on the evening before, when Fanny asked him if he had informed Julia of his feelings towards her, and ascertained hers in return. The impulse that had thus been given to his mind continued to vibrate, and he determined, before the sun that was now shining down upon him had withdrawn the light from hill and plain, to breathe into her ear the message of his love, and to hear from her own sweet lips the reply to that message. He walked on until he reached one of the outer gates of the demesne, and then passed out into the public road. The evening was calm and beautiful, and he felt as though the air was whispering to his heart sweet words of peace and hope. He turned off in the direction of Ballydine, and as he approached the village he quickened his steps, as if to shut out from his own mind the thoughts that were crowding upon it, and to economize the joys that were fluttering around his heart. He passed by the Cross, and up the Ash Grove road, until he came to the gates opening upon the avenue and lawn of Ash Grove House. He strolled quietly up the avenue, pausing here and there to hearken to the melody of the thrush and blackbird from the surrounding arbours, or to mark the gambols of the rabbits on the small green island that rose amid the placid waters of the little lake on the margin of the lawn. He had scarcely reached the end of the avenue, where it branched into the lawn immediately in front of the house, when he saw Julia passing from

the garden-gate, and directing her steps
down the lawn, as if to meet some woman
who appeared to be approaching the house
from the direction of the mountain road.
Harry at once cried out her name, when she
stopped suddenly as if checked by a string,
and then looking round she saw him, and
stepped on quickly to meet him. Her face
was glowing with pleasure, and her movement was light and elastic as a fawn's.

After they had conversed for a few minutes
she walked away towards the front of the
house, met the woman whom we have mentioned, talked with her a few seconds, and
then passed into the house. After a delay
of about five minutes she returned, with an
addition of a short light cloak to her dress,
and bearing a parasol in her hand, and, join-
ing Harry, they both passed round by the
courtyard at the rear of the house, and out
into the glade that lay stretched before them
towards the south-east.

As they walked in cheerful mood along
Harry began to relate to her all that had
passed—at least all that he thought would
interest her—while on his recent visit to
Mooloch. He gave a full and humorous
description of Joe Whitmore, his shooting

exploits, and his love passages with the ladies, especially with his sister Fanny.

Julia was greatly amused with the recital, and observed,—

"What a queer sort of person Whitmore is, especially when he talks about his own affairs, and that is pretty often; for he seems never to comprehend anything but as it bears upon himself and his concerns. At least I have never heard him converse upon any topic in which he was not the chief subject himself. I could never endure him, and I am sure your sister is much of my way of feeling in that respect."

"Oh, as for Fanny," observed Harry, "she is like a lamb in a storm when he is in her presence; she cannot stand him at all. Besides, he is making desperate efforts to win her confidence; and this annoys her beyond anything. How he hates Herbert! He believes that if it hadn't been for Herbert the fates would be propitious, and no obstruction could arise in the way of his happiness. But in that he is mistaken, too; for I believe there is nothing on earth would induce Fanny to countenance him; for her dislike of him is rooted beyond any possibility of its removal."

"I have fancied, for a long time," interrupted Julia, "that he means some mischief to Herbert. I don't know how it is, but I cannot divest my mind of this impression. He is a bad man, Mr. Moore; and I believe him capable of almost any bad act. He is always slandering people, and uttering falsehoods against them—even against those with whom he affects friendship. What worse sign of any person could there be than that? I have it from Herbert, that he has uttered the foulest calumnies against him. Herbert has heard this from persons who would not tell an untruth about it. It is shocking, is it not?"

"No one minds what he says," answered Harry; "he is too contemptible for serious notice. Anything he says about Herbert or anybody else hasn't the weight of a feather. All his infamous slanders will ultimately redound upon himself."

He paused, while Julia stepped aside a little, and bending, plucked a small flower from a bush that grew by a thorn hedge in the field. She looked at it; inhaled its fragrance; and then presented it to Harry, observing, "What a late blossom! and how sweetly fragrant!"

Harry took it, and after smelling it, placed it in the breast of his coat, saying, "I shall preserve it as a remembrance of this evening's walk. May it be to me a pleasant reminder of the hand that plucked it!"

Julia started a little, and then smiled, a slight crimson tinge passing over her cheeks and forehead the meantime.

He continued, "Do you think it strange, Miss Granville, that I should express myself so?"

"How, Mr. Moore?"

"That I wish to retain this flower as a gift, the value of which to me consists entirely in the fact that it was plucked by you, and *given to me by you?*"

Julia smiled faintly, and a slight tremor passed over her frame. She made no reply, but walked on slowly, her eyes cast down upon the ground. He walked on in silence by her side for a few minutes; and then taking her hand in his, he stopped, and said, in a low voice, "Julia—pardon me if I offend you by speaking your name so freely—I love you."

They both remained stationary and silent for some seconds; after which she bent

forward and leant her head upon his shoulder.
He passed his arm around her waist, and
pressed her to his bosom.

He then whispered, "You love me,
dearest?"

She made no reply, but pressed her hands
upon her eyes, which were moist with tears.

"Are you displeased with me, Julia?" he
asked.

She then answered, "I am happy, dear
Harry."

He pressed her to his heart, and impressed
a kiss upon her lips. They then walked on
in silence for several minutes, her arm folded
within his. At length, he said, smiling, and
looking into her eyes, "Julia, I am happy,
too. How often have I longed for this hour!
for the hour when I should tell you all that
I felt, and all that I hoped. But I hesitated;
and I did so for reasons which you can,
perhaps, appreciate now; not the least of
which was—ay, the chief of which was, that
I feared to renew within your bosom the
sorrows which fell upon you and your family
by the death of your dear father, and the
calamities which accompanied that sad event.
But, I trust that I shall be able, in some
degree, at least, to make up for that loss to

you, by my devotion to your interests and to
your happiness, which from this hour I
promise. Your family, too, shall share my
warmest affections; their welfare will be my
welfare; their happiness will be my happiness. Herbert, as you are aware, has been
always my companion and my friend; I have
loved him as a brother; and from the moment
that he left college at the death of your father,
I felt as if the blow which fell upon him then,
had reached the inmost recesses of my own
soul. It is true that even then my heart
was turned to you; yes, even then I loved
you; and though I never breathed my love
for you to him, or to any one, except, perhaps,
to my sister, yet I felt that my destiny was
entwined with yours and with that of your
family. I am happy now; and from this
hour forward, I shall strive to make myself
worthy of your love, and worthy of the
blessing which God has vouchsafed me in
securing me that love."

While he thus spoke, his voice was tremulous with emotion; and at the conclusion
he bent his head towards hers, and pressed
his lips upon her forehead. She lifted her
eyes, which had hitherto rested upon the
ground, and looked tenderly into his face.

Her cheeks were moist from the tears which had trickled upon them during Harry's recital of his love, and of the interest he had so long felt in her brother's and family's fortunes. She wiped the tears from her cheeks, and then, leaning forward, she kissed him. As she did so, she said, in soft, tremulous accents, " Dear, dear Harry ! I do indeed love you ! " As they walked on she said, "I hope you will not think it strange that I should have so readily acknowledged the feelings of my heart towards you. I have long felt, as you yourself say, my soul's affections turned to you. I wished to conceal my feelings from everybody, for I thought it would be wrong in me to indulge hopes which I had no just cause to entertain, and which, in time, must perish, leaving me more desolate than before. But I found that I could not dispel them from my mind ; they still haunted me as though they were a part of my existence ; and I sometimes thought that to destroy them would be to put an end to my life. I say, I wished to conceal all this ; but there was one from whom it was impossible for me to disguise my heart. It was Herbert. He seemed to know every thought of my mind, every throb of my soul. Whether it was that his love

for your sister had turned his thoughts upon
your family and upon everything that concerned them, or that a sympathy with me
had given him an insight into my heart, I do
not know; but he understood my feelings,
and knew, so he told me, that they were
centred upon you. I confessed the truth.
And do you know what, Harry?"—she lifted
up her face to his, with a gentle, confiding
smile, in which joy and happiness were
mixed—"from that time he appeared to me
to feel a deeper, a warmer friendship for you
than ever. And I felt so proud of it! I
had feared, at first, that if I told him how I
loved you, he would have got angry with me;
but when he knew all, when he heard all, so
far was he from showing any feeling of
displeasure, that he looked brighter and
happier than ever."

"My noble-minded Herbert!" exclaimed
Harry; "how true you have ever been to
your noble nature! Julia, I know Herbert
well; none is better acquainted with the
inmost thoughts of his soul; and this I
undertake to say, that there lives not a man
whose thoughts are purer, whose heart is
gentler and kinder, and whose mind is more
exalted and generous than his. He is the

very essence of truth, and the soul of honour ;
and if the occasion arose to-morrow, I believe
in my soul that Herbert would interpose his
life between me and death. Such is my
opinion of him, founded upon an experience
of years of college life ; and it is there, Julia,
that the character is developed, as well as
understood. Well, he would do that; he
would risk his life to save mine. Julia,
would I be worthy of the name of man if I
did not feel myself capable of performing the
same office for him ? No. Let what may
befall, Herbert and I shall walk hand in hand
along the vale of life, loving and cherishing
each other."

Thus conversing on topics immediately
connected with their own destinies, and re-
verting again and again to their early intimacy, and the first hours when they felt the
spark of mutual affection lighting up their
breasts, they passed round the wooded glade,
and returned to Ash Grove by the fields
immediately in the rear of the garden, where
the summer-house overlooked the scene.
They then passed into the lawn, and entered
the house.

CHAPTER XVIII.

DENNY MULLINS, THE PIPER, PAYS A VISIT TO
THE GLAZEMENT—NELLY CORCORAN AND HIM-
SELF HOLD HIGH DISCOURSE.

It was a dull, heavy day, in the early autumn ;
the sun lay concealed within a dusky curtain
of cloud and mist ; and the hills looked dark
and gloomy amid the vapours that lay like a
shroud around them. Denny Mullins smoked
his pipe in the chimney-corner of his own
little cabin, while the air was thick and
drowsy outside, and the old woman, his
mother, was clearing away the *débris* of the
dinner of potatoes, and pork, and cabbage, of
which herself and Denny had just partaken.
Denny smoked on, and watched with dreamy
indifference the vapour as it passed from his
mouth and moved in lazy curls up the chimney. His mind was occupied with thoughts
of jigs, and reels, and planxties, and by neces-

sary concatenation, with cheering and shouting, and high merriment. Then would follow
another train of thought in close connexion
with all this—courtship, and match-making,
and weddings—until he began to feel as if he
were actually engaged in forwarding some
great event on which the happiness of some
love-entangled pair was dependent. Then
he would take the pipe from his mouth, puff
the vapour slowly from his lips, with his eyes
half closed ; and then giving way to the ideas
that crowded upon his brain, exclaim, with a
suppressed voice and a slow deliberate movement of the head, which assisted the energy
of the expression, " By the bogs of Moonduv,
they are what you might call a likely, clever
couple.—A lovin' couple. They'll be yoked
yet as firm as Father Marshall can fasten 'em.
Believe me; that's the way 'twill be, or I'm
not Denny Mullins."

He would then replace the pipe in his mouth,
and glide on in another stream of thought,
until at length he rose from the chimney-
corner, looked out at the door, and examined
the weather. " I think," he said, addressing
the *ould woman*, as he used to call his mother,
" I'll take a ramble across the glen to see how
they are getting on over at the Glazement ;

the evenin' 'll clear up, I'm thinkin', and I may as well go and find out what's going on in the village ; for the captain, 'tis like, will be after coming out of it now."

" Don't be late, then," said the old woman. " I'll go down as far as Moll Dreelin's, if the evenin' 'll turn up ; I want to get a loan of knit-needles from her to finish thim stockins ; I broke one o' my own, and the rest are all wore out ; there's no workin' wid 'em now. I'll be back early, and get supper. So be back before the night 'll be too dark."

Denny took his hat and stick ; and having buttoned his big-coat close up to his chin, he sallied out to visit his " *ould* friend " and " *ancient* neighbour," the captain. He picked his way down the ravine, the furze-crowned hedge on either side shielding him from the *bite* of the weather, as he said to himself ; and crossing the brawling stream—for it was now very active from recent heavy rain—as it jumped and tumbled along the bottom of the glen, he turned his face upwards, and keeping by the winding hedges, as they straggled zig-zag up the side of the hill, he soon reached the comfortable and cosy cottage of the captain. He lifted the latch and entered. Nelly Corcoran welcomed him, and, lifting a

corner of her check apron, rubbed the seat of
a stool, and, placing this in the corner by the
warm turf-fire, told him to sit down. Little
Minny Rice, Nelly's granddaughter, was also
delighted to see him; but felt much dejected
when she found that he hadn't brought his
pipes. He took her upon his knees, however,
and whistled a jig for her, which he told her
was as good as if it came out o' the chanter.
He inquired for the captain; but was
informed that he had gone down to the village after his breakfast, and hadn't yet
returned. If he shouldn't be here soon, Nelly
said, she wouldn't expect him until near sup-
per-time, as 'twas likely he 'ud call at Ash
Grove, and, maybe, at Brookfield Hall. Whenever he went to the village in the morning,
'twas seldom he came home before night. So
Denny made his mind easy, and leaning his
back against the side wall of the chimney-
place, and widening out his legs so as to
receive the full benefit of the glowing fire, he
fell into high discourse with his *ould* neighbour and acquaintance, Nelly Corcoran,
occasionally giving variety and zest to the
discourse by tossing Minny on his knee and
whistling her a merry tune.

" And how does the world use you at all,

at all, Nelly," asked Denny, looking over at
his old friend, who sat on a boss (straw stool)
at the opposite side of the fire-place, patching
a pair of trousers. "You look strong and
hearty, God bless you."

"Oh, faix, there's no fear of me; as long
as I have enough to ate and drink I'll never
complain; and I have that, thank's be to
God," was the reply of Nelly.

"Well, then, 'tis a long spell now since
you and I first danced 'Cover the Buckle' in
Bill Daly's barn the time the dance used to
be there," observed Denny, rubbing his hands,
and throwing one leg over the other in the
excitement of the recollection; then throwing
himself back into his former position, he went
on, "Peg Duffy was a bouncin' girl at that
time. I was a spell at her house the other
day, and 'tis she looks well. In troth, you
might cut beef-steaks off her jaws, and she
'udn't miss 'em. God keep her so."

"She was a bouncin' girl, shure enough,"
said Nelly, "but she hadn't look or grace
after marryin' that *skial-a-velth* (rollicker) of
a man she had. Ah, then, she might get the
best match in the parish if she had sinse and
didn't take to dancin' and gallivantin' the
same as she did. 'Tisn't look or grace ever

comes o' the like. What I say, ever and always, Denny, is that any girl as goes about to dances and the like, and carryin' on wid this boy and that boy, and streelin' about with 'em, here and there, day and night, can't expect anything but shame and sorrow. Nothin' else can come out of sich doin's. Let a girl respect herself, and keep herself to herself, and mind her duty, and then God's grace will be along wid her wherever she goes. God help us, some of the girls that was goin' then, as well as now, hadn't much sinse in their heads, nor the fear o' God in their hearts, if they had 'tisn't like buttherflies they'd be goin'—big show and little substance —shiny outside and shilly-shally inside. The craturs! one would think there was nothin' inside of 'em but a cricket, makin' 'em run about without rhyme or raison, not knowin' what they were sayin' or doin'. She have a son that's no better than the father was, God help him. They say that he is now at the head of the Whitefeet, and that the war is goin' to be in the place before Christmas.

"Allelu!" she exclaimed, bursting into laughter, "what a purty commandher the people 'll have when Paddy Larkin 'll be carry-in' his sword 'efore 'em. And there's Jer

Grinnex too; they say he is goin' to be another commandher. Allelu! allelu! Jer
Grinnex and Paddy Larkin! They wanted
to make Ned Doolin and Bill Cleary join 'em;
but *they* have betther sinse. Did you hear,
Denny, that its goin' to be a match between
Ned Doolin and Peggy Cummins? And I
hear, too, that Bill Cleary and Judy Casey are
all in all. Faith then, either Ned Doolin or
Bill Cleary might go farther and speed worse.
Believe me, Peggy Cummins wouldn't turn
her back on any girl in the parish in the
regard of bein' a well-handed girl; and as for
carakther and conduct there could be no one
betther. She is seen, but not heard; that's
the way to say it. And there's Judy Casey,
as purty and as knowledgeable a girl as you'd
find in the three counties. And shure, she is
a nottable housekeeper; and so is Peggy
Cummins too. Oh, in troth, Ned Doolin and
Bill Cleary aren't blind when they're takin' to
sich girls as them. *They're* what you might
call girls; fine, and clever, and sinsible;
'tisn't all the same as the shkibs (flirts) that's
goin', that don't know the difference 'etween
a tomtit and a turkey. But, Denny, did you
hear—and shure you did, for 'tis the round
o' the parish now—about Masther Harry

Moore and Miss Julia Granville? Oh, 'tis all settled, they say. So 'tis a double match, you see. There's Masther Herbert Granville and Miss Fanny Moore to be married for certain, whatever time his property is to fall into his hands. Some say 'tis his uncle the curnel, in America, is goin' to get it for him; and some say 'tis Lord Fairborough, myself don't know which is the likeliest. Hows'ever, sea or land can't separate them, for they're dyin' about one another. Ullalu! I woudher what'll that half *liaka* (fool), Joe Whitmore, do: he's losin' his walk, they say, afther Miss Fanny. O Yia! well become of him, indeed; the likes of him of an upsthart *cummerlachaun* (ungainly person) to be thinkin' of a rale lady, wid the red blood of the Moores a runnin' in her veins. Shure 'twould be the sin of the world to see a half-cracked upsthart, widout a drop of rale blood in him —for where would he get it? to see the likes of him streched alongside of Miss Fanny Moore, wid her white skin, and her lovely blood. Ululu! God 'etween us and all harm, that we'd ever live to see the day. Faith, and in troth, they say, Denny, that Mrs. Credan is tryin' every hook and hangers to have Joe Whitmore and Miss Fanny married. There's

for you, now. Who'd drame o' that? No
less, Mrs. Credan; ay, and will you believe
me? Mrs. Moore herself is tryin' the same
thing. Well, there it is for you. Whatever
way you'll turn up your eyes, Denny Mullins,
there it is for you. Not a word o' lie in it.
Shure the world 'll soon come to an ind
when sich things is turnin' out. But, no,
O Yia! no; Miss Fanny would rather Masther
Herbert's little toe than five hundred times
the bigness of Joe Whitmore. Joe Whitmore,
eh? Arra, don't tell me; if I was a girl
to-morrow—my hand to you—I would no
more marry Joe Whitmore than I'd drown
myself in the say (sea), for all that I haven't
a drop o' blood in my veins. And then to put
him, the likes of him, alongside of Masther
Herbert! Isn't that a purty comparisment?
Masther Herbert! a man that I'd marry—
supposin' I had blood in my veins—that I'd
marry wid an inch of a candle, supposin' I
never ate a bit afther. O Yia! Mrs. Credan
indeed! We know all about it. If I was as
young to-day as I was when she was afther one
that we know—ay, and a fine blooded gintleman he was, and is to this day; but he is
altered a bit since then. Well, he was dyin'
about her, as well as she was dyin' about

him; but, the same as I was saying 'efore,
nothin' 'ud do her but to be goin' about here
and there wid every Tom, Dick, and Harry
of a gintleman that came across her, widout
as much sinse as a ninnyhammer in her head,
like; but shure she had sinse for all that, and
the blood, and everything; but she hadn't
the right sinse; she hadn't the grace o' God
to keep her in the straight road. And she
was goin' on gallivantin' wid every one, and
all the time dyin' about the one I know, till
in the long run she married a man she hadn't
love or likin' for, I may say; but a good,
honest gintleman for all that, and one of her
own blood relations. Well, the man that was
dyin' about her, and that she was dyin' about
him, never married any one since. And the
love for him is in her heart yet, and always
will be. But what's the good o' that? No
good, but harm; for she is contrairy ever
since; and she'd like every one to have a
touch o' the same sickness as herself. Yes,
she is so contrairy, after what she done agin
her own heart, that she'd fain make her own
niece, her sisther's daughter, fall out in the
same way. So, Denny, there's no knowin'
what people 'll do, high and low, when they
once lose the grace o' God, and put up wid

pride, and foolishness, and coourtin', and gallivantin, widout sinse or raison in their doin's. Ah, then, 'twas she was the fine comely girl, when she was Miss Fanny Credan; 'tis after her Miss Fanny Moore was called; and the beautiful skin and eyes she had! But Miss Fanny Moore won't go astray for any one; the grace o' God is joined to her handsome face, and her lovely skin; and she'll have Masther Herbert in spite of 'em all."

Denny had assumed a new attitude after Nelly had proceeded for a little time with her narrative; instead of remaining with his back to the side wall of the chimney-place, and his legs spread wide apart, he placed his elbows on his knees, and rested his chin and cheeks between his open palms, presenting, in some measure, the appearance of a pair of flat props supporting a ball. His two eyes, which were half closed, peered out from between his hands, and rested upon the narrator. After she had come to a pause, he said, without in the slightest way altering his position,—

"Nelly Corcoran! you opened my eyes; you incensed me in things I know'd nothin' of 'efore. And you tell me that Mrs. Credan is fillanderin' afther Joe Whitmore, to get

him for her niece, that is; for Miss Fanny
Moore. Hee-e-e! hee-e-e! Nelly Corcoran!
the longer we live the more we'll see; and
the more we'll hear too. Well, did you ever
hear the like? Mrs. Credan! the woman that
ought to rise up and say that she'd never
draw rein or bridle 'till Miss Fanny Moore
was welded, like steel, to Masther Herbert
Granville; becase why? becase they were
made for one another in love, and beauty,
and family; and becase agin, they'd never
see a day's luck, either of 'em, if they'd
marry any one else but their own four bones
to one another. And what call would Joe
Whitmore have to be lookin' afther Miss
Fanny Moore? Look now, Nelly Corcoran!
he is as much fit for her as I am for Lord
Fairborough's daughter. 'Twould be agin
natur' to have 'em joined: becase why?
they couldn't be joined; they could be no
more welded together than steel and bogash.
They'd fall asunder the minute you struck the
first blow on 'em. And Mrs. Credan, eh?
Hee-e-e! hee-e-e! I wondher will women ever
have sinse. Shure, blazes to her gizzard, she
ought to know what it is to turn her back
on the man she was dyin' about, and who
was dyin' about her; and not to be tryin'

to drag other people into the flames wid
herself.   But, I'll tell you, Nelly Corcoran,
what way it is: you never see any one in
the yollow jaunders but 'ud like to see others
smeared wid it as well as themselves.   That's
the way 'tis wid Mrs. Credan: she did a
thing she was sorry for, and is sorry for,
and will be always sorry for; and 'twould
relieve her to see others do the same thing.
I know'd the gintleman she was dyin' about,
as well as I know my right hand; and shure
enough, there's not in the seven counties
betther blood, or a comelier man: and then
she went and married another man that sue
didn't care a traneen for; and all for whims,
and notions, and foolishness.   And there she
is now grindin' her teeth for spite.   Not
but the gintleman she got is good enough
for her—he is one of the Credans shure
enough; and a noble gintleman he is.   But
what's the good o' that?   Nelly! believe
me, if you had atin' and drinkin' o' the best,
and silks and satins o' the richest and
dearest; and that your heart was troubled
and your mind on the *shaughraun* (unsettled),
'twould be all of no use.   Eh? that's as
true as if I took my Bible-oath on it.   And
you tell me that it is a match 'etween Masther

Harry Moore and Miss Julia Granville. I'll tell you what it is, Nelly; that's not one o' the seven wondhers o' the world. Did you ever see a pidgeon fallin' in love wid a drake? or a woodquest travellin' wid a crow? By course, no; becase, why? 'twould be agin sinse. If Miss Julia Granville and Masther Harry Moore wasn't in love wid one another, I wouldn't believe in Natur' no longer. Ay! ay! that's the octave of it; Miss Julia and Masther Harry; and Miss Fanny and Masther Herbert. Whoo-oo-oo! I wish the captain was come home. He'll say *de novo* to that, I'll swear. And Paddy Larkin, too. Hee-e-e! hee-e-e! Oh, I'm insinsed that Paddy is a gineral; becase he tould me so himself; and a fine bould gineral he'll make when the war'll begin. What do you think of it at all, Nelly? Only for the poor ould woman beyand—a man's mother, you know—I wouldn't half mind how 'twould go. The boys'll be strong; and they'll gather from every place round about: and if the sogers don't come blazin' on 'em of a sudden, they might carry the day. You see, there is nothin' like havin' the first blast; when you lose that, 'tis ten to one but your mouth 'll

of their courts and demesnes, and to give
'em to Moll Dreelin and Jer Grinnex. *Oh,
Yia! oh, Yia!* (Oh, God! oh, God!) Did
any one ever hear the likes? Isn't it a
wondher to me that you didn't ever larn any
sinse in your born days; and you ever and
always a talkin' and discoursin' wid the
captain, a man who travelled the world,
and was livin' in all parts, and knows every
thing from the stars down. Will you ever
have any sinse? Can you larn any sinse?
Or is it the bagpipes took it all out o' your
head, and left you as you are? Shure the
mother that reared you can't know peace
or comfort as long as you're mindin' Paddy
Larkin, and sich idle, strollin', good-for-
nothin' roolaghs (gadding fellows). Allelu!
'twould be fitter for the idle, shkampin'
blackguard to mind his work, and take care
of his mother in the latter end of her days—
the poor ould woman!—than to be carryin'
on, making a fool of himself, and earning the
gallows for himself, and others too. God
grant him sinse, and put him in the state of
grace, the strollin' gallivantin', unlucky
smuggachaun (dirty-nosed fellow). Denny
Mullins, I'm wondherin' at you. Did *you* ax
(ask) the captain about the business? If

you did he'd tell you what I'm sayin' is true. Yes, as thrue as the sun in the shky. Shure, I'd be as blind as yourself only for he tould me all; and isn't he knowledgeable, I ax you? Isn't he the knowledgeablest man in these parts? Is anything blind of him? What could a poor cratur of a woman like me know, only for he tould me? Denny Mullins, listen to him, and larn sinse."

She again rose, and taking her seat at the opposite corner, she resumed her former position and her work.

Denny, during this lecture, appeared deep in reflection. Doubt, wonder, and bewilderment took possession of his countenance in turn. But when she had concluded, and removed to the other side of the fireplace, he drew a deep breath, and appeared somewhat relieved. He then folded his arms around his legs, and looked up the chimney, with his mouth open, and his eyes half closed. In this attitude he continued for some time, but at length he turned his eyes in the direction of Nelly, and rubbing his right ear with his left hand, he muttered,—

" Troth, 'tis droll enough. Where's this I was? Ay; there's no fear of the ould mother after all. Well and good. If the

war don't come, what'll happen I wondher?
Maybe they'd take the chains off the legs of
the poor ould counthry without any fightin'
at all. Why, yes, that 'ud be the best. But,
tell me this, if Paddy Larkin ben't a gineral,
and able to conquer all 'efore him, what
reason would O'Connel have to be blowin'
undher him? That's what I'd like to know.
He tould me for certain that Dan himself
was at the head o' this business, and that
Gineral O'Doherty was his right-hand man.
There now; what'll you make o' that? To
be shure, the captain is a knowledgeable
man; and, above all men, I'd like to follow
in his track; but, then, when O'Connel, you
see, the greatest and the wisest man in the
world, is for the risin', and lays down the
law as clear and as straight as my chanter,
what am I to do, or any poor man like me?
Does the captain know how it is betther than
O'Connel? There's the question. Who'll
answer me that? Nelly, do you know what?
In troth, I'm insinsed that Joe Whitmore is
for the business, and that he tould Jer
Grinnex the same. 'Carry on, Jer,' says he,
'and gain your rights.' What do you say
to that now? And more than that Peter
Mackey tould me—Peter himself is all for it

—but he tould me that Bartley Croker, the 'torney—Bartley the Divil, you know—is of opinion that the business ought to go on, and that the risin' ought to be bould and manly. There's for you."

Nelly laid aside the work she had in hand, locked her fingers into each other, her elbows resting on her knees, and raising her eyes up towards the open space of the chimney-corner, exclaimed,—

" The Lord be praised ! Joe Whitmore, Peter Mackey, and Bartley Croker, the 'torney—Bartley the Divil—all joinin' in the risin' ! Did any one ever hear tell o' the like? Are you in earnest, Denny Mullins? or is it dramin' you are? or have you your right sinses about you ? or what is the matther wid you at all, at all? As long as I know you—and that is many a long year now— since I was the height of that,"—and she extended one of her hands about two feet above the hearthstone—" I never thought that the Lord left you without as much sinse as 'ud fit in a gandher's head. But, now, I see how it is wid you. God help you, you poor cratur; shure I wouldn't like to be hard on you, but what can any one say but that you're a holy show for the want of the

sinse. Listen to me, Denny Mullins. God
help the mother that reared you, and when
she was rearin' you, shure she thought
'twasn't an *innocent* entirely she was carryin'
in her arms. But listen to me. Joe Whitmore, Bartley Croker, and Peter Mackey, are
they the men you spoke of? are they the men
that are goin' to join the risin'? Do you
know who *they* will join? I'll tell you.
They'll join the *informer*, they'll join the
hangman, they'll join the *divil*. Do you
know now who they'll join, Denny Mullins?
If Joe Whitmore had anything to gain by it,
or any revinge to satisfy by it, he'd inform
agin every man from this to the end of the
world. If Peter Mackey could put one
goolden guinea more in his crock than is in
it already, he'd stand undher the gallows-tree,
and hidin' himself behind somethin' so as not
to let any one see him, he'd haul upon the
rope that 'ud be round his mother's neck, as
if 'twas a cat he was hangin'. And as for
Bartley Croker, O Yia! Bartley, the 'torney!
Bartley the Divil! God help us, he is not
called out of his name. Shure they say the
divil was his father. The Lord presarve us
and come 'etween us and all harm. Denny
Mullins, Bartley Croker 'udn't spare the best

man that ever walked Ireland's ground if he
thought 'twould bring a penny to his pocket.
He wouldn't pretind though—oh, no, he
wouldn't pretind that he'd crack an egg
under his foot, he's so nice and so pious.
He's in all the ordhers, they say; but when
once he finds out the scint of anything that'll
bring gain to him, he'll not stay nor rest 'till
he come at that, by lies, and by schemes, and
by deceivin', and by roguery, and by parjery,
and by murdher—yes, by murdher, Denny
Mullins. He wouldn't murdher a man wid
his own hand; but, all the same, he would
put up others to do it. And the worst of all
is this, while he'd be followin' these wicked
ways he'd have his eyes turned up to heaven
'efore the congregation, like a saint; and
he'd be givin' charity round about to the
collectors for the love o' God. Yes, for the
love o' God, that's what he'd tell 'em. God
defind us from the bad angels. They say—
whisper, Denny—they say that the divil was
a bright angel in heaven once, just the same
as a clargy. What do you say to that?
Shure I heard Father Markham sayin', wid
my own two ears, that there's no end to the
saints and to the clargy that's burnin' in the
bottomless pit—that's in hell; and that the

poorest cratur that goes about beggin' her
bit in this world is betther off than any of
'em. The most of 'em that's down in that
place is nothin' but grand people, and lords,
and ladies of honour. And shure it stands
to raison. When you're poor and honest in
this world, and when you go to your duty,
and when you don't rob, or steal, or take
anything belonging to your neighbours, and
when you give shelter and a bit to eat to the
poor craturs that's begging about for themselves and their childher, then you'll go
straight to heaven, without any danger to
sowl or body. Not all as one wid the rich :
they have their heaven here in this world,
and then in coourse of raison they have no
call to go to heaven when they'll die, but
they'll go to the bottomless pit where there's
nothin' but fire and brimstone, and all sorts
of varmint. But whath Father Markham
said in the sarmin was this, that the
grandees, that is, the rich and grand people,
can go to heaven as well as the poor, if they
attind to their duty, and be good to the
cratures that's in want, and give good
examples to every person about 'em ; and
not to be proud or conceited, or turnin' up
their nose at those below 'em. That's what

Father Markham said in my hearin', as well as I could bring it. But he spoke grand to be shure. Glory be to God! 'tis he have the tongue. You'd never be tired of the beautiful English he'd be spakin' when he'd be givin' out the sarmin.''

Denny listened very attentively; for he saw that there was much wisdom in the observations of his companion, however rudely and incoherently expressed. Besides, he had a high opinion of the experience and discretion for which she was noted throughout the neighbourhood; and was the more desirous on that account of hearing her opinions on any subject that occupied his own mind, or that was agitated among those with whom he came in contact. When, therefore, he introduced the topics of the rising of the Whitefeet, and of the part that Whitmore, and Mackey, and Croker were supposed to be prepared to take in that affair, he did not express the convictions of his own mind with reference to either the one or the other. He merely wished to hear Nelly's views on both; so that he might thereby be assisted in shaping his own views, or in modifying those which he had already formed. He did not entirely agree with her as to the propriety or effects of the rising, though he leant a good deal to the side which pointed to its folly and absurdity; but as to the intentions ascribed to the three worthies, Whitmore, Mackey, and Croker, of aiding and abetting the rising for the benefit of the people and the promotion of the public good, and also as to their real characters, he entirely concurred in the observations she had made on both these topics. Yet he did not care to tell her so : for he was a man who preferred to be thought incapable of forming shrewd opinions on passing events, to being esteemed an acute observer of them. This was his peculiarity; arising perhaps from the nature of his occupation, which brought him in contact with all sorts of people, rich and poor, high and low, Whigs and Tories, Whitefeet, and the opponents of Whitefeet.

In replying to her observations, therefore, he evaded the disputed points altogether, and confined himself to the dogmatic question as to who were, and who were not, entitled to enter heaven. He turned round on his seat, after she had closed her remarks : and, placing himself in an attitude by which his face was partly turned to the wall behind him, and his back partly turned to Nelly, with one hand supporting his head, and the other under the elbow of the former, he commenced to say,—

"I don't know but you may be partly right, and may be partly wrong. 'Tisn't every one as is able to tell how it goes on in the other world. That is, if there is any other world at all; though myself believes there is. Father Markham knows all about it, by coourse; although, Nelly, it isn't clear to me that those clargy can be depinded on when they do be makin' their sarmins. It stands to raison that they must be tellin' us somethin' or other, and if they didn't tell about the other world, 'tis hard to say what business they'd have among us at all. You see, we are able to make out this world ourselves—every one accordin' to his business. There's myself; I goes to a weddin', and to a party, and to a haulin' home, and to a grand ball, or a grand dinner, to play my pipes, and to earn a shillin'; and when I come home, the ould woman puts down the pot, and provides accordin' to manes. Well and good; all the clargy in the univarsal world don't know more anent that than myself and the ould woman, nor half as much; savin' their raverance. And so on, wid the captain and

Nelly Corcoran; and so on wid every one
else. Now thin, what sort of business would
the clargy have in the world at all, if they
had nothin' to say about some other world
that nobody ever yet seen, nor, maybe, never
would. They have a good trade, hows'ever,
Nelly. And myself don't begridge it to 'em;
God forbid. If there was ne'er a hell in it,
nor e'er a divil, myself don't know what 'ud
become of the clargy at all; the cratures 'ud
starve, exceptin' somethin' 'ud be give out to
'em by the Soupers, or some other charitable
Christians that 'ud be goin' about lookin' for
the poor. But what odds is it to me, or to
you, Nelly, or to any one that have to earn
their bit and their sup, whether there's any
other world, or any divil; shure it won't put
the value of a blind nought in our pockets.
Not all as one as the clargy; they get a good
bit, and a good sup by it; and they rowl
about on their horses and coaches, just the
same as if they were the lords of the land.
And more good may it do 'em; 'tisn't wishin'
'em any harm I am, but just tellin' how it came
about that the other world, and the divil,
and all, was invented for the good o' trade.
Nelly, did Father Markham say that the rich
would go to heaven as well as the poor?"

"He did so; and I believe him, too—that's some of 'em," replied Nelly.

"Well," continued Denny, " 'tis a droll sayin'. Ah, then I heerd a clargy sayin' the contrairy o' that; and as good and 'cute a clargy as Father Markham. I heeard him sayin' that one of 'em, that's of the rich people, had no more chance of goin' there than a camel had to go through the eye of a needle. What do you think of that now? And a camel is as big as a cow. And then, by coourse, if they can't go to heaven, there's no other place for 'em to go but hell: exceptin' purgatory: and, by all accounts, that's no betther than hell. That is, if all they say be true—and I don't know whether it is or not, Nelly Corcoran. I know I saw a spirit once: but, faith, I was afraid to speak to him. My hair stood of an end on the top of my head: and every drop of sweat that run down my body was as big as your thumb. They say, if you'd cross yourself three times, and turn up the tail o' your coat, and look under your legs, wid your back turned to him, he should speak to you, and tell you his business. But I'd fall into a faint 'efore I'd go through half that. It was when I was crossin' the pinch on the side o' the hill, comin' up from

Barnadarrag, ten years come next April. He stood 'efore me on the *cussaraun* (path) in the shape of a greyhound. The sight left my eyes when I seen him, and I had like to fall in a heap on the spot. I shut my eyes till I wouldn't see him agin, and I made back as fast as I could, till I came to Tim Murphy's, and when I went inside the door, and seen the light, I fainted like a dead corpse. That's how 'twas, Nelly Corcoran. And, believe me, I never came that way agin in the night."

Nelly appeared deeply interested in the story of the spirit, as, indeed, she did in all that Denny had said in reference to hell and purgatory. The Whitefeet and the rising vanished from her mind, and all her thoughts became occupied with the affairs of the other world. She laid by her work, and renewed the fire, telling Minny Rice to bring in some fresh sods from the linny, while she herself was clearing away the ashes, and *straightening up* the fire. In the meantime she kept dropping exclamations and broken phrases, so as to keep the train of her ideas as much as possible from entanglement. After having put down the fresh sods, and swept away the ashes, and made everything look tight and

cosy, she sat down again opposite to Denny;
and taking a ball of yarn from a hole or
recess in the wall beside her, she commenced
to patch a stocking which Minny had brought
to her from the drawer of the dresser. She
looked very grave and thoughtful; but it
was evident, from the movement of her lips,
and the occasional glance which she cast
across at Denny, that there was something of
moment agitating her mind; and that she
was struggling with her thoughts in the endeavour to put them in order, and then pour
them out in full tide upon the ear of her
companion. She coughed a low and lazy
cough two or three times; and then seeming to have gained a complete mastery over
the mob of ideas that were shuffling through
her brain, she opened her mouth, and thus
began,—

"As sure as you and myself are sittin' here,
Denny Mullins, there's sich a place as purgatory; and 'tis there the poor Christians must
go before the gates of heaven can open for
'em. Don't you believe any one that'll tell
you to the contrairy. And shure you ought
to know that yourself long ago. There's
little Minny there can tell you about it, and
she is not eight years of age yet. And 'tis

a queer thing that a man of your age, Denny
Mullins, would be without knowin' what a
little child like that have by heart long ago.
Look at your Catechism, and you'll see it
there laid down, in black and white as plain as
the daylight. Shure if there wasn't such a
place in the other world who'd ever expect to
go to heaven, where there's no one livin' but
saints and angels, without spot or stain, or
anything on 'em, but as white as the driven
snow. And poor sinners like us to think of
goin' among them is out of all raison, until
we're first cleared of our sins, and fit to show
ourselves in cleanliness and decency among
'em. Didn't I hear Father Markham sayin'
that nothin' unpure would be allowed into
heaven; and what is that, but that we must
be like a clane bleached linen shirt, starched
and ironed, 'efore we dare show our face in
sich a place. 'Tisn't all as one as goin' to
purgatory, where anyone can walk in exceptin'
robbers and murdherers, and the likes; but
they can't, since they must go to hell to suffer
for ever and ever, amen. Out of hell there's
no redemption; the meanin' of that is, when
once the poor sowls, God help 'em, are sent
there through means of their sins, there's no
back door for 'em to escape out of it, but they

must stay there, burnin' in fire and brimstone,
with sarpints and all sorts of varmin crawlin'
about 'em, 'till the end of the world, and afther
it—oh, ay, for all etarnity. But purgatory
is not all the same as that. The robbers, and
thieves, and murdherers, and the wicked
people entirely, that don't mind anything, or
believe anything but this world and their
bellies—and shure, God help us, there's
enough of them same goin'—well, hell was
made for them. But poor craturs that are
strugglin' and strivin' to do what's right and
honest, and to keep God's commandments,
and to love their neighbours as themselves for
the love of God, shure 'tisn't to hell the good
God would be sendin' them. No; He made
purgatory to send 'em there for a little while
until they were cleared of their faults—maybe
a little lie, or a little carelessness in sayin'
of their prayers, or maybe, a bad thought
runnin' in their heads, without the craturs
ever thinkin' of doin' it. Yes, Denny Mullins,
they must stay there for a while till they are
clean and sweet to be brought to heaven
among the angels and the saints, and in the
company of God Himself, and of His blessed
mother. There's poor Andy Dobbin, the
cratur who never did hurt or harm to any one,

but who was kind and lovin' to the poorest beggar that walked the road, who loved God, and kept all His commandments—when he died the other day, maybe with a little, dauny (very small) stain of a sin on his sowl, would it be fair and right that he should walk straight to hell? If it wouldn't, and that he couldn't walk into heaven either—and shure, he couldn't do that as long as there was spot or speck on him—where, in the name of raison and marcy, was he to go? That's the raison purgatory was made by the good God, who promised all of us to give us accordin' to our earnin', that is, accordin' as we desarve it. So Andy Dobbin, maybe, went there; and, maybe, he went to heaven straight. Denny, you knowed Squire Brownlow—the Lord protect us, he was a wicked man—he walked on the necks of the poor; he cursed, and swore, and drank; he ruinated every poor cratur he could lay hands on; he didn't care for the laws of God or the laws of man, and he died ravin' and roarin', that they say you wouldn't be in the betther of it all your born days. Denny Mullins, would it be fair to have him and Andy Dobbin sint to the same place, and kept in the same place for ever? I ax yourself that now? Would our good God

do the likes? Glory, honour, and praise be
to His holy name, and to His blessed mother
in heaven, for ever and ever, amin. Now,
Denny Mullins, I ax you, afther that, have the
clargy any business in this world? Shure
your own sinse 'll tell you that they're God's
messengers here, and that widout 'em the
world 'ud be upside down. Is it to the likes
of us poor ignorant craturs, that are blind to
knowledge—is it to the likes of us the world
'ud be left to do whatever we liked, and whatever the divil might blow undher us? No,
Denny Mullins, God knew betther, and so He
sent us the clergy, anointin' them with holy oil,
to stand here in place of Himself; just the
same as Lord Fairborough's agent, Mr. White-
head, is over the estate when the lord himself goes to England in the winther, and 'till
he come back in the summer agin. Nothing
'ud go right if there wasn't some one over
the estates and the tinants 'till the lord 'ud
come back. And so God 'pointed the clargy
over the world 'till the day of judgment, when
He'll come to the fore Himself, and settle
everything to His own likin'. That's the way
'tis laid out. And, Denny Mullins, you know
that as well as myself, but you must be tendin'
your humours, and contradictin' God's truth.

But don't you be givin' yourself that fashion,
for fear the divil might blow undher you, and,
may be, God wouldn't stretch out His hand
to you when you'd be in want of His help.
Think o' that."

She then paused, and blessing herself
quietly and unobserved by Denny, began to
mutter some prayers. This was evidenced
by her silent breathing, the rapid motion of
her lips, and the occasional tapping on her
breast with her clenched hand. Denny, in
the meantime, remained fixed in the attitude
we have already described, with the exception
that he had turned his face closer to the wall
—so close indeed that his nose occasionally
touched it—and gave more of his back to the
lecturer. He had also shifted his arms from
time to time, putting one hand now, and
another again under each cheek alternately.

After Nelly had paused, we say, he maintained the same attitude, and looked as
though he were unconscious of the pause, with
this exception, that he stealthily rolled round
one of his eyes, that which lay nearer to the
line in which she bore from him, as if to
inquire the cause and nature of her abrupt
termination of speech. But after this recon-
noitring movement of his eye, it fell back

again into its former dreamy inclination towards the wall. At length Nelly, having terminated her pious meditations, renewed the conversation, that is, if her own theological disquisition may be designated by the name of conversation—for Denny, as we have seen, was entirely passive under the logical flow of her eloquence.

"And was it at the pinch," she asked, "you seen the spirit?"

Denny never moved a muscle; he did not even send out his eye to reconnoitre the new position taken up by his adversary. He maintained his own position and attitude without faltering. Seeing this, and apparently pleased with it—for she made no sign that she had expected an answer to her question —Nelly went on,—

"'Tis many a year ago I heeard of that same pinch bein' haunted; and good raison why. Did you ever hear tell o' the blind pedlar that used to be goin' about long ago? Oh, you weren't much good then, nor I either. Well, one night, a dark, dreary night that you couldn't see your hand, and the wind blowin' the same as if 'twas the end of the world was there; and the rain was goin' wid the wind, enough to blind a

saint. That was the night; and 'twas near
Christmas. I heeard my father tellin' it, many
is the time, and the neighbours gathered
round the fire, of a winther's night. I was
small myself at the time; and I remimber I
used to run between my father's knees, afraid
o' my life that I'd be caught by the spirit.
Ah, 'twas a woful time then. No one 'ud go
out afther sunset for fear they 'ud be murdhered. And where they buried him was
down at Kildobbin churchyard. And no one
'ud pass by there afther, for the world; since
he used to be seen goin' over the stile of the
churchyard on his rounds, wid the pack on
his back, and the same stick he had when he
was alive. And then he'd go up to the pinch
where they murdhered him, and stop there
till near midnight, when he'd come back to
the churchyard agin, and go over the stile,
and across through the graves till he'd find
out his own coffin; and lie there for the rest
of the night. Peg Duffy could tell you how
her uncle was comin' home from the fair of
Corrigcastle one night, and when he was
comin' towards Kildobbin churchyard what
would he see just risin' over the stile but the
pedlar, and his pack hangin' down on his back
and his stick on the top o' the stile—in the

shape of a goat. As soon as he seen him, he
lost his walk, and fell down on the middle o'
the road, just the same as a corpse ; and he
never rose out o' that spot till the men were
goin' to work early in the mornin', and found
him there, wid just the life in him, and that's
all. They took him up, and brought him to
the next house, that was Paddy Sheehan's,
near the turnpike road, until his brother
came down wid a horse and car, and carried
him home ; and there he was stretched on the
broad of his back in the bed for six long
weeks 'efore he recovered his sinses, I may
say, for he was as weak as a child in the
bed. So, you see 'tisn't right to be out in
the night."

Denny, who was constantly shifting
his position, during this recital, and occasionally drawing the sleeve of his coat
across his forehead, which became covered
with perspiration, moved farther into the
chimney-corner when she had uttered the last
words repeated above. And then looking
tremulously around him, and fixing his eyes
on Nelly, asked her what time would the
captain be home?

CHAPTER XIX.

THE ART OF ROGUERY—PIETY ASSISTS IT.

WHEN Denny Mullins inquired of Nelly what time the captain would be home, he was swayed solely by one feeling, and that was the fear of spirits.   While Nelly was relating the accident that had befallen Peg Duffy's uncle when he had seen the pedlar's ghost on the stile in the shape of a goat, Denny's heart was undergoing a series of oscillations, inspired by fear, which caused him to reflect on the best mode of securing his safety against the dangers which he felt gathering around him.   It is true that no ghosts had ever been known to appear on that line of communication which lay between the Glazement and his own cabin; yet, how was he to know that the spirit of the pedlar should not, on that particular evening, take a freak, and stroll into the glen, to meet him on his way home.   And what further aided this rising apprehension in

his mind was, that while Nelly was advancing
in her narrative, the evening was advancing
in gloom and sullenness. The shades had
thickened around the mountain side, and
the wind began to rise, and to puff in sudden
gusts down the chimney; and all this was
accompanied with a pattering of rain against
the window-panes. In short, a night of
elemental uproar appeared to be approaching;
and Denny was not a man that could allow
such doings to go on without speculating as
to their consequences to himself. He had
often heard, and indeed it was a point of
faith with him, that stormy nights, when
gloom and weird shadows settled down upon
the earth, and when wind and rain held high
carnival in the air, were especially selected
by the spirits of the dead to walk abroad,
and visit those haunts around which in the
days of their earthly pilgrimage they were
wont to saunter. If the hour of twelve
o'clock at night, that is, the midnight hour,
had passed he should feel safe; because at that
hour all wandering ghosts retired to their
resting-places, and the way lay clear for live
men travelling to their homes; but before that
hour no man in his senses had any business
to be out, especially in any place where it

was known spirits paid their visits. When, therefore, Denny inquired what time would the captain be home, he was influenced by his knowledge of the law which regulated the movements of the dead; and he felt that if he had to remain till midnight,—for, before that hour, his return home was not to be thought of, unless the captain accompanied him—and that there should be no one in the Glazement but himself and Nelly, and the "little *cratur* of a child, Minny Rice:" and if the night instead of getting better should become worse, and that in consequence he should be obliged to remain till morning, he should be caught doing *two* things which were not at all agreeable to him, namely, keeping his mother up waiting for him, and exposing the "*charakter*" of Nelly Corcoran. The question then was one fraught with interest to his physical and moral welfare. The idea of being thrown into a corpse by the sight of a spirit, or of being the cause of ill-repute to the character of a decent woman, was by no means agreeable to the feelings of Denny. He couldn't stand it. And who should blame him?

Whether Nelly understood the full drift of the question thus put to her or not we have no means of ascertaining, inasmuch as her

reply was of that curt and double-handed
nature which precludes the possibility of
arriving at any definite conclusion as to its
precise meaning. She simply replied "It
depends." He then wheeled round to his
former position, turning his back upon Nelly,
and his face to the wall, and became silent and
motionless as a statue. We shall leave him
so for the present, and permit Nelly also to
go on with her darning without further ques-
tioning.

At the time, or, at least, about that time,
when Denny addressed the question to Nelly
as to the time of the captain's return home,
that gentleman was engaged in investigations
of high import; or, at least in the unravelling
of certain mysterious and ominous proceedings of vast consequence to the interests of
some of his friends. The night, as we have
said, had set in with very gloomy forebodings.
The sky became one impending mass of
black, heavy, sluggish clouds; the rain fell,
and was borne along on the wings of the
rising wind, that flew in wild and fitful gusts
through the air, and rattled amid casements,
doors, and chimney-tops, making a strange
uproar. At that time, we say, a consultation
was progressing in a warm and well-appointed
apartment, not many miles from the Glaze-

ment; and, strange to say, some of the topics there discussed were precisely the same as those which had occupied the attention of Denny Mullins and Nelly Corcoran. This must be regarded as a remarkable coincidence, but what made it still more worthy of notice was, that the individuals—and they were only two in number—who carried on this consultation were of an entirely different class from that to which those of the Glazement belonged. They were no less distinguished personages, indeed, than Joe Whitmore and Bartley Croker; and the apartment which afforded them its comforts and its retirement for the purposes of their high deliberations was the library of Castle Whitmore. Here they sat, up one pair of stairs; the window-shutters closed and bolted, and the crimson-coloured drapery throwing its heavy folds along the entire window front. A table lay between them, partially covered with books and papers, with a whip, a pair of gloves, and a few other objects of incongruous charac-ter lying and scattered among them. The fire blazed in the grate with a bright and cheering lustre, and the chandelier that lay suspended above the table flung its flickering rays along the shelves and book-frames which covered the walls around. The table was placed longitudinally from the fire-place towards the opposite wall; and on the end next the fire were placed two decanters, and two wine-glasses, the latter sparkling with the juice of the grape. The two gentlemen sat on either side, with their feet resting on the fender, and their bodies thrown back in the luxurious recesses of soft-cushioned arm-chairs. At first, they appeared to talk indifferently upon topics which accidently presented themselves to their observation; sipping their wine occasionally, and looking through their fingers at the gentle quivering of the blaze that played around the grate.

We have said that some of the topics which engaged their attention were identical with those which Denny Mullins and Nelly Corcoran were discussing at the cosy fireside of the Glazement. And so they were. Whitmore asked Croker, just as they had entered the library from the dining-room, where they had parted with one or two other gentlemen, who had been dining with them— he asked him what he thought of ghosts. Croker smiled a curious smile, and then twisted his mouth towards one ear. He next assumed a sort of solemn aspect, and looked up to the ceiling, playing with, or counting his fingers, as if abstracted in deep thought. Whitmore, in the meantime, took his wine-glass, and lifted it to his lips; and having just tasted it, he laid it down again. Impatient for the reply of Croker to the very important question which he had put to him, he ventured upon an opinion himself; which was to the effect that he had some misgiving on the point; and that, in fact, he was rather inclined to think that there were ghosts. He referred to his memory for passages of Scripture which would seem to justify the belief he entertained; and after a confusion of ideas, created by his quotations from memory, he came to the sage conclusion that "there might be ghosts; and that there mightn't be ghosts, after all." Croker smacked his lips, and yawned; then he took his wine-glass and sipped it, and laid it down again. After this prelude, he twisted his right eye, that is, the eye on the side next to his companion, and fastened it on him for a moment; but it was only for a moment, for he instantaneously withdrew it; and none save the closest observer could have detected the slightest movement in it. He then, with a face that

lengthened as he spoke, and with a voice
and air that mimicked the tone and mien of
extreme sanctity, observed that "it is our
duty in all cases of doubt and difficulty,
where spiritual things are concerned, to submit ourselves to those whom the Great
Jehovah has set apart for the investigation
of such matters. It was the very essence of
wise and judicious conduct to adopt this
rule, nay, to obey this law; just, as in temporal affairs, the Great Power, the high
Moving Authority, the Omniscient Being,
has, in His infinite and loving wisdom, set
apart men learned in the law, that is, the
temporal law, for the purpose of directing
all persons in the line of duty which they
should pursue, with due regard to their
personal safety, and personal welfare here
below. These then" (he was alluding to
those learned in the law) "are the only safe
guides in all our temporal difficulties; they
are the only persons who know how to
extricate us from danger, from difficulty, and
from error; and to these, therefore, are we
bound, in wisdom and in prudence, to subject
ourselves. They are, as it were, the *tempo-
rarily* anointed of the Lord; just the same
as clergymen are the *spiritually* anointed."

Whitmore heard this exposition of spiritual
and temporal authority with absorbed attention ; but yet, at its conclusion he appeared
by no means satisfied about the existence or
non-existence of ghosts—that is, of ghosts
visiting this earth. And so, after another sip
from his wine-glass, he said that " it appeared
to him, from the explanation which his friend
had made, that the lawyers were the best
judges of the matter—that is, of ghosts,
inasmuch as they, the lawyers, were the
anointed of the Lord for earthly purposes,
and it was to earthly ghosts he was alluding; that is, to the ghosts that showed
themselves on this earth."

Croker looked through his fingers, while a
dark shadow passed over his brows, and his
mouth curled upwards. After a brief pause,
he said, " As to whether ghosts—disembodied
ghosts—visit this earth or not, I am not in a
position to assert. It is a question admitting
of much debate. At a first glance I would be
disposed to say not ; because the affairs of this
world are unsuited—must be unsuited to the
condition of the soul when divested of its
earthly trammels, and transferred to a state
of being of which we can have no conception,
but which we must now believe to differ

essentially from that with which we are con-
versant here. I say this, reasoning upon the
matter, and assuming for argument sake that
there is such a thing as another state of
existence. If there be, I repeat that it must
be one so unlike to this which we enjoy
here, that the concerns of the world cannot
possibly affect the spirits of those who have
once shuffled off the coil of flesh and blood
with which they had been encumbered. But
I cannot say that I believe in any such
state." Here he tossed off another glass of
wine, and then resumed, " I say, it is no part
of my belief, of my real internal convictions,
that there is such a thing as a future state.
You know, my dear sir, that the necessities
of society, and our own individual aspirations
here, require us to assent to, nay to become
supporters of this wholesome belief. Yes, I
say, *wholesome*, because it keeps the ignorant
and the unlettered, and the weak-minded,
within convenient bounds for us to operate
upon them. So it is *wholesome*. If all were
capable of understanding the mystery of life;
if they knew that it was a period of being
which was limited to personal gratification
and enjoyment in this earthly sphere, what
should become of you and me ? what should

become of the few who are like us—the superior portion of the great mass of humanity, who direct all things to their own individual and wise purposes ? Sir, I tell you," —and he struck the table with his clenched hand—" Sir, I tell you that the doctrine of *a hereafter* is a consummate farce. But, as I have observed, it is a useful doctrine, notwithstanding. And I have always considered it as a most important portion of the duty which I owe to myself, to encourage it by every means in my power, by externally complying with those practices its teaching involves. In point of fact, I am most punctilious in that regard ; and 1 am therefore regarded in society as a devotee of the first water. Once declare yourself a non-believer in a future existence, and what becomes of your hopes of wealth and power ? What becomes of that magnificent field which is presented to your ambition, and which consists in the credulity, the conscientiousness, the simplicity, and the unguarded openness of those who are influenced by this frippery of belief ? Why, the gates of advancement towards the goal of all real blessing would be closed against you. *All real blessing*, I repeat, because there is no blessing either here or hereafter, whatever that hereafter may mean—*no blessing* save that which is derived from wealth and power, and which consists in the gratification of the senses. Yes, the part of wisdom is to go with the teachings and practices of the Church—what is called the *Christian Church*—amongst us, to go the full length with them; for then you have free scope to advance your interests by every mode and practice that your sagacity and ingenuity can suggest. The Church will sustain you in all your acts, provided you do not openly commit yourself—that is, that you do not expose yourself to the grasp of the law of the land. What would your father have been, I ask you, if he had been swayed by the influences and compunctions of this superstitious doctrine of *a world to come?* What would *he* have been, Whitmore? And what would you be now, had *he* been a drivelling idiot of that sort. But he was a wise and a sagacious man. He saw the right thing, and he did it. He clothed himself with the piety of the time and the age; he followed in the path of Church doctrine; he submitted to its practices : but in his wisdom and his prudence he realized a fortune. How? by availing himself of the folly of those who really believed in the superstitions they practised, and by making that his own which would otherwise have passed into the hands of others. Conscience, and honesty, and charity; truth, and justice, and honour; heaven, and hell, and purgatory—pshaw! There is no reality in this chaotic jumble of ideas; it is a mere fungus overspreading the rotten structure of this belief of a future state. No, Whitmore, there is no such thing as a future existence. The first and greatest philosophers, those men of lofty and vigorous minds, who in the springtime of humanity, I may say, with the freshness and expansion of the intellect to direct and guide them, could not fail to grasp the destination of the principle of life, they derided the doctrine of a future state. Their successors, it is true, dreamt of such a state. Socrates, an old driveller, led on this later brood of dreamers; but when the hour of dissolution arrived to him, how did he treat his own doctrine? Did he adhere to it with the unflinching tenacity of belief? No; he fell back into the prevalent doctrine of his time, a doctrine which admitted of no determinate *first cause*, and consequently of no sustaining power of immortality. To be sure, there have been systems of religion at

every period of the world's existence; but
what do they avail in the way of argument
to support the doctrine of a future existence?
Nothing. They prove one thing, and only
one thing, that is, that it is in the nature of
man to *desire* a continued existence. But
that is only a principle, a mere elementary
sensitiveness inseparable from the human
composition, which preserves it from immediate extinction, and guards it against
those dangers which surround it on every side.
And a very necessary element of life it is;
for without it man would not exist an hour.
The desire of existence is what preserves and
promotes existence. Then, from this principle
religion sprang up; and every people gave to
this such shape and form as was suited to
their peculiar views of the prolongation of
life. Some had one system, some another.
Each people established an array of gods and
goddesses in accordance with their ideas of
what was best calculated to lengthen out
their days, and to afford them the greatest
amount of enjoyment in the longest time.
The lower animals are impressed with the
same desire of immortality; they have their
religious systems, too, according to their respective capacities. That is, they seek to pro-

long their lives by the adoption of a system of care and protection suited to their various instincts, or *beliefs*, if I may so term them. This is as much a principle in the nature of beasts as in the nature of man. Mark the absurdity of this doctrine of a future state. If there is such a state in reality, how is it that man was not impressed with that un-failing conviction from the beginning, and with the means of arriving at it with an un-erring aim ? So far from this being the case, we know that men and nations in all ages of the world differed in their views on the sub-ject, and in all their proceedings aimed only at the gratification of their senses and the indulgence of their passions. If there be what is called a self-existent Being, who created the world, and who is capable of destroying it, He could have no other design in its formation than the indulgence of a whim, to amuse Himself and to sport with His own power; otherwise He would have im-planted in man, who appears to have been the highest manifestation of His creative will, an inflexible determination to accomplish the end of his being, if that end was to arrive at an endless existence hereafter. But we know that such is not the case ; for all men, at all periods of the world, have pursued different courses, according to their different interests, and all tending in different directions. There is no fixed system to justify a belief in a future existence. All is at variance; all is a chaotic mixture of antagonistic interests, limited to the pleasures and enjoyments of this world. Such are, in brief, my views of the nature of man and of his province in the Creation."

He filled himself another glass, and took it off at a breath. Whitmore listened in a sort of dreamy mood to this exposition of the nature and end of man; occasionally nodding assent to the positions laid down by his companion, and affirming them by the expressions, "I believe that," and "that is my view."

We feel that we ought not to proceed further in recording the views of this brace of godless rascals, before offering a few remarks on the nature and tendency of those views. Bartley Croker, as we have more than once intimated, was a low attorney, who by means of a species of cunning peculiar to men of his character, and of an external piety, succeeded in obtaining the agency of Lord Milford's estates in that part

of the country where he (Croker) resided.
Lord Milford was, unfortunately, an absentee
landlord, and hence the power assumed and
exercised by the attorney-agent over the
estates and tenantry was unlimited.   He
made and unmade leases, imposed fines,
ejected tenants, received and disposed of
rents just as it pleased him.   He trans-
mitted such sums of money as he thought
proper to Lord Milford at two periods of the
year, these being at the gale days when the
rents were collected.   On those occasions he
also forwarded a statement purporting to
be a succinct account of the state of the
tenantry, their habits, their punctuality in
the payment of their rents, and their in-
debtedness, as the case might be, or rather
as he represented the case.   Lord Milford
received the rent and the statement at some
temporary abiding-place in England, or
France, or Germany, or some other country
where his pleasure or his ease happened to
transfer him.   His lordship took the money;
and the statement he invariably threw into
the fire.   Hence it happened that Bartley
Croker became so absolute in his authority
and power over the tenantry of Gurtroo, and
of the other townlands embraced within his

jurisdiction, that he ruled them as serfs, and
with an eye solely to his own advantage and
aggrandizement. He became possessed, as
tenant of course, to his principal, of several
small farms on the estate, from which he
had driven the tenants by means of ex-
orbitant exactions : but his great acquisition
in this way was the large property held,
under a lease of lives renewable for ever, and
at a nominal rent, by the late Greoge Granville of Ash Grove. His mode of accomplish-
ing this was of the simplest kind. He
studied Mr. Granville's character (this was
an essential part of his system of roguery),
which he found to be easy, confiding, and
credulous, as well as careless, extravagant,
and improvident. He then became his intimate friend and flatterer. Next, he encouraged him in every species of reckless
extravagance, such as betting on races;
purchasing extraordinary horses at extraordinary prices; giving great, frequent, and
expensive entertainments; speculating in all
sorts of bubble companies; and in short,
running risks of every kind which involved
a large and wasteful expenditure of money,
with a remote and very doubtful expectation
of a return. He furnished him with sums

of money from time to time, in furtherance
of these speculations; and he never, of
course, troubled him for rent; on the contrary, he begged him never to speak of it;
'twas so insignificant, so paltry, Lord Milford
would not hear of it.

It is scarce necessary to say that Lord
Milford was wholly unacquainted with those
proceedings; and that after a certain convenient period he was carefully informed
that that portion of the property held by
George Granville was going to ruin, and that
not only there had been no rent paid on it
for years, but that it had been actually
mortgaged for several thousand pounds.
The consequence was that George Granville
was dispossessed of the property, and Bartley
Croker became its proprietor on the same
terms as it had been held by Mr. Granville.

How this was effected the reader may
easily imagine when he is reminded that
Bartley Croker produced an account of mort-
gages against Mr. Granville of five times the
amount of the sums he had actually lent
him; and that this account was supported
by the acknowledgment, in writing, of Mr.
Granville himself. How this happened can
be accounted for simply by the fact that

Bartley Croker made it a point to obtain Mr.
Granville's signature to any paper he deemed
of importance, only when they sat in jovial
humour and abounding glee over their wine.
Indeed, Bartley Croker manifested, from a
boy, the most astonishing skill in everything
that comes within the province of roguery.
To this he owed his present position. He
was the son of a poor cobbler; and was
early trained to a life of lying and stealing
among the streets and alleys of Cushport.
He was first launched into a sort of fixed
employment by an attorney, of no good
repute, in the town, who took him to sweep
his office, light his fire, and run about with
messages. He acquired increased skill in
roguery, as well as increased pay, and pre-
ferment, in the office, in the course of a short
time; and at length he became an articled
clerk to his employer, having, in the meantime, acquired a knowledge of reading and
writing and figures. Thus the tide favoured
him; and he rode upon its crest into the
agency in which he was now flourishing.

This was the man, then, who so pompously
declaimed against the existence of a future
state, and the providential arrangement of
the powers and destinies of mankind. To

hear him speak one would be inclined to
believe that he was, at least, possessed of
great learning; and that, however unblest
by the light of faith, he was not unacquainted
with the testimony of unbelief as handed
down to us in the philosophy of the heathen
and the frenzied ravings of the atheist. But
no; he was as ignorant of anything like
learning as it was possible for any human
being to be who had never entered its pre-
cincts. His education was a blank; his
reading was confined to the mere mechanical
routine and technical formalities of his profession; and his thoughts were all directed
into those channels of deceit and fraud and
perjury which are regarded by men like him
as the true destination of a great mind, and
the direct pathway to wealth and honour.
He was, therefore, altogether outside his
province when he undertook to speak upon
any subject connected with the domain of
science and literature. Of these he literally
knew nothing; yet of subjects embraced
within their range he would talk with as
much confidence and assurance as if he were
really capable of understanding them, and
as if they were matters as light and as easy
to manage as the concoction of an attorney's

bill. But, as in everything else, he had his
one motive operating even here. He wished
to make something out of it. He knew that
the great bulk of men were little competent
to judge of a man's real knowledge or real
ignorance; and that whatever he might
venture to assert, he should stand very little
danger of being detected as an impostor.

There is a sort of disposition on the part
of mankind generally to be imposed upon.
They seem to like it; and especially where
religion is concerned. If we only look abroad
upon the world and mark the diversity of
sects and of creeds—some in direct hostility
to every principle of moral virtue—we must
come to the conclusion that mankind may
be easily led away by the superficial plausi-
bilities or demoniac ravings of any impostors
or madmen who may set themselves to traffic
upon them.

Bartley Croker, low-reared and uneducated
as he was, knew by a sort of vicious in-
tuition, as well as by experience, that all he
had to do with such a man as Joe Whitmore
was to repeat in plausible language the cant-
ing phrases of a sort of philosophical theo-
logy which freethinkers, and atheists, and
deists, and every species of vagabond and

thief have written and spoken, in order to impress upon him not only his own importance and cleverness, but also the folly of being restrained by the teachings of a Christian church. He knew Whitmore was a silly man, as well as a rogue. He wished, therefore, to tear away from his mind and feelings any apprehension that might be lingering there as to a future state; and thus to embolden him in the perpetration of any act of villainy which he believed would be attended with advantage to himself.

Therefore it was that, on the present occasion, when he had an object in view, which will appear immediately, he flung the sacred Scriptures aside; he trampled upon history; he sneered at the Christian dispensation; and substituted his own vicious vagaries for the wisdom of ages, and the sacred inspirations of heaven. He revealed his real character too; he felt himself safe with his half-idiot companion; and gave vent to the hypocrisy which constituted the leading feature in his mental composition. He declared himself as practising all the external duties of a Christian, while he internally disbelieved the doctrines which inculcated them; and as being prepared to

commit any act in violation of those doctrines, provided that it was of advantage to
him, and that he escaped detection by the
law.

Joe Whitmore, we have said, listened with
a sort of dreamy attention to all this denun-
ciation of the doctrines of Christianity, mani-
festing occasionally his assent by brief mut-
terings, such as, " I believe that," " It is my
opinion too." But when Croker had ceased
speaking, and leant lazily back into his chair,
Whitmore roused himself; and filling his
glass from one of the decanters, proceeded
to unfold his mind, which he seemed to do
without reserve, to the view of his companion.

" I don't know exactly," he said, " what
to think about a future state of existence,
but, cracko ! I like to enjoy myself in this
world as far as I am able. I am a true blue,
in that respect, Croker; and I don't envy
the man who doesn't feel as I do in that way.
Men may say what they like, but if the veil
were drawn aside, I just imagine that it is of
this world, and not of any fanciful one, they
would be found thinking. Now, Croker, my
dear fellow, it is not for us to be wasting
words upon those things that don't concern us;

I wish to have your assistance in that affair
which immediately affects myself, ay, and
you too. I want to clip the wings of that
aspiring bantam, that presumptuous beggar
who is crossing my path. I want, too, to
take down that little impertinent monkey
from her stand, and teach her how to appreciate my character and feelings. Cracko! I
am not to be trifled with by such contemptible butterflies. I am a man of property and
position in the county, and I must not be
insulted with impunity. Not that I care a
rush for the little jade; but I have fixed my
mind upon possessing her, and I must not be
baulked. And to think that such a fellow as
Granville, the sneaking beggar, should pre-
sume to come between me and the object of
my desire, is a thing not to be quietly en-
dured. Then he is making his calculations
on the influence of his friend Lord Fairborough."

Here Croker gave a sudden start, and,
turning quickly to the table, filled a glass of
wine, and drank it off. Whitmore continued,
"I care not a rush for Lord Fairborough;
I'm independent of him and of the whole
British Government. I say, Croker, how do
Lord Milford and Lord Fairborough stand?

Are they friends ?" Croker evidenced some
uneasiness again at this question, but he
made no reply; and Whitmore continued,
" Well, I say that I care not for the influence
of Fairborough and Milford united, not I. But
what have they to do with the prosecution of
my design? I want to possess Fanny Moore
—that is my object. I don't speak of love in
the case. Cracko! I am no milk-sop of that
sort. I have one object to achieve ; no, I
have two objects to achieve—I have to pull
down the pretensions of that upstart coxcomb,
Granville—the presumptuous scoundrel—and
I have to teach that little chattering monkey,
Fanny Moore, that she cannot insult me with
impunity. These objects are worth attain-
ing, and I have the power to attain them. I
shall send the cur whining to his lair, and I
shall have the gratification—yes, it will be a
gratification in a double sense, I admit that
—of compelling that little pea-hen to acknow-
ledge me her lord and master. Cracko!
what a delightful prospect. Look here,
Croker! confound me !"—and he here struck
the table with his great clenched fist, which
caused the decanters and glasses to dance
and ring—" confound me if I would not
sacrifice half my property to accomplish this.

Now I am still of opinion that the plan I
submitted to you the other day for this purpose is the best. There is a decision about
it that pleases me, besides the *éclat* of the
thing. Cracko! what will the people say? To
be sure they'll say that it was a manly, cou-
rageous, noble act. But listen, Croker—"
he bent over towards his companion until
his lips nearly touched his ear—"listen;
Miss Moore is an heiress, and old Moore
is wealthy. Put that and that together,
and then say if Joe Whitmore knows what
he is about." He here leant back in his
chair, and fell into a fit of laughter, which continued for several minutes, and during which
he glanced over at Croker two or three
times, as if to ascertain whether that gentleman fully appreciated the extent and depth
of his genius. Then he resumed, "Yes,
Croker, my boy, I am a man who keeps
awake while others are asleep. You know
the arrangement I proposed. Peter Mackey
at the Cross will direct the movement. He
is to engage Jer Grinnex, and three others
from the town of Cushport, friends of
Grinnex, on whom he can rely, and who are
unknown in these parts. They are to effect
an entrance into Moore's house a little after

midnight, say, between one and two o'clock, and to take her by force from her bed. I am to remain with my carriage and servants at the outer gate of the demesne, on the public road. She is to be gagged, so as to prevent all noise, and make the thing pass off smoothly. I then take her into the carriage with myself, and the thing is done. We drive to Cushport, arrive there before day, or at least by dawning, and going on board at once, set sail for Liverpool. The craft shall be employed for my own special service. That's the plan; it admits of no failure. I shall have Fanny marked with the Whitmore arms, eh? cracko! and I shall have the satisfaction of knowing that beau-Granville will be sucking his thumb in idiotic helplessness, while his heart will be lacerated with the tortures of defeated love. Love! The milksop! the goose! Ha, ha! I shall have my satisfaction then for his impertinence and silent insults, and for *her* open and public scorn." Here he ground his teeth together, and drew up and extended one side of his mouth until it nearly reached his ear. "And her brother, too—the little sparrow-hawk—his pride shall be pulled down, and his languishing lady-love—the exquisite Julia—oh, how she will fret and pine! Ay, Croker, I shall play confusion among the whole cursed set of them, and propitiate at the same time the offended genius of my race for the insults and the outrages of years. Ho! ho! I'd crush their head beneath my heel, if only one head contained the lives of the whole of them. I'm not a man to be crossed in my purposes; I'm not a man to be treated with scorn; I'm not a man to permit myself to be trampled upon; ay, like a worm. No! no! no!"

Here he started up from his seat, and walked rapidly up and down the room, brandishing his arms in the air. Croker meantime turned around in his chair, and eyed him curiously, while his face assumed a grin which seemed to indicate the internal satisfaction which he felt at the prospect of using for certain selfish and diabolical purposes the man whom he now saw unveiled before him.

After having exhausted his temporary rage, Whitmore returned to the table, and again filled himself a glass of wine, which he swallowed at a breath; he then threw himself into his chair, closed his eyes, and drew a deep sigh. He then leant back, and fell into a state of reverie; during which his lips kept constantly moving. Croker still kept his eye turned upon his companion; and appeared to enjoy his abstraction; if a grim smile which played around the corners of his mouth and the involuntary opening and closing of his nostrils afforded evidence of his feelings. He said, at length,—

" Now, Whitmore, my dear fellow, we must look carefully at this plan of yours. I have thought it over several times since you first mentioned it to me; and though I see a good deal in it which I can approve, yet, I would not act too hastily upon it. It requires a great deal of deliberation. I would not adopt it as a first step; I would rather reserve it for future action, in the event of other methods failing.—Now I have a plan which, I think, ought to be tried in the first instance; and it recommends itself to my mind on two grounds; first, it is more safe; and second, if successful, it will be more effective, more radical. Now, let me unfold it to you."

Whitmore opened his eyes, and sat upright in his chair. Then looking, with a fiery glare, at his companion, he said,—

" Out with it, then—let me hear it at once. Come, what is it ?"

"My dear fellow," resumed Croker, "you must be patient, and attend calmly to what I say. Great events can be brought about only by coolness and diplomacy. Passion won't do. Reason, unclouded judgment, calm reflection, and deliberate action—these are the requirements, in all cases where difficulty and danger are involved. Now, hear me calmly and dispassionately. This Whitefeet organization, you are aware, is spreading pretty generally through the country—at least through this part of the country; and some mischief has already sprung from it. The public mind is a good deal disturbed by its acts and proceedings. Several attacks have already been made upon private residences; and fire-arms have been forcibly taken from them. Some persons, too, in resisting this violence, have been wounded, and nearly deprived of life. Very well; you say—that this jackanapes, Granville, is in your way; and so he is. I look upon him as a dangerous character, not only as regards you, but as regards the peace of society. He is a cool, plotting, unprincipled scoundrel. He would sacrifice you, and me, and everybody, in furtherance of his own schemes of ambition. He wants this Fanny Moore's fortune; he

wants a position in society, in order to tram-
ple upon his betters;—and if he had secured
his ends to-morrow, how should you and I
be treated by him? We know that; it is not
necessary to dwell upon it. I have no doubt
myself that he is engaged in this unlawful
organization, though he pretends otherwise;
of course he does; such villains are always
double-faced. He wishes to secure the confidence or friendship of Lord Fairborough,
for the purposes of ambition; and, hence he
assumes an appearance of attachment to the
British Constitution, and of allegiance to
the Sovereign of these realms. That's all
pretence. He cares nothing for either constitution or sovereign, but as they are
calculated to promote his selfish designs. I
have reason to believe that he is this moment
endeavouring to influence Lord Fairborough
to interfere, with regard to the arrangements
of some properties in the county; and that
his lordship has actually written to Lord
Milford in connexion with this matter. What
do you think of that? Is property, is the
right of property to be canvassed and disturbed at the instance of a beggarly scoundrel
like this fellow, Granville? If such things
are permitted, what security have you—what

security have I—what security has any man,
that his property will not be tampered with
by every low ruffian who may fancy he has
some claim to it? These wicked designs
must be nipped in the bud. Now, sir, how is
this base intriguer, this beggarly pretender
to the hand of a woman who should—and
who would, were it not for this vile intriguer
—feel honoured by your devotion to her—
how is he to be met, and counteracted?
First, it is not necessary for me to say that
no measures should be kept with such men;
they should be regarded as a curse, as a
plague-spot, to be swept away as soon as
possible. And again, the most effective course
should be taken to accomplish that end.
What I would suggest is this;—and I have
thought the matter over, as I have said,
many times, with the view of arriving at
some definite plan to effect the object in
view—now, you can get Peter Mackey to
act in this matter in whatever way you may
think proper. He is intimate with some of the
principal members of the Whitefeet organization;—I believe you told me that he was
one; or, at any rate, pretended to be one of
the organization himself. Let him get this
fellow, Jer Grinnex, and his comrades from

Cushport, to arrange an attack on Granville's house, for the purpose of obtaining fire-arms. Do you understand? In that attack, shots will be exchanged, no doubt; for that base cub, Granville, will resist, if only to give himself *éclat* in the county. Very well, you understand the rest;—a stray shot from Grinnex, or one of the others, may cool the ardour of his love for Fanny, eh? and put a gentle climax to his ambitious aspirations. What do you say?"

He rubbed his hands together, with great apparent glee; and then, turning round, slapped the table with his hands, exclaiming, at the same time, "Genius is the highest prerogative of man—what do you say, Whitmore, my blade?" Then he leant back in his chair, and laughed immoderately.

Whitmore seemed lost in meditation. After a little time, however, he said, with a gravity of expression which sat clumsily upon his features,—

"I never thought of that, Croker. But, do you think it is better than *my* plan? You see, my plan, if well carried out, would torture the fellow's soul. He would be alive, to envy me; and to feel all the pangs of jealousy and madness; and that would be a great luxury to me. But, according to your plan, it would scarcely be a triumph at all. However, I must take a little time to reflect upon it."

CHAPTER XX.

THE CAPTAIN HAS HIS EYE TO WINDWARD—THE PLOT DISCOVERED.

AFTER Joe Whitmore had delivered himself of the grave reflection contained in the concluding part of the last chapter, he and his companion separated for the night; but before separating they agreed to meet again in the course of a few days for the purpose of determining upon the line of conduct that might be considered best under all the circumstances. By that time Whitmore would be able to make up his mind as to whether or not he should adopt Croker's plan, or adhere to his own, or combine the two, or devise some other that might appear best calculated to carry out the end in view.

The reader will have borne in mind that Denny Mullins, the piper, felt a good deal of anxiety for the return home of the captain on the night in question. This anxiety was manifested after Nelly Corcoran had related the story of the pedlar's ghost appearing in the form of a goat. Denny then sat closely ensconced in the chimney-corner of the Glazement, whilst the wind and rain were careering amid the gloom outside. Nelly was unable to give a satisfactory reply to Denny's question as to the time when the captain might return; in point of fact she was herself as ignorant upon that subject as Denny himself; for it was rarely the captain deemed it necessary to inform her of his business, unless it was of such a nature as rendered it desirable that she should be made acquainted with it. But such was not the case on the present occasion. The captain had gone out early in the day, and had said nothing as to the business he was intent upon, or the hour at which his return might be expected. Indeed he knew nothing of this himself. He had no particular design in his setting out, and he had no particular concern as to the hour when he might come back. It was his wont to stroll down to the village every day, at least every day that did not require his presence at home about the management of his garden, or of his house, or of anything else connected with his domestic arrangements. He did this, that is, he strolled down to the village every day, for the purpose of seeing and hearing what was going on there, and of lending a hand in any work or business that was going forward among his friends, and that required his aid, particularly at Ash Grove and at Brookfield Hall. He was, moreover, interested, as the reader must be be aware, in the proceedings of the Whitefeet; and he wished to make himself acquainted with every new revelation connected with them, in order to prevent, as far as he was able, any mischief that might arise from them, especially to his friends. On the present occasion, then, he walked out early in the day, and directed his steps, as usual, towards the village. He visited Brookfield Hall, where he remained for an hour or so, and cracked a few jokes with the old steward, complimented Miss Fanny on her good looks, as he had chanced to meet her just as she crossed the avenue, and had a word or two about the weather with the master of the mansion, old Mr. Moore, as he was crossing the courtyard on his way cut. He then crossed over the fields, and out on the mountain road, and down towards the Cross. He

went into Moll Dreelin's on his way, and had
a long talk with her, he sitting on a stool
near the fire, and she on a box in the corner
mending her gown. She told him the news,
said that her husband was working at Peter
Mackey's, and that Anty was up at the big
house, that is, Ash Grove House, helping
about the kitchen. But the most important
piece of information, that is to him, which
she gave him, was, that Bartley Croker
passed in his gig through the village a little
bit ago on his way to Castle Whitmore.
There was no one with him but a servant,
and when he had come to the Cross he
alighted and went into Peter Mackey's. He
hadn't stayed there long when he came out
again accompanied by Peter, who walked
down a bit of the road with him.

The captain listened to all this with a
good deal of interest, for he knew that
Bartley Croker's movements about that part
of the country did not forebode much good
to some persons at least.

After resting himself for a considerable
time, and after learning all the news that
was of any importance, the captain rose,
and, wishing Moll a good evening, took his
way towards the Cross. He met one or two

persons whom he knew—and whom did he
not know about Ballydine and its neighbourhood?—and he stopped to talk with them
about the season, and the threatening aspect
of the afternoon, and other matters of equal
interest to country people. They were coming
up from the direction of Castle Whitmore,
and they told him that as they were passing
the gate leading up to the castle who should
they see but Bartley the Devil driving up the
avenue. This was news to the captain, and
so he put it up in a corner of his mind, to
have it to hand when it should be required.
He then wished his friends a good evening,
and proceeded towards the Cross.

Having reached it he paused for a moment,
and then muttering to himself, " Yes, that'll
do; I want to buy snuff," he turned into
Peter Mackey's shop. The captain was not
to say a snuff-taker, but yet he carried his
box, and occasionally offered a pinch to a
friend. It was to him a sort of companion,
as well as a pledge of friendship; it was
even more than that, it was a sort of *familiar*
or attendant spirit, for he conversed with it,
and imbibed inspiration from it when sitting
alone in the Glazement, or rambling among
the glens and hills in silent meditation on

things present, past, and future. He, therefore, kept his box always by him, and had
it ready for every emergency. So he went
into Peter Mackey's shop to recruit it, not
that it was empty—indeed it was nearly
half-full—but he wished to go in, and he
wished to have an excuse for going in.

While the little boy behind the counter
was measuring the quantity of snuff required,
Peter Mackey, who had heard the voice of
the captain, stepped out from the room
behind the shop, and accosted him with his
usual show of friendship. Having passed a
few ordinary remarks on the weather, and
the appearance of the clouds, he asked the
captain to step in with him and rest himself
awhile. So they went into the room together,
and sat down by the fire, and joked, and
laughed for some time.

At length Peter made allusion to the dis-
turbances that were taking place in some
parts of the country through the activity
and zeal of the Whitefeet. He approved of
them, and he didn't approve of them, and
he wished to have the captain's opinion
upon the subject. Not but that he already
knew what the captain generally thought
of the new organization and its aims, but

yet he wished to talk about it, and to *sound* him.

The captain just glanced along the surface of the subject, for he, too, wished to *sound* Peter.

" I have no great belief in them," observed the captain. " I am afraid that their ballast is not well stowed ; and, besides, the rigging is not of the best, I think; and as to the crew, I fear they are not exactly first-class at steering, or reefing, or any other neces- sary work required on board."

This was not *very* condemnatory of the movement, and so it afforded an opening to Peter to try his hand on the captain.

" By jing," he observed, " I'm half of your opinion. The boys are not, as you might say, perfect knowledgeable in the business; but still and all something ought to be done to sarve the poor counthry. I don't believe myself that anything worth spakin' of can be done 'till the gintry join in it. I wish they were all like Masther Herbert Gran- ville; then we'd soon have our rights, and we'd have no slavery or the like. He is a noble gintleman, only for he's so poor, and more is the pity. I wondher does he go out wid the boys any night ; if he did he'd show

'em how to act, for, you see, he has the
learnin', besides the spirit of the ould stock.
There's nothin' like it, by jingo. But tell
me, captain, is there anything for certain
about himself and Miss Moore goin' to be
married ? "

He asked the question in a low, confidential
tone of voice, bending over towards his
companion at the same time.

The captain pleaded ignorance on the subject, but, nevertheless, replied with a tone
and manner that were intended to convince
Peter that the captain had so much confidence in him that he would readily communicate to him everything he knew, either as
regarded the matter inquired into, or any
other matter whatsoever.

Peter felt all this, but yet he was wary,
and advanced in his inquiries and communi-
cations with slow steps.

" Well," he said, " I'd like to see the same
couple married, for, by jing, they look like
two that were made for one another. Miss
Fanny Moore is a noble cratur, not more so
in the barony ; and as for Masther Herbert,
show me his equal in all Ireland, in mind
and body. That's what I always say. Mr.
Whitmore, they say, is afther her too ; but

what chance could sich a *gommeril* (half-foolish fellow) have near Masther Herbert? not a bit, no more than myself. I wondher will they be married before he goes to see the uncle, the ould cornel, in Canada; or will they put it off till he come back. Likely they'll put it off. But, maybe, he wouldn't go at all. Some say Lord Fairborough is workin' hard to get back the property again for him—the property that Bartley Croker took from ould Mr. Granville. I wondher is it thrue? By jingo, 'twould be a good deed if Bartley lost it, afther all. They say there was foul play in it; but myself don't know much about it. The ould man, that's Mr. Granville that was, was careless about signin', they say; and so he gave papers for more than he owed. And now they say Lord Fairborough is bringin' it to light. And there's a great deal more said about Bartley keepin' the rents that the ould gintleman paid him, and tellin' Lord Milford that he never received 'em at all. Myself don't know how it is, by jing. But I'm tellin' you all I know about it; since I'd keep nothin' from you, knowin' you to be a sinsible, know-ledgeable man, that 'ud keep to yourself what-ever I'd tell you. And I'm the same way wid you. If you tould me about the killin' of a man, by jing, no man or mortial 'ud ever know it from me. That's the sort I am, captain."

The captain saw that he was not likely to obtain from Peter any information that he had not already been possessed of. However, he resolved upon a hit; and having cursorily replied to the several questions and insinuations so dexterously thrown out by Peter, he observed,—

" Mr. Croker is a clever man, and knows how to handle the tiller with any boy in the ship. It will go hard with him if Lord Fairborough or any one else go to win'ard of him. He is a 'cute man, Mr. Mackey. And Mr. Whitmore, too, knows the stem from the stern of a ship. They're very smart, handy men; and it wouldn't be easy for you or me to find out their bearings. If any man could do it you are that man, Mr. Mackey. Although, Bartley Croker 'ud try to twist you and me, and every one else round about to every point of the compass to serve his own turn, I am thinkin' that he'd find out soon that *you*, at any rate, aren't a man to be put into a strait waistcoat. He makes his boast, so I am tould, that he could make use of

any man he ever cocked an eye on; and that
he could handle you like a top at any hour he
liked. But I always said, 'twas never born
with him to handle Peter Mackey that way.
Well, some people 'ud put their finger in my
eye for sayin' so; but I stand to it, for all
that. And, moreover, I heard people sayin'
that Mr. Whitmore made his boast that he
was able to knock his dealin' thrick out o' you
any day; but I stood up against that, and
tould 'em to their teeth that Whitmore was
never able to handle a rope-yarn with Peter
Mackey of the Cross of Ballydine. I hear a
great deal, Mr. Mackey, among the people,
but I always stand up for you, so I do; and
why not? Aren't you one of the old stock
o' the place, and thrue to the people, like all
your family before you. Not all the same as
some that come among us, and who have
nothing sound in 'em. I wondher how does
Bartley and Whitmore stand now?"

The captain flung out his line at last. The
reader will notice that he was only removing
obstructions from his path in all that he had
said up to the last sentence; but the moment
he said, "I wondher how does Bartley and
Whitmore stand now;" he hurled his eye at
Peter, and pierced him to the very soul.

Peter, however, bore the question and the scrutiny well. He was taken a little by surprise, it is true; the question came suddenly upon him, while he was intent on pursuing the winding thread of the captain's observations, not exactly knowing what they were leading to; so he received a slight shock, but rallied immediately.

There is no doubt that the captain's movement was exceedingly dexterous; he made his approaches under cover, and without any noise; and had he been dealing with an ordinary man, even with a rogue of ordinary calibre, he could not have failed in flooring him. But Peter Mackey was no ordinary man, he believed himself fully able to cope with any knave on Irish ground; and to do him justice, he came up to the mark, or nearly so, of his own estimate of himself. We say, although he was a good deal staggered when the blow was dealt him, of " I wondher how does Bartley and Whitmore stand now?" yet the readiness and adroitness with which he recovered his level again were worthy of all praise, at least in the eyes of men of his craft. He looked the captain straight in the face, returning glance for glance; then his eye quivered a little, and he dropped it just on the toe of one of his feet. But it was no sooner down than up again, and stuck upon the captain, who watched its movements carefully, speculating on the final result.

The difficulty with Peter lay in this: he was acquainted with the black designs of Bartley and Whitmore, nay more, he was a party to them; he naturally wished to have them kept as secret as possible, and any attempt on the part of anybody to trace them out he felt it his duty and his interest to foil at once. Besides this he knew that the captain was aware of the intimacy subsisting between himself and the persons alluded to. Here, then, we may see that when the captain threw in the question sidelong, "I wondher how does Bartley and Whitmore stand now?" he (Mackey) found himself at once hurled upon a dilemma, and struggling between its horns. He couldn't deny his intimacy with Bartley and Whitmore; and if he were led away by the insinuations of flattery, or by any weakness whatever, to let in any light upon their hellish schemes, he would be at once captured in his own snares, and committed to the mercy of the captain. How then to escape from his difficulty was the cause of the unsettled condition of his eye. We say it,

the eye first rushed into the captain's face,
and after settling there for an instant,
bounded to the ground, and perched on the
toe of his (Mackey's) shoe; but this position
it abandoned after a second, and darted upwards again, and fixed itself upon Mackey's
nose. Then it hopped to his right shoulder,
and then to his left, and at length it lodged
in vacancy, when he thus began :—

"By Jing, captain, the way it is—and I'm
sure I wouldn't mention it to any one but
yourself, since, between you and me, 'tis
enough for every man to mind his own little
business, bekase why? You see the times are
not very good, as you might say, though
nothin' to complain of. And for the matther
o' that, a man has no business to mix or
meddle in what doesn't belong to him. The
way 'tis, the gentry and the people dale
in my little shop, and I thry to pass every one
in civilty; and shure 'tis our duty to pass one
another, as you may say, civil and Christian-
like, glory be to God! But about the gintry,
'tisn't our business to mind 'em or meddle
wid 'em when they're cross or contrairy to
one another; or when their blood is up, and
nothin' but djuels 'll satisfy 'em. By jingo,
I don't know how 'tis between Mr. Croker and

Mr. Whitmore; 'tisn't to me or the like of me they'd tell about their djuels. Isn't it a wondher they'd be fightin' with those pistols, and not have a blow of a fist at one another like common min? And so you heard that there's a djuel to pass 'etween 'em?"

The reader will perceive at once the skill and judgment manifested in this reply of Peter's. He advances carelessly and loosely, as if he had seen no point at all in the captain's question; but when he comes to a certain stage in his remarks he discharges his piece with force and precision, "And so you heard there's a djuel to pass 'etween 'em?"

The captain felt the full effects of the blow, and the more so that it came unexpectedly upon him. He could never have anticipated such a reply. In point of fact, it was no answer to his question, but yet it was an inquiry which evolved itself from that question, leaving the captain not only in the position which he had occupied before putting the interrogatory as regarded information, but also in the further predicament of being put upon the defensive.

When the captain put in the blow, " I wondher how does Bartley and Whitmore stand now?" he could never have expected that the reply to his blow would be, "And so you heeard there's a djuel to pass 'etween 'em?" The captain, as we have said, was taken aback; or, as he himself said when talking of it, "he was brought up all standin'." He looked at Peter as a mere object of curiosity, and without any intention of replying to him. He saw his eye resting in apparent quiet beneath his shaggy brow, which all but covered it, leaving only a small streak of light glimmering in the very centre. His great red nose was expanding and contracting like the nostrils of an over-heated beast. His mouth was drawn aside towards his left ear, with a hideous gape, as if his soul was struggling to escape from that orifice; and his two hands pressed convulsively down upon the bench whereon he sat, one on either side, as though he were relieving his buttocks from the piercing of nails or of some sharp instrument that was stuck in them. The captain couldn't help smiling, but he made no reply. After a little time occupied in eyeing each other, the captain rose, and said that he must be moving. Peter immediately relaxing from his state of torture, rose up too, and asked the captain if he would take a drink. The captain declined, but Peter continued to press him, recommending his "lovely *ale*," his "foamin' *pale butt*," and his "splendaceous *double X*," to his notice. The captain still declined, and passed on to the shop-door, where he stood and looked out. Peter stood by his side commenting upon the weather, which promised to be stormy.

" 'Twill be a rough evening," observed the captain.

" 'Twill be bad for travellin', I'm thinkin," said Peter.

" 'Faith, I'm afraid you'll have to give shelter to Bartley to-night on his way back," rejoined the captain.

Peter started as if he were struck, and then replied in the flurry of the moment, "Oh, yes—why—no—who tould you ? "

The captain laughed outright at the unguarded response of Peter, and felt secretly at a loss to understand how he could possibly have shown himself so much off his guard, especially when he had but just a moment before manifested such impenetrable security. He wished Peter "good-bye," and passed out. He turned, not in the direction of Castle Whitmore, but off to the right at a considerable angle from that line. He did this purposely to elude the vigilance of Peter, intending, after he had proceeded some distance, to cross over the fields and strike out on the Castle Whitmore road, that is, the public road leading to the town of Corrigcastle, and by the demesne of Castle Whitmore. As he tripped along he fell into a train of meditation on the conversation and scenes of the last hour. He passed before him in mental review the appearance, language, and physical contortions of Peter Mackey. He rested particularly on his hideous and beastly aspect when he replied to his question, "I wondher how does Bartley and Whitmore stand now?" by the corresponding question, "And so you heeard there's a djuel to pass 'etween 'em?" But when he came to review him at the door, at the time he committed himself by acknowledging his acquaintance with Bartley's movements and intentions on that day, he became quite puzzled; he felt wholly incapable of accounting for it. And that was a wonder, for the captain, though no physiologist or metaphysician, was, nevertheless, a shrewd and keen observer of men as well as of passing events. The fact, however, was, that Peter having undergone such a struggle in the room in the endeavour to escape from the trying question put to him by the captain, became somewhat exhausted; the tension of his mind was so great in shaping the necessary answer, that after the extraordinary exertion had passed away, the mental powers became relaxed; and hence when they were tried again, they were found unequal to a reiterated effort. So that when the captain said, without one note of warning, " Faith, I'm afraid you'll have to give shelter to Bartley to-night on his way back," Peter broke down suddenly, and exhibited his weakness by the miserable drivel, " Oh, yes—why—no—who tould you ? "

The captain proceeded on his way, thus entertaining himself with philosophical reflections on the character of the publican, until he had reached a turn in the road, at the distance of about a mile from the Cross. At this point he turned into the fields, and inclined towards the Corrigcastle road. In the space of half an hour he emerged upon this road, and after advancing upon it for a quarter of an hour he came to the gate opening upon the demesne of Castle Whitmore. He passed in through the gate, and winding to the right by the wall of the demesne, and under cover of the elms that lined it, he reached a covert of underwood by the side of a large pond,

and into this he entered. He seated himself
in the fork of a sycamore-tree, and began to
arrange his thoughts. When he had left the
Glazement in the early part of the day, he
had no particular aim beyond that of learning any news that might be going the rounds
of the village; but when he had been informed by Moll Dreelin that Bartley the
Devil had passed by the Cross, and that he
had been in conversation with Peter Mackey,
the publican, his mind began to work, and
he felt that there was some occupation before
him. He then saw and conversed with Peter,
and he no longer hesitated as to the course he
was bound to adopt under the circumstances.
The leading idea in his mind was that he
should proceed without loss of time to Castle
Whitmore, or, at all events, to that neighbourhood; and there endeavour to obtain all
the information he could with respect to the
movements of Bartley. Why he became thus
interested in this gentleman's actions the
reader must be already aware, from the fact of
the disreputable character which Bartley had
established for himself in the country round,
and especially from the circumstance of his
being so mixed up with the calamities which
had befallen the Granville family. He was,

therefore, looked upon by the people generally as a bird of ill-omen, and every eye was
turned upon him whenever he appeared on
the wing. The captain sat on the fork of the
sycamore-tree in order to arrange his thoughts.
The housekeeper at Castle Whitmore was an
old friend of his. Indeed, if the truth must
be told—and it is right that in this instance
it should be told—passages of love had passed
between them in their younger days; or, as
Nelly Bryan herself—that was her name—
used to say, " many a bar of coortin' they
had in their time." He had no doubt upon
his mind that she would do him a service if it
lay in her way, for she never forgot old times,
" and happy times they were," she often said.
He concluded, therefore, to walk up to the
Castle, and to make his mind known to Nelly
Bryan "in regard to what was troublin' it
now."

So he left the sycamore-tree, and by a
circuitous movement approached the back
premises of the Castle, and made his way to
the servants' quarters. Nelly Bryan was
delighted to see him, as she "ever and.
always was, and would be." He "should
come now," she said, "and sit in her own
room, and make himself at home; and

she'd get a nice glass of somethin' to warm him."

We have said that Joe Whitmore and his friend Bartley Croker sat in the library of Castle Whitmore while discussing the question as to which would be the best plan of obtaining the " hand and heart," if we must so express it, of Fanny Moore for Mr. Whitmore, and at the same time of torturing the bosom of Herbert Granville. This room was situated in the front of the Castle, that is, on that side of it which looked out upon the avenue leading to the main entrance, and was up one pair of stairs. Behind this was another smaller room, which was entered by a door on the right of the landing at the entrance of the library. This was the house-keeper's room, where she used to make her friends snug, when any of them visited her, and that was pretty often, especially of a Sunday. It was plainly but comfortably furnished; and for its better accommodation, it was furnished with a buffet, or closet, which contained, besides the " tay-things," a bottle or two of " choicest spirits," and a " nice decanter of port wine for the ladies." This closet stood in the partition wall between the room and the library; in fact, it had been once a door, communicating between the two rooms, but it was afterwards closed up and converted into a closet, as we have seen. The back of this closet consisted of a single board only, which was painted dark blue on the side of the library, but was covered with old newspapers on the other side. It may be easily conceived that a person standing inside this closet might easily overhear any conversation that was carried on in the library.

When the captain had arrived at the Castle, the dinner was over, and the gentlemen had retired to the library, that is, the two gentlemen with whom we are concerned; the other gentleman or two having gone home. The housekeeper was therefore at leisure to enjoy herself, and to make much of her friend; and so, after a short chat in the servants' hall, she and the captain retired to her own room to spend an hour there in "peace and quiet." The captain, of course, unburdened himself to his friend shortly after he had taken his seat in the snug armchair beside the cosy fire. He told her all he wanted to tell her as to his apprehensions regarding Bartley. She was already aware of much, indeed almost of everything con-

nected with his character and proceedings;
and she was also aware of her own master's
penchant for Miss Moore. So the captain
hadn't much trouble in putting her in possession of everything that was then occupy-
ing his mind with respect to these matters.
She made him "a nice little warm drop, to
comfort him after his walk;" and she filled
herself a *small glass* of the port wine, with a
little deechy drop of hot water in it, and a
bit of loaf sugar. They talked on about old
times, and how those were better than the
present times—"indeed, 'tisn't the one day
they ought to be compared." And then the
captain threw in a sly hint of former feeling,
and said how the "heart that was once
touched, never forgets answering to its
helm," and so on, until Nelly Bryan—her
face was naturally red and her eyes soft—
glowed very much about the cheeks and
neck, and melted charmingly about the eyes.
She now began to fear that they might be
heard talking, though it was difficult to perceive whence the apprehension could arise,
as the room door, as well as the door of the
closet, was closed, and there was no other
aperture through which sounds could escape,
even if there were any persons outside try-

ing to catch them, as there were not. At all events, she said, "maybe, we might be heard;" and, as she said it, she drew over closer to the captain, and putting her face nearer to his, began to talk in a soft, low voice. The captain, following suit, dropped his voice too, and spoke soft and low. And the housekeeper put her hand on the captain's knee—she should do this in order to ease her bent posture—and the captain put his hand upon her hand, and began to count her fingers.

At length she stood up, and opened the closet door, and listened. She became apparently interested, for she continued to listen for at least ten minutes before she stirred from her position, her ear being all the time inserted between two plates which stood upright against the back of the closet. At the end of ten minutes she returned to the captain, and whispered something into his ear, as though she feared that the air would hear what she had to say. The captain then stood up, and went into the closet, and put his ear to the back of it, and he soon became very interested, too. He just caught Bartley's speech as he was developing his plan for achieving success in the case of Whitmore and Miss Moore, by the destruction of his (Whitmore's) rival, Herbert Granville. The captain listened with breathless attention until Bartley concluded his speech with that remarkable peroration—which he rounded off with a rap of his clenched hand on the table —"Genius is the highest prerogative of man! what do you say, Whitmore, my blade?" The captain then withdrew his ear from the wall, in order to straighten himself and breathe a little freely. But he was too anxious to catch every syllable that might be dropped inside in the library, to keep his ear long from the wall. So he applied it again, and kept it there, notwithstanding the housekeeper's earnest entreaties to "come and sit by the fire, and not be perishing himself there." But he heard nothing further of any importance.

Soon after Bartley Croker left, and the captain had no further business in the closet. He therefore resumed his seat at the fire, and after about half an hour's friendly and confidential conversation with the housekeeper, he took his leave of her; but in doing so his head happened to come in contact with hers, and he couldn't help just touching her lips with his, for the sake of old times.

CHAPTER XXI.

HERBERT GRANVILLE PREPARES TO JOIN HIS
UNCLE IN CANADA—VARIOUS COUNCILS HELD,
AND VARIOUS OPINIONS OFFERED IN CON-
SEQUENCE.

It was now some time since the Ash Grove
family had received a letter, or any intelligence
from Colonel Brown; and they began to
grow uneasy on that account. Uncle Ben
could not make out the cause that influenced
his brother Felix in maintaining so long a
silence, and felt greatly puzzled about it.
Mrs. Granville thought that perhaps he was
sick; and people who are afflicted in that
way do not generally care to trouble themselves about writing; though still she knew
that it would not be the case with herself,
for she always liked to acquaint the various
members of her family with any illness, or
other calamity that might befall herself or

any one of her household. Miss Julia
Granville supposed that her uncle Felix was
getting careless in consequence of his old
age; for she thought that old people found
it difficult and troublesome to be writing
letters. But then, on the other hand, he
might employ an amanuensis, unless he was
unwilling to commit private family affairs to
the secrecy of a stranger. Herbert, however, feared that his uncle was huffed in
consequence of his own procrastination; for
he had more than once told him in his letters
that he would join him shortly. He failed
to fulfil his promise, however, in consequence
of the appointment of which Lord Fairborough
had spoken to him, but which had not yet
turned up. His lordship might have got
him one in Australia, or India, but then he
preferred it in Canada, chiefly on account of
his uncle residing there; but also on account
of the superior advantages of that country,
arising from climate, soil, geographical position, and the character of its inhabitants.
His uncle was not aware of this cause of
delay, though he (Herbert) had mentioned,
in one of his recent letters to him, the kind-
ness and generosity with which Lord Fairborough was endeavouring to promote his

views, by obtaining for him an appointment
in Canada. He therefore felt very uneasy
about his uncle's silence; and determined to
set out, without further delay, and join him.
Uncle Ben shrugged his shoulders; and did
not at all seem satisfied with his nephew's
decision. Mrs. Granville and Julia were
equally dissatisfied. But yet they were all
unwilling to throw any obstacle in the way
of Herbert's prospects. They were unani-
mous on one point, namely, that he should
call upon Lord Fairborough, and acquaint
him with the state of things, and with the
resolution he had formed; and that he should
also see the Rev. Dr. Markham and Sir
Michael Carey, his particular friends, on the
same subject. Herbert concurred in the propriety of this proceeding, and also of modifying his own opinions in accordance with their
views. He accordingly called first upon
lord Fairborough, who became very grave
and thoughtful as soon as he was informed
of the decision of his young friend. His
lordship spoke a good deal upon the subject,
viewing it from all points; but at length
concluded by saying that it could not, at all
events, do any harm that Herbert should
visit his uncle; that he himself would not, in

the meantime, relax his efforts to serve him
in the way he thought best; and that if anything should turn up in accordance with his
views, he would communicate it to him in
Canada. This was satisfactory, inasmuch
as it enabled Herbert to act upon his own
decision without incurring the risk of losing
any advantages which Lord Fairborough's
interest might procure for him.

He then called upon the Rev. Dr. Markham.
The doctor expressed his great regret at his
young friend's decision, and said that he
ought to pause before carrying it into effect.
He did not like to see any of his parishioners
going away, particularly persons of education
and character, like Herbert. Such persons
should remain in their own country to
strengthen and adorn it. He understood
very well, that for a certain class of persons
emigration was desirable, for agricultural
labourers, for instance, or for mechanics, or
for small farmers with a little capital; but
as to gentlemen of a liberal education, and
of character and family, he could not see the
advisability of their emigrating. They were
not fit for the colonies; and the colonies
were not fit for them. It might possibly
happen, in some cases, that such persons

would succeed; but those cases must be
necessarily rare. The colonies required
physical labour, and little else. Education,
talent, character, family, all were thrown
away in the colonies. At least, this was his
view of the matter; and, therefore, he could
not advise his young friend to emigrate.
But then he might go and see his uncle, and
return again; that was another thing. He
shouldn't dissuade him from that. What he
was opposed to was his settling down in a
colony, and expending himself in it. That
would be preposterous.

Herbert was rather pleased with the
doctor's views, for they accorded with his
own feelings; and they also squared in a
great measure with the ideas expressed by
Lord Fairborough. His decision, therefore,
was not shaken. He next paid his visit to
Sir Michael Carey; and laid his plans open
to that gentleman. Sir Michael knew a good
deal about the colonies, and had always
taken an interest in their advancement. He
was particularly taken with the promising
aspect of Canada. He called it a noble
country; and prophesied that it would yet
hold a position not inferior to any country
in the world. Its lands were capable of

maintaining as large a population as the whole of Europe; and its climate was unexceptionable. It would be, in the course of time, the grand receptacle of the overflowing population of these British isles; and of a great portion of that of the other countries of Europe. Its situation, its extent, its fertility, ay, and its climate, were all favourable to this view. He encouraged his young friend to go there ; and said that if he were a young man himself, he would prefer it as a place of residence to any country he knew of. At the same time he could not conceal from himself the regret he should feel at the absence of his friend ; but yet this regret would be modified by the reflection that he (Herbert) would be placed in a position which could not fail to advance his interests and secure his happiness.

This representation of Canada and of its future prospects gave a spring to Herbert's spirits, which caused him to cling more ardently than ever to the decision which he had taken. The family at Ash Grove discussed the various opinions which had thus been offered, each regarding them in the light which accorded best with his or her private views and feelings. Uncle Ben was rather inclined to the opinion of Lord Fairborough, because, while it favoured a visit, on the part of Herbert, to brother Felix, it did not imply a perpetual residence in Canada. The fact was, as regarded Uncle Ben, he would wish that both brother Felix and Herbert were settled in Ireland, and just in that portion of Ireland where he could visit them every day, and talk to them about hounds, and horses, and coveys of partridge. His opinion was entirely shaped in accordance with that one idea. Prosperity in Canada was a matter of no importance to him; they might be as rich as Crœsus there, or as exalted as the sovereign of Britain, for what he thought or cared; but their presence in his own house, or, at all events, in his own neighbourhood, was the great thing with him. Indeed, he never approved of the step taken by brother Felix in going to live in Canada; he couldn't see what he did it for, or what was to come out of it. No man in his senses would do it, he thought. And the sooner he left it, and came to live among his own, where everything was Christian-like and natural, the sooner he would show himself a man of common sense and of proper spirit.

Such was the channel in which ran the

thoughts of Uncle Ben. Mrs. Granville nearly agreed with him, but not entirely. She saw nothing unwise or unworthy in Felix's going to Canada, because he went there for the purpose of taking possession of a large tract of land offered to him by the Government; but she thought that he should have sold that, and then returned home. This was her view of the matter; and she always told her brother so in all her letters to him. What did he want to remain there for, she should like to know. He was unmarried, and had no one to look after him either in health or in sickness. He must be very wretched, she thought; and this idea was ever present to her mind, and gave her a great deal of uneasiness. Julia thought, with the Rev. Dr. Markham, that a colony was not a nice place for a gentleman to live in. She should like dearly, though, to visit her Uncle Felix, with Herbert; and then to return after a few months. This would be pleasant, she thought, unless the travelling by water should make it disagreeable. She did not think that she should like to be in a ship; she never was in one; and the appearance of it, rocking upon the water, always made her feel uncomfortable when she thought of Herbert being in it. She was very confident, though, that Lord Fairborough would not encourage Herbert to do anything that was not right; and this thought reconciled her in a great degree to the idea of her brother going away for a short time. She held Sir Michael Carey in high estimation ; and his opinion had great weight with her; but this was owing to his great knowledge of the colonies, as well as to his character for good sense and a kindly disposition, for which he was so much esteemed by all who knew him. Still, notwithstanding all this, she rather feared that he was an enthusiast on the colonies ; and that he might, in the present instance, be mistaken. Altogether she could not reconcile herself to the idea of her brother going away, unless on one condition, which was that she should herself accompany him. So that, looking at the state of things from every point of view, it was evident to any impartial observer, that the family at Ash Grove was not of one accord as to the advisability of Herbert's emigration. All that could be fairly assumed was, that a short visit to Uncle Felix would meet with no serious objection from any of the family.

However, it soon went abroad in the village and neighbourhood that Mr. Herbert Granville was about to set out for Canada to visit his uncle. Some said that he intended to settle there for ever, as his uncle, the colonel, had settled all his property upon him on that sole condition; and that he was taking Miss Moore with him. With regard to Miss Moore herself there was a considerable divergency of opinion; for some said that she was to be married to him before they left; some others, that she was not to be married until they arrived in Canada, and obtained the colonel's consent; and there was a third party, and it was a strong and confident party too, who maintained that they were already married, and that the colonel was aware of it, and even pleased with it. These were the chief representatives of opinion upon that particular point; but there were thin streaks of opinion, or rather of conjecture, which is about the same thing, running between those various opinions, like small stripes between wide bars, on a piece of printed cotton. One of these was that he wouldn't marry her at all, because she was not of sufficiently high blood for him. Another was, that she wouldn't marry him,

because she was in love with Joe Whitmore.
And another, that Herbert looked forward to
a matrimonial alliance with the family of
Lord Fairborough; and that that was the
reason why his lordship took such an interest
in his fortunes.

We shall mention only one other conjecture, and it was held with great tenacity,
and an amount of plausibility which it was
almost impossible to resist; it was to this
effect, that Sir Michael Carey intended to
bestow one of his daughters upon Herbert—
in fact, that he had already proposed the
matter to him, and that Herbert had assented. In corroboration of this, it was
asserted that Sir Michael and his whole
family were going out to Canada, for the
purpose of establishing themselves there;
so that nothing could be better adapted to
meet all the exigencies of the case:—the
remaining portion of the Granville family
were to follow, including Uncle Ben.

But amid this rainbow variety of public
opinion, there were two persons at least who
were not misled; and who, therefore, relaxed
nothing in their exertions to effect their own
particular purposes; these were Joe Whitmore and Bartley Croker. Joe knew but too

well that Miss Moore was not in love with
him; and not only that, but he further knew
to his utter despair and madness, that she
and Herbert Granville were in love with each
other: he knew these two facts; and he
cared not for any other news. Bartley
Croker, too, with the shrewdness which accompanied his innate villainy, was thoroughly
satisfied that Herbert Granville was not a
man to waver in the pursuit of any laudable
object, or to permit a stain of dishonour to
settle upon his escutcheon. He knew besides,
that Lord Fairborough was in communication with Lord Milford on the subject of
the property held for centuries by the Granville family under the latter nobleman and
his family, but wrested from Herbert's father
through his (Bartley's) own fraudulent and
swindling conduct. This he knew; and it
was this that goaded him on to the destruction of Herbert, if he could only accomplish
his fell purpose through any possible instru-
mentality, no matter how high or how low, or
in what manner or form.

There was a third person, too, who knew
that the reports afloat in connexion with
Herbert's decision to join his uncle in
Canada were ill-founded; and that person

was Peter Mackey, the publican at the Cross.
He was cognizant of all the villainous designs
of Whitmore and of Croker; and his own
personal interests induced him to furnish
himself with all possible information respect-
ing the intentions and movements of Herbert
Granville. Peter, as the] reader is aware,
was a selfish and avaricious villain. Like
most persons of this character, there was in
his composition a prying and inquisitive vein
which kept him constantly on the alert in
the endeavour to discover everything that
was occurring or likely to occur in the families
around him. Like all scandal-hunters he
was frequently imposed upon by persons
who wished to put him on the wrong scent,
knowing the baseness of his character, and
detesting him accordingly; but still, he generally succeeded in ferreting out such information as was essential to his dark and
treacherous designs. He knew everything,
almost, connected with the movements of
Herbert; he was aware of his] attachment to
Miss Moore; he was cognizant of his intention to join his uncle in Canada; he was
aware of his aim to get back his father's
property from Bartley Croker, through the
exertions of Lord Fairborough : he knew all

these things well; but he never pretended
to this knowledge to anybody but to Joe
Whitmore and to Bartley Croker. To these
he communicated whatever he discovered in
reference to these points; but he also took
care, at the same time, to mix up this information with as much falsehood as he deemed
necessary to arouse their hopes or fears, as
the case might be. In short, Peter was not
a tittle inferior in villainy to Bartley himself;
while, as he sometimes insinuated, he could
twist Joe Whitmore on his little finger, since
he was no more than a *gom* (a dribbling
fool). So, when Peter thought it would
suit his purpose he was prepared to inform
Bartley or Whitmore that Herbert was a
member of the Whitefeet organization for
he "made it out, when no other man could."
In fact, Peter, knowing the deep feeling of
hatred which both these gentlemen entertained for Herbert, never ceased inventing
lies of one kind or other about him, to suit
the hour and the occasion.

In the present state of opinion, as regarded
the intentions and movements of Herbert,
Peter was very active, sometimes inclining
to one opinion, and sometimes to another,
and sometimes inventing an opinion, and

putting it on the wing. He visited Bartley at his residence at Gurtroo, one very dark night about this time. He was armed cáp-à-pie to encounter him. The two scoundrels understood each other well; but being of mutual advantage one to the other, they had to disguise their feelings, and assume a friendship and a confidence of the most ardent and unshaken kind. Peter spoke of the different opinions that were abroad, that is, of the opinions which he had himself forged, with a thin sprinkling of the actual reports.

" There's no time to be lost, by jingo," he said; " for 'tis known for certain that he (Herbert) is goin' sthraight to Lunnun (London) to see Lord Milford himself, wid strong letthers in his pocket from Lord Fairborough. That's what's said now; and 'tis thrue, for I heeard it, by jing, in a way that no mortial man could find out but myself. And another thing that's said is, that when he'll come from Lunnun he'll be agent over all Lord Milford's estates, in this and every other county they're lyin' in. There's no mistake at all about that. And besides, when he'll come back he'll not mind marryin' at all. Myself don't know how Mr. Whitmore will

like it; but 'tis said for certain that Miss
Moore and Herbert Granville are separated
for ever, by consint of both.   Oh, that's as
thrue as you're there. *I know it.* So Mr.
Whitmore 'll have no trouble at all in gettin'
her now."

He threw his eye slyly across at Bartley,
to mark how he took the news, as he called
his own lying invention.

Bartley looked, or pretended to look, troubled; as if he saw a chance of losing the
co-operation of Whitmore in his designs on
the life of Herbert; and Peter saw, or
thought he saw, that he hit his mark.   He,
therefore, said no more; for, as he observed,
when he related the circumstance to Jer
Grinnex a day or two afterwards, " I thought
it a pity to spile the sthroke, by jing."   The
truth is, that Bartley did not believe one
word of all that Peter had told him; but, as
we have said, he *pretended* to be troubled
about it, in order to deceive Peter and throw
him off his guard.   Bartley knew precisely
how far he had to fear the interference of
Lord Fairborough; he knew well that his
lordship had not interfered at all in Lord
Milford's private arrangements, and that it
was not at all likely he would do so.   It was

not fear, so much as hatred, that influenced
Bartley; though there is no doubt that a
certain fear was mixed with his hatred; a
fear, however, which did not proceed from
any apprehension that Lord Fairborough
would meddle with the affairs of Lord Milford's estates; but from the consciousness
that he had inflicted a great injury upon
Herbert, which injury might, in some way or
other, be discovered and avenged. In one
word, he injured Herbert, and he therefore
hated him. So that when Peter Mackey
chuckled at the idea of having made a good
sthroke, as he called his lying story, he was
only deceiving himself. And he was equally
deceiving himself when he fancied that the
story of a separation having taken place
between Herbert and Miss Moore would
influence the action of Bartley. Bartley did
not believe one word of this either. In fact,
he believed nothing of all that which Peter
had told him. He *saw* at once the channel
in which Peter's mind was running; which
was simply to rouse him (Bartley) to immediate action against the life of Herbert, and
thereby to promote the views of Joe Whitmore without exposing the latter gentleman
to any danger arising from a participation in

such action. Bartley, therefore, *pretended* to
be troubled, in order to carry out his own
plan of inveighing Joe Whitmore into the
perpetration of the deed which he felt so
anxious to see accomplished, that is, the
removal of Herbert Granville from his path,
either by fair or foul means. Bartley having
now, by his *pretended* uneasiness, thrown
Peter off his guard, commenced to ply him
as follows,—

" I must say, Mr. Mackey, that this news
disturbs me very much. I cannot entertain
a doubt that you have been thoroughly
informed ; and therefore I consider it necessary not to lose a moment in guarding myself
against any probable danger that may arise
from the circumstances you have mentioned.
It strikes me now that I should lose no time
in determining on the best course to be
adopted in this emergency. My first idea is,
to proceed immediately to London, and have
an interview with my Lord Milford. I shall
then inform myself correctly of everything
touching that portion of your information
which has respect to Lord Fairborough's
intermeddling with my Lord Milford's affairs ;
and as to the other matter—I mean that
which relates to Herbert Granville and Miss

Moore—it doesn't concern me. But, as I apprehend that my Lord Milford will not be found in London at the present moment, I shall, very probably, have to proceed to the Continent ; and this will take me a considerable time before I shall be able to be back here again — not unlikely six months, or more. So that by that time Herbert Granville and Miss Moore will have had ample space and opportunity to settle their little differences, whatever they may be ; or failing this, Mr. Whitmore will be, perhaps, in a position to claim her as his own."

Peter Mackey looked a little chopfallen, his eye fell, and his tongue swept round his upper lip, as he laboured in thought. He felt that the victory he had calculated upon only a few seconds before was in danger of being lost. His tongue went round and round his lip ; and still he failed to evolve anything from his mind that was calculated to meet the crisis. If Bartley should go, and remain away six months, it was difficult to say what turn things might take. One thing only appeared certain to him in such an event, and it was this, that he himself would be left alone with Joe Whitmore to manage matters which required the utmost skill and daring of the most unscrupulous and most practised villain. He did not like this idea. Although he was not at all doubtful as to the amount of the bribe which he would be able to command from Whitmore, yet he did not feel so safe in acting alone with Whitmore, as if he had the co-operation of Bartley. Whitmore would act, he was aware; but then Whitmore was not a man to be relied upon, in point of sagacity or skill. Besides this, Peter expected a trifle from Bartley, in addition to the bribe he knew he would be able to extort from Whitmore. So that, taking everything into consideration, the idea of Bartley's absence from the scene of action was grating to the sensibility of Peter Mackey. His tongue still went round and round his upper lip, and his eyes remained half closed. He appeared to be nonplussed. Bartley seemed to enjoy his discomfiture, for he eyed him keenly, whilst a grin of the most savage description settled in one corner of his mouth.

At length a bright idea seemed to flash across Peter's mind, for the tongue was drawn in, and the eyes opened gradually, and rested upon the crown of Bartley's head. He saw the only chance now was to hasten

the catastrophe as much as possible; that is,
to bring about the attack upon Herbert's life
within the briefest space consistent with due
and careful preparation. Keeping this idea
in view, he observed,—

" What I was thinkin' of, Mr. Croker, was
as this ; that 'tis hard to believe everything
a body hears these times—God help us !—the
people are givin' to lies in sich a way now,
that, by jing, 'tisn't easy to know what to
believe, and what not to believe. Maybe,
after all, there's not much truth about Lord
Fairborough botherin' himself at all about
Lord Milford's estates. How the Jericho
could any one know one way or t'other?
What I suspects now is as this,"—and here his
eyes began to twinkle with a lurid glare—
" that some people would like to have you go
away, so as to let young Granville have full
scope to make his own plans widout any one
to spile (spoil) 'em on him. That's what I
suspects. And now, Mr. Croker, are you the
man to allow a brat of a pretindher to cross
your path, widout puttin' your heel on his
nick ? "

He started to his legs as he began to utter
these last words, and walked up and down
the floor, brandishing one of his arms, the

other arm being plunged into the waistband
of his breeches. After concluding, he stood
before Bartley, and threw his eyes with a
fierce glare into his face. Bartley never
shrunk for a second, but bore the assault
with all the cool and rigid indifference of his
nature. After a brief space he quietly observed,—

"As to crossing *my* path, I care very
little about that. He can do me no harm—
not the least. It is my friend, and your
friend, Mr. Whitmore, for whom I feel concerned. We all know that Mr. Whitmore is
a man of probity and of high honour; that
he abhors everything low and mean—in
short, Mackey, Mr. Whitmore is a Christian
gentleman. Very well, when a man is a
good Christian, like our friend; when he
fears God and obeys His laws, and when his
mind is fixed upon the eternal salvation of
his soul, his views and interests ought to obtain the support of every good man. It is
for the interests of society that it should be
so. On that account, therefore, you and I
concern ourselves about the personal matters
of Mr. Whitmore. We are not ourselves
personally interested; the utmost that can
be said in that respect is, that we participate

in the general advantages of society, and so
to that extent we are of course interested,
but no farther. You understand me, Mr.
Mackey. Now I would urge upon you to see
Mr. Whitmore, and to use all your influence
with him—for I know you possess influence
with him, and very naturally, on account of
your superior intelligence and your Christian
morals—to lose no time in maturing any
plan that he may determine upon for the
benefit of society. These troublous times,
my dear Mackey, admit of no delay on the
part of those who desire the stability of the
British empire, and the general peace and
welfare of society. Those Whitefeet must
be arrested in their dangerous machinations
—I mean, of course, the leaders of them—
you understand me; the dupes of these men
it is impossible to blame very much; poor
creatures, they know not what they do. But
such men as Granville—you understand me
—they are a pest, sir; they are a pest that
should be removed radically—yes, *radically*,
my dear Mackey, *radically.*"

As he thus spoke, he rose; and taking
Peter Mackey gently by the coat-collar, he
breathed a very gentle breath into his ear;
and the breath bore these words : " See to it,

my dear fellow; see to it. Delays are dangerous."

Peter scarcely knew what he should do. He saw clearly enough that further conversation at that time would profit nothing, and therefore he resolved to take his departure, leaving it to future reflection to strike out a new plan of action. He accordingly wished Bartley a good-bye, assuring him in the most earnest and energetic manner that he would be always his *thrue* friend.

CHAPTER XXII.

GENERAL DOHERTY IS PUT IN MOTION—A PLAN
OF ATTACK IN TWO DIVISIONS.

IT was now generally known throughout
Ballydine and the neighbourhood all round,
that Herbert Granville was about proceeding
to Canada to join his uncle Felix; and, as
we have seen, people were variously affected
by the intelligence. Joe Whitmore was im-
merged in doubt as to the precise part which
Fanny Moore was disposed to act, or would
be compelled to act, on this occasion. He
heard that she had no intention of getting
married to Herbert, and of accompanying
him to Canada; but he had no idea as to her
or his ultimate views with regard to marriage.
Some persons told him that they were engaged to be married upon his return from
Canada, which would be in a brief period;
and others informed him that they had been

already secretly married, and that it was her
intention to join him in Canada in the course
of a few months. This latter intelligence,
however, he disregarded upon the assurance
of her mother as well as of her aunt, Mrs.
Crcdan. His great object, therefore, was to
prevent their being united at any future
time ; and to accomplish this he directed all
his energies, calling in the assistance of his
ingenious friends, Bartley Croker and Peter
Mackey. We have seen how these two last-
named gentlemen were endeavouring to over-
reach each other, and to shift the responsibi-
lity of their portions of the drama from the
shoulders of the one to those of the other.
Bartley was anxious for the destruction of
Herbert, but wished to avoid, by all possible
means, his being identified as participating
in the act. Peter Mackey, on the other
hand, was desirous of placing Bartley in the
foreground, and thereby covering himself
from view, while he clutched the double
bribe—one from Bartley, the other from
Whitmore. His intention was to use Jer
Grinnex in the conduct of the business, by
placing him under the patronage of Bartley,
and thus securing himself against the consequences of a miscarriage. Joe Whitmore,

however, had not yet given up his favourite plan of a forcible abduction, and was only waiting to see how events might develop themselves from day to day.

Fanny Moore was greatly affected when Herbert broke to her his final decision to join his uncle, though she was somewhat prepared for it from their former frequent conversations on the subject. On this occasion they were sitting in the summer-house of the garden at Ash Grove, after he had returned from his visit to Sir Michael Carey, which we mentioned in a former chapter. He told her where he had been, and detailed to her everything that had occurred at the interview, as also at the other interviews with Lord Fairborough and the Rev. Dr. Markham. She listened to him with a sad and pale countenance, occasionally putting her pocket-handkerchief to her eyes, and wiping away the tears which were silently rolling down her cheeks. After he had concluded, her fortitude abandoned her, and she flung herself upon his bosom, throwing her arms around his neck, and bursting into a loud cry. He soothed her with all the endearing tenderness prompted by his deep love for her, and endeavoured to rouse her from her dejection, by assuming a cheerfulness which he but little felt, and by referring to the very brief interval that was to intervene before his return. After a little time she became composed, and expressed herself as being prepared to endure anything for his sake.

"Dear Herbert," she said, " I cannot help feeling, not so much for myself as for you. I shall be safe, and—" she was going to say "happy," but she could not belie her heart, so she substituted "resigned." "I shall be safe and resigned at home; but you will be exposed to the dangers of the ocean, without a friend to cheer you; without any of the comforts to which you have been accustomed. And then, when you arrive in a strange land, your days will be lonely; and you will be thinking, with a sad heart, of those whom you left behind you, and who would be so happy—oh, how happy—to be at your side, and to cheer your solitary hours."

Here she burst into tears again, and bent her head upon his bosom. He, too, was deeply affected, and wiped away the tears from his eyes more than once while she spoke. He said, after a while, " I trust, my dear Fanny, that you will not permit yourself to indulge in any gloomy forebodings while I am away from you.

Remember that I am yours; and though I am obliged to part from you for a time, I shall again return to you with redoubled affection, and we shall be happy together for ever. The time of our separation shall not be long, for I am resolved to return after I have spent a few months with my uncle, no matter what may arise. If he should insist upon my ultimately settling in Canada, I shall at all events return, and take you back there with me, after we shall have been married here. So there is no reason why either of us should feel disheartened; on the contrary, we should feel comforted from the consciousness of our mutual love, and in the prospect of a life which my heart tells me will be one of pure and unalloyed happiness. After all, we could not have expected to have our path in this life clear of obstruction from beginning to end. To suffer is inseparable from human existence. And those who pass through this condition in the early part of life are better prepared to meet the vicissitudes which may arise in its succeeding stages. At least, let us hope for the best. I cannot, at the same time, conceal from you, or from myself, the feeling of loneliness which oppresses me when I think of being separated from you, even for

a short time; but then we must be brave.
Yes, to use your own expression, so often
addressed by you to me on other occasions,
we must be brave. I know you will always
think of me when I am away; but let me
request of you to mingle those thoughts of me
with the bright hope of our meeting again in
joy and happiness. In this way our separation will be relieved of the sadness which
would otherwise hang around it, and the hours
and days will pass away in the sunlight of
peace and hope. I shall write to you the
moment I shall have landed in Canada, and
shall continue to do so at every opportunity.
I shall expect you to do the same. So you
see, my sweet little woman,"—here he patted
her playfully on the cheek—" we shall not be
altogether miserable while away from each
other's society. But, by-the-bye, I have no
doubt that you will sometimes be obliged to
hear some evil things said of me while I am
away. But do not be troubled on that
account. You know that this is one of the
things we sometimes have to endure in this
life. Indeed, it could not be otherwise, unless we
were to suppose that there is no evil on earth.
But we cannot deceive ourselves by any sup-
position of that sort. Let us—if we may use
the divine name of our Saviour without irre-

verence when speaking of ourselves—let us
always remember that He suffered the stings
of the evil tongue during His short sojourn
here; and let us not forget, either, that His
chosen successors shared a similar fate. It
matters little what may be said of us in the
way of reproach by evil-minded persons; our
safeguard, our consolation, and our antidote
lie in our consciousness of rectitude. You
will not, therefore, mind what evil they may
speak of me. Some will speak kindly of me,
I have no doubt, and to these your ears will
be turned with gladness. You see there is no
evil without its antidote. Well; I am
fatiguing you now. We shall have other
opportunities of telling our thoughts to each
other before I go. So we shall now speak of
something else. Let us walk through the
garden."

Such was the manner in which Fanny
Moore received the account of Herbert's
intended departure from Herbert's own
lips. Her feelings were deeply affected; she
was sad and sorrowful. But not so did she
bear herself when, some days afterwards the
subject was brought under her notice by her
mother and her aunt, Mrs. Credan. They
wished to probe her feelings with reference
to Herbert, and to turn her attention away

from him altogether, by representing any friendship, as they expressed it, which she might have felt towards him, in the light of a childish fancy.

Mrs. Credan said, " Now, my dear Fanny, you must allow me to be a judge in these matters; I have been a girl once like yourself, and I had my fancies, too, like you. But these things pass away with our years ; and you will be surprised, in the course of time, at your own folly in pursuing mere shadows. No, my dear, you must look to the substance of things, and doubt your own judgment when you are troubled with fancies. To be sure, no one questions that Mr. Granville is a very proper man, of good presence and ancient family, and all that; but you must know— and you will hereafter discover—that these mere outside attractions are not what con- stitute our happiness in this world. As I have said, you must learn to doubt yourself, and be guided by the experience of those who know the world, and who know what is best for you. Your father and mother are the persons most interested in your welfare ; and I am sure you will allow that next to them I feel the deepest interest in your happiness. Well, we are all opposed to your throwing

your life away upon a person like Mr. Granville, who has no means of making you comfortable, or of giving you that position in
society to which your birth and your family
entitle you. You ought, my dear, to attend
to what our experience points out to you as
the most desirable course to follow." In this
strain she continued for some time, while
Fanny listened with respectful attention, but
with an evident disapproval of the advice
tendered by her aunt. Mrs. Moore followed
up the same line of observation, and endeavoured to win over the mind of her daughter
to a calm and rational view of what her best
friends considered her true interest. But
although Fanny was respectful in her attention to all that was urged both by her aunt
and her mother, her feelings remained wholly
unmoved by all that they said. She felt not
the slightest inclination in favour of their
views ; nor was the deep spring of her affection for Herbert Granville in the slightest
degree disturbed by their representations.
At the same time, she was unwilling to unveil
the sanctuary of her heart to the profane gaze
of even her mother and aunt. That was too
sacred a spot for any, save her own Herbert,
to look upon. She therefore confined herself

to a mere passing commentary on the advice that was tendered to her, without entering seriously upon the subject which was dearest to her heart. She said, "Well, really I have no intention at present of getting married; but that I do intend to get married some time or another is, of course, true; but I cannot say when that time will come. I am quite sure that you, my dear aunt, as well as my mamma, have no other desire than the promotion of my happiness. Of that, indeed, I cannot entertain a doubt. But I believe also that you would not wish to force me into any marriage contrary to my own feelings. I have no desire to marry at present, nor can I really say at what time I shall be in a condition to take that step. But this I must say at once, so as to prevent any further conversation about it, that I shall never marry Joe Whitmore. Nothing on earth could induce me to marry him. I have more than once expressed myself to this effect before, and I now repeat it. And, further, I say, that rather than marry him I would beg, or starve, ay, or die. There now is the solemn declaration of my soul. I trust, therefore, my dear aunt, that you will never again mention his name to me; and, dear mamma, I am sure that you will not, now that you know the feelings of my heart on this subject, annoy yourself or me by referring to it any more. I shall be content with the suggestions of my own heart, and for my happiness I shall rest upon the providence of God. Here my faith is fixed, and I feel that I shall not be disappointed." She then stood up and walked over to her mother and kissed her cheek. She did the same with her aunt, and then left the room.

But while this agitation was going on among the ladies, Joe Whitmore and Bartley Croker, with their understrappers, Peter Mackey and Jer Grinnex, were not idle spectators of passing events. The two first-named gentlemen met by appointment, and discussed the subject nearest to their heart, each contending for his own view of the course to be adopted just as it suited his own particular interest. Joe was, at first, very tenacious of his original purpose of abducting Miss Moore by force, since he saw in this the proudest triumph he could achieve over Herbert Granville, for, as he urged, "it would cut him to the very centre of his heart." This, he thought, would be better than murdering him; for if he were once dead he could suffer no more; but by being alive, and seeing the girl of his heart in the possession of another, he would be suffering a repeated death, that is, a continuous death in life. And Joe gloated over this idea.

Bartley Croker, however, thought otherwise; and he was not a man who would permit an inferior villain to himself, like Joe Whitmore, to overrule him. He accordingly took up Joe's arguments seriatim, and "thumped them to powder," as he afterwards said. He pointed out the folly of supposing that Miss Moore, even in the event of her being abducted, would be reconciled to her abductor. So far, he thought, would Whitmore be from establishing a triumph over his rival, Mr. Granville, by such a course, that he should only expose himself to derision, perhaps to ruin. But there was the probable failure of the enterprise to be considered. It might not be so easy as Whitmore imagined to take Miss Moore forcibly from her father's house. Even if her parents and her aunt, Mrs. Credan, favoured the design, there were other difficulties in the way. Would her brother, Harry Moore, who loved her so dearly, and who was so deeply and tenderly interested in the fortunes of the Granville family—would he be ineffective in his resistance to any outrage offered to his sister? But was it likely either that old Mr. Moore would assent to any arrangement touching the abduction of his daughter, no matter what his wife or sister-in-law might think about it. Was it not most probable that he would not listen to such a thing, and that his wife and sister-in-law would not dare to mention such a thing to him? Then, look at the personal danger to Joe Whitmore himself which this matter involved. The probabilities were all on the side of the opinion that his ruin would be the inevitable consequence of any attempt of the sort contemplated. Thus Bartley reasoned, placing Whitmore's plan of operation in every point of view that was calculated to influence its rejection and the adoption of his own. Whitmore at length began to waver in his purpose, notwithstanding the great *éclat* which he had promised himself from the abduction; and the terrible torture which he believed it would inflict upon the heart of Herbert Granville. Joe Whitmore was a vain villain; indeed we are not sure but that all villains are vain; for vanity would appear to be a part, and no small part, of the natural constitution of the generality of villains to be

met with in ordinary life. But be that as it
may, Joe was doubtless afflicted with a large
share of vanity; and therefore to be deprived of the " glory," as he termed it, of
carrying off Miss Moore, was in no small
degree painful to him. It was hard to make
up for this in any other way. As to Herbert
Granville's destruction, he didn't much care
about that, one way or another, except that
he wouldn't go to the trouble of having any
active hand in it himself. It might be done,
for aught he cared; but he did not set his
heart upon it. He wished him to be removed out of his way, to be sure; that was
an important object with him ; but he should
as soon have it done by transportation, or
hanging, or any other way as by murder.
Bartley Croker, however, was of a different
opinion. He was not a man of half-measures.
He held it as a fixed principle from which
there should be no deviation, that any man
who stood in the line of your ambition or
your interest should be removed from it in
the most effectual way; that is, in such a
way that no apprehension need ever be
entertained of him. To effect such a removal,
then, there was but one way, and that was
his absolute destruction. Bartley, too, was

a pious man—we do not mean, of course,
that he was actually so, but we mean that he
assumed the outward expression and sem-
blance of piety, and made it a most important
portion of his system of villainy to impress
an opinion of his piety upon every person
with whom he came into contact. His being
an attorney by profession, too, added greatly
to the advantages which he hoped to derive
from this deception; for his being known
and spoken of as a "pious attorney" would
be regarded as one of the wonders of the
world, and could not fail to surround him
with overflowing confidence and all its consequent benefits. It is true that he assumed
this piety at the time that he had been a
practising attorney, and before he became
agent to Lord Milford; but as it was a wise
measure then, he had no reason to think that
it would not be equally wise and beneficial to
continue it through every ramification of his
career. At all events, he *did* continue it;
and he still endeavoured to be recognized as
the "pious attorney." To be sure, Joe
Whitmore understood him pretty well, that
is, as far as his inferior degree of roguery
enabled him to penetrate the more extensive
regions of Bartley's villainy. He knew him

well enough, at all events, to see that on the present occasion he was anxious only about his own property and character, and desirous of removing every possible chance of having either of them sifted or disturbed. But Whitmore had his own turn to serve, and he was incapable of effecting anything without Bartley's assistance; so he was obliged to submit to his fate, and to adopt the course marked out by his friend's superior ingenuity. It was therefore resolved between them that an attack should be made, in the shape of a Whitefeet invasion, upon the Ash Grove House, and that the attack should be so arranged as to provide for the greatest possible probability of Herbert's being shot. They could not of course devise any plan that would ensure his certain death, since there was no doubt that he would defend himself; but the greatest probability of arriving at that end was all that could be aimed at in the arrangement, and to this they applied themselves. Who was to lead the attack? This was a question which presented some difficulty. They saw at once that Paddy Larkin was not the man to suit their purpose in that respect, since his devotion to the interests of the Ash Grove family was well known. Then there was another difficulty, which was equally insurmountable; it was this, that Paddy being the chief officer of the "Army of Freedom" in his own district, no operation could be planned or carried out there without his concurrence and superior control. In fact, they saw that Paddy was not available for their purpose; and that in order to be successful they must hide their design altogether from that gentleman. What then was to be done? Bartley Croker struck out the plan at once, that is, after they had determined upon ignoring the services of Paddy Larkin.

The plan was this : Jer Grinnex was to be employed to enter into an arrangement with the General of the Ballydine Division of the Army of Freedom, with the view of effecting the purpose in hand. The general, through Grinnex, was to be informed that a certain sum of money was to be placed at his disposal in consideration of his acting in conformity with the views of a certain party, to him unknown, but who, he was to understand, were equally interested with himself in promoting the cause of Irish freedom. The part which he would be called upon to act was this: on a certain night, and at a certain hour, he was to order a combined attack on two points within the district of Ballydine; that Ash Grove House was to be one of these points; and that the other would be left to his own discretion. He was to appoint Jer Grinnex commanding officer in the movement upon Ash Grove House; while Paddy Larkin was to be placed in command of the other attack. It was determined that four men should be detailed as the force which Jer Grinnex was to lead in his part of the attack, and that these men should be strangers, that is, that they should not belong to the village or immediate neighbourhood of Ballydine. It was suggested that Cushport men, or Corrigcastle men would be the best suited to the purpose. Furthermore, the general was to be instructed not to acquaint Paddy Larkin with the second portion of the combined attack, that is, that portion which had Ash Grove House for its object.

This was, of course, essential; for otherwise Paddy, instead of pressing on, and carrying the fortress, assigned as his portion of the work, at the point of the sword, would most probably fall back; and in place of aiding, would throw his whole force into a resistance to the whole plan of operation. Bartley Croker next suggested that Jer Grinnex should be placed in immediate communication with Peter Mackey, the publican, who was to act as the mainspring to the whole machine.

" You see, my dear fellow," said he, addressing Joe Whitmore, and taking him soothingly by the coat-collar at the same time, " You see, my dear fellow, that it would never do for us to be *seen* in this affair. We must be as if we were not. Mackey will transact the whole business; he is a shrewd, keen fellow, and alive to his own interest—i' faith! for that matter I'd back him against the kingdom," and here he chuckled with great self-complacency, drawing himself up, and placing his arms akimbo. He then resumed, " We must place a fair sum of money in his hands, so as to set him in motion. Promises would be of no avail with him; for he seems to have a low opinion of mankind; not like you and me, Whitmore, whose confidence in our fellow-men is beyond suspicion, eh?"— and he winked and smirked at his companion, who returned the intelligence in a sort of faded echo; " yes, Mackey will re-

quire a sum of money to grease the springs
of the machinery and put it into motion."

" But," interrupted Whitmore, " does
Mackey know who this general is? I think
it is important that we should be informed
upon this matter before we put our hands
in our pockets. If he is ignorant upon this
point, and if it must be that he has to depend on Grinnex for information, I should
not, for my part, venture to spend any
money on the affair."

" Bless your soul," replied Bartley, " he
knows him as sure as he knows his right
hand. Know him? why whom does he not
know? If this general be not a myth—if
he really exists, Mackey knows him, you may
depend upon it. But if he do not exist, if
he be a mere imaginary creation; a voice, a
name, a rallying point, a *shibboleth*, in a word ;
still, our purpose can be served quite as effi-
ciently as if he were an embodiment of flesh
and blood. Let Mackey alone for that. Now,
look here," he pressed up closely to Whitmore, placing his hand upon his shoulder,
and his lips to his ear, and whispering very
gently, "place a hundred pounds in Mackey's
hands, with suitable instructions, and then
let the thing work itself."

He then drew back his head, and looked half-smilingly into Joe's face, as if to mark the effect, the soothing effect, as he believed of his whispered words upon him.

But Joe did not seem to be quite charmed with the words of his friend; for instead of appearing pleased, as was expected, his face became shaded with a passing cloud, through which his eyes looked out rayless and muddy.

Bartley saw this at once, and at once proceeded to rectify his error.

" Now, Whitmore," he said, " you understand this hundred pounds is only a loan, a temporary loan. Mackey is to return it— we shall have this in writing, observe—as soon as he is compensated, at least to an equal amount, for his services to the Government in striking the first blow at this gigantic conspiracy." His eyes twinked with a lurid glare as he spoke: " And," he continued, " look at the exalted position you shall have attained in the estimation of the king, when his Majesty shall have been informed, as he shall have been, of the noble part you had taken on behalf of the Crown."

Bartley waved his hand in confirmation of the soundness of the view he had thus placed under the eyes of his companion; and then seated himself; folding his arms across his breast, and looking up to the ceiling.

Whitmore appeared somewhat stunned with the new idea; and could make no reply for some minutes. He paced the room, up and down, and then looked out at the window; and then rubbed his eyes. After that he appeared to brighten up; and the next evidence of returning sagacity was a smile which quivered sluggishly over his face. He then sat beside his companion, and said in the most confidential manner possible,—

" My dear Croker, I leave the management of this business altogether in your hands; I am now ready to carry out with you any arrangement which your superior judgment suggests. I shall place the necessary funds in your hands, to be disposed of in the manner best calculated to effect our purposes."

Having delivered himself of these very sagacious observations; and feeling a flow of spirit which operated very kindly upon him, he slapped his hand upon his companion's knee, exclaiming,—

" Cracko! you are a man of genius, Croker. I never doubted your great qualities; and I now see that heaven has stamped them with its power. Croker!"—here he took his companion by the hand, and shook him warmly—"if you and I only stood, for even once, in presence of the king, and heard him say, 'Mr. Whitmore, I thank you for your services to the Crown,'—eh, Croker? If I heard these words addressed to me by the king—yes, by our sovereign lord, the king—cracko! there, Croker; cracko! I say." He sprang to his legs, and paced the room with rapid strides, waving his handkerchief and muttering something about majesty, sovereign, glory, realm.

Matters having been thus far adjusted between the two chief plotters, it only remained now to engage the services of Peter Mackey, the publican, and Jer Grinnex, the patriot; and to put the plot in train for execution. Peter Mackey was accordingly sent for by Bartley Croker a day or two after this last interview between himself and Joe Whitmore; and the arrangement mentioned above was submitted to him. He hesitated for a moment about accepting the part assigned to himself; but after Bartley had developed the plot in all its minutiæ, and shown the advantages which were sure to flow from it to the public interests generally, and to Peter himself in particular, the latter waived his objections, and entered heartily into the views of his employers. He stipulated, however, that he should receive the sum of fifty pounds immediately, and before he proceeded a step in the execution of the plot; "because," as he said, "I must grease the hands of Jer Grinnex before I can make him stir an inch. And another thing, Mr. Croker, I must tell you—if you don't know it a'ready—that there's no man in the county able to handle the same Jer but myself; but, so itself, I could never make any cloth out of him widout puttin' the ready rhino into his fist. So you see it stands to reason to give me the fifty pounds. I'll take care of it, and make it go far. You know me, Mr. Croker, to be an honest man that 'ud niver deceive a friend or keep a shillin' that didn't fairly belong to me. I'll settle for the hire o' the men; and do everything that's needful. Four men will be enough, besides Jer himself; because, you see, the fewer the betther. There'll be less noise, and surer work. There's no one, you may say, in Ash Grove House to be afraid of, exceptin' Herbert himself; for ould Ben ain't able to do anything; and the two ould

men that's sarvants there, instead of fightin'
or the like, will crawl undher the beds to
hide themselves. To be sure, Herbert 'll
stand out like a lion; but so much the
betther; since the men 'll have a fair open
aim at him. Lay the money on my hands;
and then name the night for the work."

Bartley saw that it was useless to attempt
to enlist the services of Peter without giving
him the sum he asked; he therefore placed
the money in his hands, with the injunction
to spend only as much of it as was necessary
to engage the services of Grinnex and the
four other men who were to be employed.
Whatever amount remained over this was to
be accounted for and considered as a portion
of the sum which should be determined upon
as his (Mackey's) own reward for his successful execution of the plot. Now, although
Bartley accompanied the money with this
injunction, he had not the least idea that
Peter would give an honest account of it;
on the contrary, he felt quite sure that he
would place the whole of it, or nearly the
whole of it, in his own purse; and that the
only payment he would make to Grinnex and
his four assistants would be a few pints of
whisky, and perhaps a few shillings in their

pockets after their work of blood was done ; yet he wished in this covert way to intimate to him that a farther sum was to be given him, for his services in the faithful and effective discharge of the task assigned to him.

Peter Mackey, having put the fifty pounds in his pocket, and having agreed to acquaint Bartley with the completion of the necessary arrangements, and the time when he would be prepared to act in the final execution of the plot, took his leave, and proceeded homewards. But he had not gone more than a mile when he met Jer Grinnex approaching him on the road. Jer told him that he had called at his house ; and finding that he had been absent, and that he had gone on the Gurtroo road, he strolled along that way in the hope of meeting him. They walked along together ; and Peter told him that a good time was coming, and that his (Jer's) fortune would be made very soon unless it was his own fault. He told him in the strictest confidence that the Government would give any money to have Herbert Granville put out of the way, because they had heard that he was a very bad and dangerous man, and that he plotted their overthrow.

That, moreover, they had heard that he (Jer Grinnex) was a good and loyal subject, and in every respect a worthy and deserving man; and that they believed he was the only person they could rely upon to put Granville out of the way. If he did this service for them, they said, in the presence of the Lord Lieutenant of Ireland, that they would make a man of him, and give him the finest house and farm in the county. In this way Peter went on to ply his companion, as they walked along.

Jer felt greatly elated at the idea that the Government held him in such high estimation, and that there was such great luck in store for him as to become the proprietor of the finest house and farm in the county. He was, therefore, ready to do anything, and to run all sorts of risk to serve the Crown, without taking further thought than that of the future reward that was held out for his services. So he agreed at once to employ the four best men he could get either in Cushport or Corrigcastle to join him in the proposed undertaking; and he further agreed to speak to General Doherty (for he was one of the general's right-hand men), for the purpose of getting him to order an

N 2

attack on any night that would suit (it
should be, of course, on the same night on
which the attack was to be made on Ash
Grove House), on some other point, and to
place Paddy Larkin in command of it.

Having arrived at the Cross of Ballydine,
Peter Mackey took his companion with him
into his house; and having treated him to
a glass or two of his best whisky, he dis-
missed him on the business in hand, enjoin-
ing him not to allow the grass to grow under
his feet until he saw General Doherty, and
did everything necessary for the accomplishment of the great design on which his
fortune now hung.

A day or two passed over, during which
all parties interested in the forthcoming dis-
play of the great Army of Freedom were
busily occupied in the necessary preparations.
Several interviews took place between Bartley Croker and Joe Whitmore; and also
between Peter Mackey and Jer Grinnex; and
the night for the combined attack was ap-
pointed; and the two *corps d'armée* with
their respective commanders were detailed
for this double service. The night would
be dark, for the moon was on the wane; and
the hour of one o'clock in the morning was

deemed the most favourable ; this was the hour fixed for the attack on Ash Grove House : but the hour for the other attack, which was intended upon a police-barrack about a mile and a half distant from the Cross of Ballydine and at the foot of a hill lying to the west of Glen Corril, was left to the decision of General Doherty, who was to direct Paddy Larkin in that behalf.

On the morning of the day preceding the contemplated attack, Peter Mackey and Jer Grinnex breakfasted together at the house of the former; and this they did according to arrangement, in order to keep fresh in their minds the method and manner of the advance, assault, and retreat. The ostensible object of the assault was to take possession of the fire-arms at Ash Grove House for the use and benefit of the Army of Freedom; but the real object, which was kept from the knowledge of the rank and file, and only known to their commander, Jer Grinnex, was to shoot down Herbert Granville.

" You are to bring up your men along the avenue," said Peter, repeating the order of advance, " until ye reach the little pond by the side of the lawn. Yourself and two of

your men will then take a stand between the
upper edge of the pond and the corner of
the house in a line with the hall-door, and
under the shade of the beech-tree; and the
other two men are to steal along by the wall
till they come to the hall-door, where they
are to knock as loud as they can with the
butt-end of their carbines, and demand admittance in the name of the Army of Freedom. Then 'tis like that Master Herbert
will show himself above at one of the
windows, and ask what is wantin'. If he
opens the window, and stands fair front, a
shot would be the best answer to give him;
for, you see, that would silence him, and
make the business easy for the men to enter
and take the fire-arms. But, maybe, he
wouldn't stand fair front; if so, the hall-
door is to be burst in with the sledges; and
that'll either bring him down, or make him
put out his head at the window to fire. If
he comes down, a bould rush at him in the
hall, wid a pike or two will do the job; but
if not, and that he puts out his head to fire
down, two slaps together at him, wid two
carbines, will be shure to splinther him. If
not, in together with ye all, and pound away.
When 'tis all over, away wid ye then, and

never rest ham till ye reach the hill beyond Corrigcastle; and there ye can hide in the woods until the next night, and no one 'll be the wiser."

CHAPTER XXIII.

THE ATTACK—ITS CONSEQUENCES.

WE showed in a former chapter that John Gorman, the captain, became acquainted with the designs of Bartley Croker and Joe Whitmore through the medium of his friend and former lady-love, Nelly Bryan, the housekeeper at Castle Whitmore. This information, as the reader is aware, was obtained on the evening when the captain was entertained in the housekeeper's room in the rear of the library. On that occasion the housekeeper overheard the conversation of her master and Bartley Croker, as she happened to enter the closet which stood in the partition which divided her room from the library. With all that occurred on that evening the reader is already acquainted, with the exception of this, that before the captain parted from Nelly Bryan on that evening, he had exacted a solemn promise from her that she would always keep her eyes and ears open whenever Bartley Croker visited Castle Whitmore, and especially whenever those two gentlemen sat together in the library inside her own room, where the closet lay so conveniently situated for overhearing their conversation. Nelly Bryan was faithful to her promise, and never failed to acquaint the captain with all that transpired since that evening of a nature to interest him, whether it was a conversation between Joe Whitmore and Bartley Croker, or any other information, of whatever shape or form, which appeared to her to be desirable for him to be furnished with.

It so happened, then, that on the night preceding that on which the attack on Ash Grove House was to take place, Bartley Croker paid a visit to Joe Whitmore, and they both sat together in the library, and talked the subject over. Nelly Bryan thus acquired a considerable amount of information through the medium of her "nice little closet;" and of information, too, so interesting and so important, that she concluded no time should be lost in communicating it to her friend the captain. We should have ob-

served that the captain had informed Denny
Mullins, the piper, of all that had transpired
at Castle Whitmore on the evening of the
interview in the library, that is, in reference
to the affairs of the Granvilles and the
Moores. Of course the captain did not
think it necessary to tell him of the tender
passages of love that took place between
himself and Nelly Bryan. Denny was therefore on the alert to take note of everything
that turned up which bore upon the interests
of his friends at Ash Grove and at Brookfield Hall. He never allowed a day to pass
without visiting both houses, and also ex-
tending his rambles in the direction of Castle
Whitmore. He sometimes called in to the
Castle to see the housekeeper, and to play a
tune for her, for he was an old acquaintance
of hers, too; and besides, it was understood
between herself and the captain that she
was to communicate to Denny whatever information she might deem of importance
under the circumstances. The captain himself, we need scarcely say, allowed his brain
but little rest from the moment he had discovered the fell intentions of the two villains
upon the peace and happiness, as well as
upon the life, of his friend, Herbert Gran-

ville. He was out early and late in quest of information. His visits to Castle Whitmore were short and not frequent, for the obvious reason that he did not wish to attract notice. But with Denny, the piper, there was no need of such caution, inasmuch as it was in the course of his profession to call at the houses of the gentry everywhere, and at all times. No notice therefore was to be taken of him.

When Nelly Bryan, the housekeeper at Castle Whitmore, had arrived at the knowledge of the attack that was about to be made upon Ash Grove House—and this knowledge she had obtained, as we have stated, on the night preceding that of the intended attack—she became very anxious, and sought every opportunity to make the captain acquainted with what was going forward.

Denny had not made his appearance at or about the Castle on the following morning; and Nelly Bryan knew no one whom she could trust with a message to either the captain or the piper. She waited, and waited, until the afternoon of the day on which so much depended in the way of making the necessary preparation to defend Herbert Granville from the approaching assault upon his life. She grew more and more restless and distracted when she found that the time was getting short, and that neither the captain nor the piper had made their appearance.

It was now evening; even the shadows of night were beginning to fall, and yet there was no appearance of any person to whom she could communicate the important information with which her breast was burdened. She became almost desperate. At length, throwing her cloak over her shoulders, she rushed out of the house, resolved to find the captain, and inform him of the danger of his friend. She passed hastily down by the edge of the lawn until she got into the winding of the avenue amid the embowering trees. Here she heard footsteps advancing up the avenue. She paused; and after a moment she beheld Denny Mullins advancing towards her with his pipes under his arm. She hurried forward to meet him; and taking hold of his arm, she communicated to him in broken sentences, but in a sufficiently intelligible manner, all that she had overheard in reference to the projected attack upon Ash Grove House. With reference to the movement against the police-barrack she was not so clear; all that she could tell on that point

was that Paddy Larkin was to lead it, and
that it was to take place at twelve o'clock
that night, that is, an hour before the attack
upon Ash Grove House. Denny appeared
greatly excited; but he endeavoured to elicit
from her every particular that occurred to
him as necessary to be known, by putting all
sorts of questions to her, and attending to
the answers she returned. He then left
her, and commenced retracing his steps towards Ballydine; for it immediately crossed
his mind that Moll Dreelin was the first person
whom he ought to see and question with
reference to the movements of Paddy Larkin.
It was getting late, and no time was to be
lost. He pushed on with great alacrity,
shifting the green bag from arm to arm, in
order to promote his speed.

Having arrived at Moll Dreelin's, he took
that lady into the back room before he spoke
a word, thereby causing her, as well as her
daughter Anty, to feel not a little alarmed,
especially when they noticed the excitement
and trepidation which accompanied his beha-
viour. Having slammed back the door as
they entered the room, he flung the green
bag upon the bed; and then taking her by
the arm, which he pressed and shook in his

excitement, he asked her, in a series of rapid questions, " Where was Paddy Larkin ? when had he left the village ? what was he doing ? when would he come back ?" which he followed up by other questions, and by observations expressive of his astonished and indignant feelings.

After she had taken time to draw her breath, she asked him why he was in such a state of excitement, and what had happened to him at all that he should behave himself in the way he did. He then became a little calm, and told her about the attack that was to be made that night upon Master Herbert Granville. It was her turn now to become alarmed ; and so she clapped her hands together, and began to give vent to her feelings of sorrowful apprehension. She then called in Anty, who, when she heard the news, began also to clap her hands and to ejaculate her sorrow.

Time, however, was not to be wasted in idle regrets; so Denny demanded at once all the information they could give him with respect to Paddy Larkin. Anty, from whom her betrothed was not wont to conceal any of his movements, then related all she knew. She said that Paddy left the village early in

the evening; that he went to Corrigcastle to
see General Doherty; that he was to leave
that town at half-past ten o'clock with a
party of Whitefeet to attack the police-
barrack at Skark, and that he was to be back
at their (Dreelin's) house again between one
and two o'clock in the morning. He told
her before he went that the general expected
him back to Corrigcastle as soon as the business should be over at the barrack; but that
he would not return there, but would return
to her immediately. This was the substance
of her information, and it was enough for
Denny.

Leaving his pipes in the care of Moll
Dreelin, and taking a stout blackthorn stick
in his hand, he sallied forth in search of
Paddy Larkin. But before he passed outside
the door, he directed Anty Dreelin and her
mother to lose no time in finding out the
captain, either at his house or elsewhere,
and telling him how things stood. He then
went on his way, down by the Cross and
along the road to Corrigcastle. His intention
was to meet Paddy Larkin at Corrigcastle
before he had set out for the attack on the
barrack, and there inform him of the intended
movement against Ash Grove House. He

knew that Paddy, as soon as he should have received this information, would hasten back to defend the family under whose roof he had been sheltered from his earliest boyhood, and for whom he entertained the deepest affection.

No sooner had Denny, the piper, stepped outside the door of Dreelin's house than Anty, taking her shawl and wrapping it around her, went forth in search of the captain. She had not gone far, when she met Ned Doolin and Bill Cleary coming down against her on their way towards the Cross. She stopped them; and at once informed them of all that had just transpired. They were greatly astonished; and told her to return to her house, as they would go immediately and tell the captain, for they knew where he was. She accordingly returned home; and they, retracing their steps, passed up the mountain road for a short distance; and then, crossing over the fields, proceeded in the direction of Brookfield Hall. They found the captain there, seated before a blazing fire in the servants' hall, and cracking jokes with the fat butler. They took him out into the farmyard, and there communicated to him the intelligence they had received. He comprehended the whole matter at once; and telling them to hasten down to Ash Grove House, and to acquaint Master Herbert with the news, and to stop there with him until he should join them, he returned into the Hall again for the purpose of seeing and speaking with Master Harry Moore.

This gentleman, as soon as he had heard from the captain that danger was impending over the Granville family, hastened to afford them all the assistance in his power. He got together some of his men—house and farm servants—and armed them with blunderbusses, carbines, and pistols : then giving his double-barrel fowling piece to the captain, and taking a case of pistols under his own arm, he, and the captain, and the men hastened down to Ash Grove House. They found Herbert Granville and Uncle Ben, with Ned Doolin and Bill Cleary seated in the parlour, talking over the news, and speculating as to the probabilities of its correctness or otherwise. After some conversation between all the parties, in which the captain took the chief part, it was determined to take immediate steps to guard against a surprise, and to put the house in a state of defence.

It was now between ten and eleven o'clock, and consequently it was time to make the necessary arrangements to repel any assault that might be made upon the house and premises, in case there was any truth in the news received to that effect. It was true that no great reliance should be placed upon a statement made by Anty Dreelin; but then Denny, the piper, was not a man that could easily be deceived upon a matter which had latterly so much occupied his attention. This latter consideration, coupled with the information possessed by the captain, whose shrewdness and penetration no one could question, left scarcely a doubt that some movement of the kind mentioned might be made. Every possible preparation was, therefore, made to resist the apprehended assault. All the lower windows were strongly fastened and bolted. Barricades were erected against the doors, front and rear. The upper windows were to be manned; that is, as many of them as there were men to guard, two men being stationed at each window; the rest were to be fastened and barricaded. Some men were to be stationed on the outside as sentinels, who were to give notice of the approach of the assailants, and then retire within the house. By the time all these arrangements were effected, the clock struck twelve. All the front lights in the house were then put out; and the party held themselves in readiness to take their posts as soon as the sentinels, who had now taken up their assigned positions outside, should report the approaching attack. The clock struck one; and there was no alarm from the sentinels. But within fifteen minutes afterwards they came in quickly, and reported that there was a suppressed murmur in the avenue as if of many persons stealthily approaching.

All now took their places. In a few minutes Jer Grinnex was seen creeping towards the beech-tree in front of the house, where he crouched beneath its branches. Two or three other men appeared gliding among the trees between the pond and the house, while some others were seen moving off towards the end of the house and in the direction of the courtyard. The night was rather dark, a few stars only twinkling here and there between the black masses of cloud that spread over the sky. But yet there was sufficient light to permit the outline of objects at a short distance to be seen.

Herbert Granville and Ned Doolin occupied one of the windows in front of the house; and Harry Moore and Bill Cleary occupied another at a little distance from them, one window only intervening between the two parties. Scarcely had they marked the movements we have just mentioned when a loud voice was heard at the hall-door demanding admittance in the name of Captain Whitefoot and the Army of Freedom.

Then there was a pause of a few seconds; after which two or three blows, as of a sledge-hammer were heard resounding against the door. Harry Moore lifted the window-sash near which he stood, to the height of some eight or ten inches, and delivered a pistol shot at those who were endeavouring to force the door. Immediately two men rushed back from the door, flinging aside a sledge-hammer and a crowbar, and made for the avenue by the edge of the lawn, both crying out at the same time, with bellowing voices, that they were " kilt, and murdhered, and batthered to pieces entirely."

In the midst of this uproar Jer Grinnex was observed lifting himself up beneath the shade of the beech-tree, and levelling a carbine towards the window whence the pistol had been fired. Ned Doolin perceiving this, immediately raised his blunderbuss, and levelling it at Grinnex, fired; the two shots went off simultaneously, and appeared to have both produced effect; for Grinnex was whirled round to his right side, and then flung upon his face, while Harry Moore staggered back from the window, and dropped upon a couch that lay near him. No sooner, however, had the report of the two last shots died upon the air, than a shout was heard in the avenue, followed by tumultuous sounds, as if of a number of men rushing forward. In a few seconds more, a voice, which was recognized as that of Denny Mullins, the piper, was heard high above the rest, exclaiming,—

"Hurroo! Granville aboo! Follow me, Paddy Larkin! follow me, men! Clear the way! Granville for ever! hurroo!"

This exclamation was followed by a rapid succession of shots, near the pond, and along the avenue; after which a dead silence ensued.

Herbert Granville, followed by Ned Doolin and Bill Cleary, then descended the staircase, and presented himself at the hall-door, where he was met by the captain and some of his

own men, who were carrying between them
the apparently lifeless body of Denny Mullins.
Paddy Larkin was also with them, accompanied by half a dozen strange men. As
soon as Herbert spoke, Denny lifted himself
up between the men's arms, and attempted
to brandish his arm and raise a shout, but
he failed; the arm dropped, and the words,
" Granville for ever," died away in a low
murmur on his lips. He was carried in and
laid upon a couch in the back parlour. The
men stood around; while Herbert Granville,
stooping over him, endeavoured to discover
the seat of his injury. After a little time he
detected a drop of blood upon his right
breast just below the shoulder. He then
gave orders to have the family surgeon
brought immediately, giving a small scrap of
pencilled paper to the messengers to be presented to him.

Old Uncle Ben and the ladies, who had,
according to arrangement, been placed in a
retired room upstairs under the protection of
three or four of the men, now came down,
and were deeply affected at the prostrate
condition of poor Denny. Uncle Ben talked
of duels, and wounds, and scratches, and
fractures, while Mrs. Granville and Julia

busied themselves in providing whatever
they thought was calculated to soothe the
sufferings of their "poor, dear friend."
While they were thus employed, Denny
opened his eyes, and recognizing Mrs. Granville and her daughter, he made an effort to
extend a hand to each of them; but his
strength failed him; his hands fell back
upon the couch; and two tears rolled down
from his eyes and spread over his cheeks.

While waiting for the arrival of the
surgeon, we shall take leave to lead the
attention of the reader back to the proceedings of Denny Mullins from the time he had
left Moll Dreelin's until his arrival upon the
scene where he met with his disaster. He
went on with all the speed he could command until he reached Corrigcastle; and as
he was crossing the Fair Green of that town,
it occurred to him, for the first time, that he
was wholly unacquainted with the place of
residence of General Doherty. This caused
him great uneasiness; but he still pressed
on in the hope that he might meet some
person from whom he might obtain the desired information. He entered the labyrinth
of streets; and passing on from one to
another he looked about himself, but in vain,

for some clue to direct him to his object. He called into two or three small shops whose owners he was intimately acquainted with; but he obtained no information available for his purpose. Despairing now of meeting Paddy Larkin in the town, he concluded that his best course would be to proceed at once towards the barrack of Skark, keeping on the road that led thither from the town; for thus he hoped either to meet him on the road or somewhere in the vicinity of the barrack. So he returned to the Fair Green; and crossing it, he passed out upon the high road to Skark. On he went without meeting any one that could afford him any satisfactory information, until he came within a mile of Skark, when he met a man who told him that he saw a party of men standing inside the hedge by the roadside within a couple of hundred yards of the barrack. This information afforded assurance to Denny that he was now in a fair way of effecting the object of his journey. So he hastened forward until he reached a turn in the road at the distance of less than one quarter of a mile from the barrack, when he heard a shot; then another; and then a volley, as if a dozen shots had been fired together. He

jumped across the ditch on his right hand,
and, keeping close to the hedge on the other
side, he soon perceived a number of men
rushing down the road from the direction of
the barrack. He looked out through the
furze on the top of the hedge, as the men
rushed by; but he recognized none of them.
At the same time he heard a voice some
distance above him on the road, which he
knew to be that of Paddy Larkin. He kept
his attention fixed on the point whence the
voice had proceeded; and he discovered by
the murmur and tramp which reached his
ears that another party was coming down
the road. He still listened as the sounds
drew near; and having fully satisfied himself
that Paddy Larkin was amongst the party,
and was probably leading his men away after
an unsuccessful attack upon the barrack, he
came out from his hiding-place, and hailed
him. Paddy knew the voice, and asked in
an angry tone, what brought him there?
Denny then jumped out upon the road,
and advanced towards the party. Having
, reached them, he took Paddy aside, and
talked with him for a few minutes. Paddy
made a few impatient gestures; and ordering his men to halt, he addressed them in a

few words, informing them of the state of affairs in reference to the contemplated attack on Ash Grove House, as communicated to him by Denny, and asking them to accompany him for the purpose of repelling that attack. They unanimously assented. The party consisted of six men exclusive of Paddy Larkin. They immediately crossed into the fields, and hastened on towards Ballydine.

At this time it was about half-past twelve o'clock, and there was a mile and a half of distance between them and Ash Grove House. They accordingly walked on with rapid strides in order to reach the house if possible before the attack commenced, which, according to Denny's information, was to take place at one o'clock precisely. As they went along Denny learned from Paddy Larkin, in answer to questions which he continued to put to him every now and then, that the inmates of Skark Barrack had had information of the approaching attack upon them from some quarter or other; and were, therefore, prepared to repel it. When Paddy had brought up his men, which were twelve in number (six of whom had scampered away upon the first fire), he disposed them in two divisons, one

in front and the other in rear of the barrack.
He had scarcely done so, however, when a
rifle ball fired from the barrack whizzed by his
ear. He returned the shot immediately, but
he had no sooner done so than a dozen shots
were fired from front and rear. The six men
whom he had ordered to the rear rushed back
in a panic without firing a shot, whilst himself and the six men whom he had with him
crouched behind a wall which ran partly in
front of the barrack. Here they remained
for a few minutes unable to do anything.
They knew that if they put their heads above
the wall they would be fired at, and that to
return the fire would be perfectly useless.
They therefore crept along the wall until they
came to an angle which took them out of
range of the barrack. They then crossed a
field or two under cover of the hedges until
they came out upon the road on which Denny
had met them. Such was the substance of the
information which Denny elicited from his
friend as they passed along over the fields.
They were now close upon Ballydine Cross,
but instead of passing through it they crossed
over into the fields, and came out upon the
mountain road, a little above the main entrance to Ash Grove House. They passed on

until they reached the gate, where they stood for a moment to listen for some sounds, but not hearing any they passed in at the gate and up the avenue. They had not proceeded twenty yards, however, when they heard the first shot, and then they rushed up quickly. The two next shots were immediately heard, when Denny, advancing in front of the party, burst into a cheer, and called upon Paddy Larkin to follow him, as we have already recorded. Just as he had reached the lower end of the little pond by the side of the avenue, he saw two men moving in a crouched attitude beneath the trees, and holding each a gun poised in his hands as if prepared to discharge it; he rushed at them, and before they had time to place themselves in position to fire at him he struck down one of them with his blackthorn stick. Just as he did so the second man fired, but without effect. Two or three other men who were rushing across the avenue exchanged shots with the advancing party, and it was from one of these that Denny received his wound. Just as he fell a man was seen retreating from the avenue towards the trees on the edge of the pond, carrying a gun in his hand; one of Larkin's men fired at him, and evidently struck him, for he staggered near the edge of the pond and fell into the water. This was the last shot that was fired. The captain and two or three of the Granville party then came up, and after a brief conversation with Paddy Larkin and his men, they took up Denny and carried him to the hall-door as before stated. About an hour had passed since Herbert Granville had sent for the family surgeon to attend Denny, and now that gentleman arrived. He examined the wound; and although he shook his head and looked ominous, yet he did not apprehend that it would terminate fatally. He then proceeded to extract the shot, a task which he performed with great skill and care. He then dressed the wound, and gave some general directions for the treatment of the patient. Denny had now considerably recovered from his exhaustion, under the gentle care and kind treatment of Mrs. Granville and her daughter, and was able to converse a little with those around him. But we must not omit to state here that Harry Moore was all this time in Mrs. Granville's private sitting-room, receiving the most tender attentions from that lady, and also from Julia. He had not been much hurt when he staggered back from the win-

dow after Jer Grinnex had fired at him. His
face was barely scratched by the broken glass
which was blown about by the shot, and the
corner of one of his eyes was cut slightly. So
that when he dropped back upon the couch, it
was merely with the intention of loading his
pistol again in case of his being required to
use it. Paddy Larkin and his men retired
immediately after the surgeon had pronounced
Denny out of danger, and so did all the others,
save Harry Moore, who remained with the
family. The captain went over to Brookfield
Hall to inform the family there of what had
transpired, and to relieve them of any uneasiness that they might have felt from the
absence of Master Harry. The day was now
breaking, and in the course of another hour
several persons appeared on the scene of the
recent conflict. Among others Sir Michael
Carey and the Rev. Dr. Markham rode up the
avenue. They were followed shortly afterwards by a party of police from the Skark
Barrack, and a large number of the neighbouring peasantry soon followed. In short, the
day had not advanced many hours when the
report of the attack upon Ash Grove House
had spread far and near, coupled with that on
the barrack at Skark. The lawn and sur-

rounding grounds were now examined by the
police, followed by the peasantry, when the
following results came to light : Jer Grinnex
was found under the beech-tree, lying on his
face, with a carbine resting under his breast.
He was quite dead. At the edge of the little
pond near the lawn was found a man with his
head and shoulders buried in the water and
mud, and his legs resting on the bank; when
he was taken up and exposed to view, he was
at once recognized as Peter Mackey, the publican at the Cross. He, too, was quite dead,
and a blunderbuss was immersed in the mud
beside him. No other person was found on
the grounds either dead or wounded : but
several indications of the fray were discovered
here and there, such as carbines, pistols, hats,
and one or two overcoats. And thus terminated the combined attack of the Ballydine
Division of the great Army of Freedom.

CHAPTER XXIV.

AN UNEXPECTED ARRIVAL—GREAT REJOICING AT
ASH GROVE HOUSE.

IMMEDIATELY after the captain had told the
news of the night's affray to the old butler
at Brookfield Hall, the whole household were
astir with excitement. Mr. Moore sent forth
a volley of puffs and exclamations, as he
rolled himself out of bed, that grated dread-
fully on the nerves of Mrs. Moore, who,
bustling amid the blankets and sheets, was
endeavouring to steady herself before com-
mencing to dress. The servants kept up a
continuous clatter and gibber throughout the
house ; and the captain, seated in front of
a roaring fire in the hall, was renewing the
narrative of the night's adventures to servant
and straggler, as they succeeded each other
in trembling excitement to " hear the whole
truth about it." The captain closed his eyes,

and repeated the story over and over, and over, to the great admiration and amazement of each succeeding news-seeker. At length Mr. Moore thundered and rolled down stairs; and puffed and rumbled his way into the hall; and seating himself in the fat butler's armchair, desired the captain to tell him all about this affair; and the captain renewed his story again :—

" Well, squire," he commenced, " as soon as we had the hatches battened down, and the decks cleared for action, and everything tight and snug; when every man was placed at his post, and all stragglers were forbid to pass up or down on either deck; when the ship was prepared at all points to go into action, the enemy was sighted. He came on slow and slouching, like a great lubbard, that wasn't well up to his business. He divided his fleet into three divisions; one rounded off on our quarter, keeping at a safe distance, and covered by the fog, so that we could neither reach him with a flying messenger, nor exactly discover the proper direction in which to despatch a messenger with our compliments; the second division took up a position a short distance in front of us under cover of a dark and hanging cloud; this

consisted of a single craft, strong, short, and
rakish, and showing an earnest desire to
close with us, at the first fair chance; the
third was made up of two rough-looking
crafts, carrying heavy metal, and determined
upon quick action. This last division came
sneaking up at first; but no sooner did it
come within close cuffs of us than it began
to pummel away at our ports ; I did not like
that, I tell you, squire. It was ugly looking,
and contrary to the true principles of naval
science."

Here Mr. Moore became impatient; and
requested to be informed of the affair in as
few words as possible. The captain resumed :—

"You must observe, squire, that I am
called on to give a full, true, and faithful
account of this first great battle—I suppose
it may be called the first—this first great
battle fought between the Army of Freedom
and their enemies. This is the more necessary for this reason, that the first authentic
history of every great event is used as a
model and store-house by every succeeding
historian, and thus sent down from generation to generation, until it becomes a sort of
sacred deposit, which it would be a sacrilege

to touch. So you see, sir, that the facts must be clearly stated, and arranged in shining order ; then the language must be such as to preclude every possibility of mis-apprehension—clear, plain, precise, simple. I am now repeating the words of a book I once read, which described the duty of an historian; for I always wish to flank myself with sound authority. Well, squire, this being the case, I hope you will permit me to go on in the proper historical order."

" Order be hanged ! " exclaimed Mr. Moore. " Are you not talking to me about this attack of the Whitefeet as if it was a naval engagement you were describing? What has this scuffle to do with decks, and ports, and quarters ? I want to know how many men were there ; and what they did; and who is hurt; and if any one is killed. How is my son ? Are the Granvilles unhurt ? "

" Now, squire," resumed the captain, " there is no honest man killed or hurt except one, and his name is Denny Mullins; but he is not in any danger. He was exhausted from long fasting and fatigue ; and having received a slight wound in the engagement, he was brought to a low ebb at first ; and when his excitement passed off, he seemed the same as dead, but he is recovering fast.

"How are the womenkind there?" asked Mr. Moore; "I suppose they are frightened to death. Why didn't they send for me?"

"All well and hearty," answered the captain. "Your son, Master Harry, is paying them the best attention; or they are paying it to him, I don't exactly know which; but I suppose it comes to the same thing in the long run."

"Oh, the scapegrace," exclaimed Mr. Moore, "I didn't think he had so much forethought as to attend to the requirements of any person."

"You may make yourself easy about that," observed the captain; "there's one person, at least, whose requirements he'll attend to."

"Who is that?" asked Mr. Moore.

"One of the sweetest angels that walks upon two legs; and her name is Miss Julia Granville," replied the captain.

"Julia Granville?" said Mr. Moore. "True, a nobler and fairer girl does not tread upon Irish soil. I am glad to hear that my son can appreciate what is fair and noble. Well, how is poor Mrs. Granville? and my old friend, Ben Brown?"

"They are right well," answered the captain, "we put them under convoy, and sent them to the rear, where they stood off and on until all was over. Now, sir, I must be off, and see how all stands at the Glazement; then I must see Denny's mother, and tell her how the world goes. She might be fretting, poor woman; especially if any bad news came to her ears." He then rose, and set out for his house.

While the preceding conversation was taking place between Mr. Moore and the captain, Mrs. Moore and her daughter were on their way to Ash Grove. After they had arrived there, they were shown into the drawing-room, where they were received by Herbert Granville and his sister Julia. Harry Moore was also there. Mrs. Granville came in immediately afterwards; and the whole party remained in conversation for some time, Mrs. Granville and Julia describing the fearful events of the night, and the state of alarm into which the whole family were thrown, and bewailing the sad consequences which followed. Fanny looked pale and tremulous, and yet a happy smile lighted up her face as from time to time she glanced over at Herbert, who appeared quite cheerful as he talked with Harry Moore. At length she glided softly over, and bantering her brother on his scratched cheeks and wounded eye, she said, looking up to Herbert, " I don't see any marks of the affray upon you, Herbert. How did you escape ? "

" I had so many friends at my side," replied Herbert, " that danger was not able to approach me. Besides, there may have been some invisible agency guarding me." And here he looked significantly at Fanny, who smiled, and said,—

" Perhaps some good spirit hovered over you, and preserved a life that was deemed too valuable to be so early cut off."

" You pay me too high a compliment," rejoined Herbert. " The fact is, I was in no danger throughout the whole affair. But the life of your brother here was in imminent danger; and I believe it was preserved through the watchfulness and activity of Ned Doolin. He it was who prevented a person named Jer Grinnex, from shooting him; but, unfortunately the wretched man himself, I mean Grinnex, was killed."

A slight tremor passed over Fanny's frame, as she looked towards her brother. She then said with grave solemnity, " Thank God, that you all have escaped so well. Oh, how wretched it would have been if anything serious had happened to any of you ! ''

She then joined her mother, and Mrs. Granville and Julia; and they four went to see how Denny Mullins was. Denny was sitting upon a couch when they entered, and looked pale and exhausted; but as soon as he saw Mrs. Moore and Fanny he rose, and extended his hands to them, saying, " Master Harry is not a bit the worse, ma'am, for the touch he got, not a bit, Miss Fanny. We had great ructions, ma'am; but 'twas nothin' to spake about. 'Twas all over when I came, Miss Fanny. So I was just comin' up the avenue, and I got a little scratch here on my breast; but 'tis nothin' to spake about.'' He then cast down his eyes upon the floor, and said in a low mumbling voice, " I don't know yet what way the ould mother is gettin' on.''

" Don't you be troubled,'' said Mrs. Moore, " about your mother. I saw her last evening; and she was quite well. And I suppose the captain will bring her an account of you, and make her mind easy. We left him at the Hall as we came away, and I suppose he has gone up the Glen by this time.''

The ladies then retired. Many visits were made to the family during the day, by the neighbouring gentry; as also by the peasantry, who were continually coming and going, and expressing their sympathy for the several members of the family, as well as for Denny Mullins. The Earl and Countess of Fairborough drove up at an early hour; and remained a considerable time. His lordship was particularly anxious to discover some clue to the perpetrators of the outrage; and examined Denny Mullins as to his knowledge of the origin and motives of it. Denny's account of it was not very explicit, as he did not like to commit himself in any way that would tend to involve the name and reputation of Nelly Bryan. At least, he would keep everything close in his own mind until he had an opportunity of conversing at length upon the subject with his old friend and confidant, the captain. So his lordship left, without eliciting any definite information as to the cause of the attack. There was a probability, however, in his own mind, that it originated with the Whitefeet. There was one thing that puzzled him very much, namely, the presence of Peter Mackey on the scene of the outrage; and with fire-arms too.

This was a mystery to everybody who knew Peter, and he was a man who was widely known.

For days and weeks there was scarcely any subject spoken of in the country round save this assault of the Whitefeet upon Ash Grove House; and what gave a peculiar zest to the topic was the fact of Peter Mackey, the sensible, peaceable, prudent, loyal, conservative Peter Mackey, being among the perpetrators of so foul and heinous a transgression against the laws of his country and the well-being of society. It is true, there were some who knew Peter well, and consequently experienced no surprise when they heard of his being mixed up in the affray, who knew him to be a vulgar knave, without principle, without religion, without scruple; but always planning his own benefit, without caring how or by what means that benefit was secured, or what evil consequences might result to others from its remorseless pursuit. But those were few among the many who carelessly regarded his exterior, and took him at the surreptitious value he put upon himself. He was, accordingly, looked upon as a proper and respectable man, and a worthy example for imitation by all who desired to maintain a decent position in society, that is, a decent position for a man of his class. These persons were, therefore, greatly surprised at the appearance of Peter among a lawless gang of depredators and robbers; and endeavoured to account for it in some way that was consistent with their former opinion of him. It struck them, then, that he must have been up late that night; and finding, somehow or other, that something unusual was going forward, he remained on the look out until he found that Ash Grove House was going to be attacked; that then he armed himself, and set out to aid the Granvilles in repulsing their assailants. This was a very plausible mode of settling the matter with themselves. But it happened, unfortunately for this theory, that a slip of paper was found in one of the pockets of Peter's waistcoat after he had been removed to his own house, and previously to the holding of the coroner's inquest; and this paper purported to be a receipt for ten pounds given by him to Jer Grinnex in consideration of the said Grinnex performing a certain mysterious duty in connexion with Ash Grove House, which, when coupled with what had actually transpired, could leave no doubt upon any disinterested mind that the attack in question, with the view to murder, was the duty indicated. This receipt was in the handwriting of Peter Mackey, while the signature was in that of Jer Grinnex. It ran as follows :—

"Ballydine, October 17th, 18—

"This day I received from Mr. Peter Mackey the sum of tin pound on condition to do the work settled betwune us, at Ash Grove, so as to pick down the bird. Purvided, if the bird eshkapes this turn, he is to be purshued ontil he is done for.

"JER GRINNEX."

The date of this receipt was the day previous to that of the attack upon Ash Grove House. So here was very strong circumstantial evidence that Peter Mackey's presence on the occasion in question was not accidental, nor yet prompted by any benevolent motive. However, a variety of conjectures and speculations in connexion with the whole affair were bandied from mouth to mouth, and went the circuit of the whole country. Magistrates, justices, and police officers were busy everywhere round about

Ballydine; and some suspicious characters, found prowling about the country, were arrested and placed in confinement; but no material information was elicited, so as to afford the slightest clue either to the party who attacked the barrack, or to those who attacked Ash Grove House. Still fame was on the wing; and the names of Bartley Croker and Joe Whitmore began to figure in the narratives that continued to circulate around the country. Somebody heard that somebody saw Bartley Croker coming down the mountain road late that night, and saw him passing the Ash Grove gate, where he met a man who came out from behind one of the piers; and he saw him speak with the man for a few seconds, and then saw him pass on. Another person assured his auditors that on the same night there was a man returning from the town of Cushport; and that when he was coming up towards the Cross of Ballydine, thinking of nothing, but looking up at the sky to see what way the clouds were going, he heard a horse trotting down the road against him; that as soon as he did, he turned into the ditch, under the trees, to let him pass; and that when he was passing he saw Joe Whitmore

on the horse's back, as far as he could judge
in the darkness of the night. But the climax
of all the popular narratives that found birth
on the occasion was this : that two men were
crossing over the hill above Glen Corril the
same night; and when they came out on the
road leading over to Skark, who should they
see but two gentlemen in a gig a little above
them on the road. So they went behind the
hedge, and crept along quietly, so as to obtain a near view of the gentlemen ; and who
should they be—for they knew them well—
but Dan O'Connel, the champion of Ireland,
and one Tom Steel. This story ran rapidly
through all the highways and byeways of the
country, and jostled out every other narrative bearing on the subject.

It now began to be generally believed that
the combined movement against the barrack
and Ash Grove House was the work of
O'Connel, and that it was merely preliminary
to the great rising that was so long anticipated. The captain, as the reader is aware,
was the oracle of Ballydine, and was always
consulted upon matters of high political import by the peasantry all round. In the
course of a few days after the Ash Grove
affair, he was passing down towards the

Cross of Ballydine, when he saw Ned Doolin and another man coming up against him. They appeared to be engaged in some conversation which greatly interested them, for they every now and then, as they were approaching the captain, would stand and gesticulate as if they were endeavouring to convince each other of the views which they respectively entertained. As soon as they met, the captain asked them what it was that they seemed to be so earnest about; when Ned Doolin replied that his companion wanted to persuade him that O'Connel had given the word for Ireland to turn out, and take back her own from the *Sassanagh* (Saxon). But he (Ned Doolin) was showing his companion the nonsense of all that talk, since it didn't stand to reason that O'Connel would do anything that would be so foolish, or that any man in his senses, not to speak of O'Connel, would think of the like. So when they saw the captain coming down against them, they said to one another that they would leave it to him to decide which of them was right and which of them was wrong. The captain listened to the speaker with an appearance of grave humour; for though he kept his eyes fixed attentively on

him while he spoke, yet there was in those
eyes a twinkling of drollery which showed
that while he respected the good sense and
honest manliness of Ned Doolin, he could
not help entertaining a feeling of ridicule for
the opinion which he set forth as that of
his companion—an opinion which he knew
was shared by the great bulk of the peasantry throughout the country. He said in
reply to Doolin, "Your canvas is all square,
Ned; neither too light nor too heavy for the
craft. When a man's brains are light, his
senses are wheeled about every way, just
like a weather-cock; and when they are too
heavy, there's no moving him at all. So you
see between the two the right gauge is stationed; neither too light nor too heavy is
the proper thing. You are right, my boy,
when you say that O'Connel is against anything and everything that would put the
people in the way of being destroyed. He
is too wise a man, and too good a man for
anything of that sort; his canvas sits too
snug and tight on him to drive him about
'like a whirligig in that way. 'Tis only your
flyblows that like rebellious weather. It
warms them into life; it gives them a chance
to flutter about for a little while. They are

good for nothing as long as the weather remains clear and wholesome; but when clouds and rain, and bursts of sun between 'em, happen to come along, then your fly-blows flourish and buzz about the same as if the world was their own; until the sun shines out again and drives away the dirt; then they can't be seen any longer. That's the way the thing is, Ned. The best man in this world is he who does his duty in whatever corner of life God places him. The worst man in this world is he who is always waiting for chances. To conquer the Saxon, indeed! You might as well try to turn the hill of Glen Corril there upside down as to conquer the Saxon. And besides, if you were able to conquer him to-morrow, what good would that do you? No good at all; but a great deal of harm. Ned Doolin! and you, my good man, listen to what I say; for I wish you and all Irishmen to know the truth, and to follow where it leads; and never to give heed to falsehood, and to the brood of delu-sions, and conceits, and mockeries that are born of falsehood. Well, here is the truth for you. It is far better for this country of ours to be governed by the Saxon than by anybody else. Who is the Saxon? He is a steady, sensible, hardworking, honest-minded man, who knows how to take care of his business, and who is ready to give a helpin' hand to any man that deserves it. He won't help the idle stroller, to be sure ; and why should he ? But he'll help the honest, striving, peaceable man, and put him in the way of helpin' himself and rearin' his family, and of doin' like himself. He doesn't want to be bothered with idlers, or *boolamskiaghs* (swaggering bravadoes), or such vermin, and flyblows that are a disgrace and a curse to every country they're in. He sweeps those out of his way, as in duty bound, before God and man; and he takes to his breast the good and sensible men who, like himself, are willing to earn their bread by honest ways. Now, that's what the Saxon is; and I ask yourselves—I ask every sensible man, which is better—to have this man govern us, or one of those idle rakes and flyblows that are goin' about the country from post to pillar, lookin' for a chance to pick the pockets of every honest man they come across ? Which 'of these now, I ask you, would you like to be head steward over you—the honest, peaceable, good-minded, sober, industrious Saxon, or the swaggerin', dirty, lazy, schemin',

thievish rake? Sure, I needn't ask you, or
any man with a grain of common sense in
his head. O'Connel, indeed! to try to upset
the country, and turn it into a den of
thieves! He is the last man in the world
who'd do the like. Oh, no; he is too knowledgeable and too good for that. What does
he ever and always say? Here are his
words: 'Obey the laws of the land, and be
sober and industrious; and above all things,
don't attempt to shed a drop of blood.'
That's what he teaches, and that's what our
holy Church teaches, from the Pope of Rome
down to the curate of the smallest village in
the country. And sure we know, too, that
it is the same thing that God's holy Bible
teaches; and didn't the blessed Apostles and
holy martyrs teach the very same thing?
Well now, I ask you, who are we to listen
to? Is it to the rakes and boolamskiaghs
(swaggering bravadoes), the idle, lyin',
dirty, schemin', mean, sneaking thieves and
vagabonds, or to O'Connel, the Pope, the
Apostles, the martyrs, the Bible, and the God
of heaven? The Saxon, indeed! Sure 'tis
a blessin' from heaven that we have such an
honest, steady man to guard us against the
thieves and the rakes. God forbid that we

should ever have one of these skialavelts (loose-livers) over us. How well, indeed, we should be off then; our lives, our properties, and our liberties at the mercy of all the wanderin' ragamuffins in the country. No, my friends, this must never happen; the people are gettin' to open their eyes now, and they'll be no longer led away like blindfolded creatures that saw nothin' and knew nothin'."

As the captain was thus sensibly enlarging on the state and prospects of the country, a distant cheer came faintly upon his ear. It was also heard by the two men who were standing with him. It came again with increased volume; and again; till at length it burst in a storm upon their ears.

The three men then proceeded together towards the Cross. A crowd of men and women and children came up from the Corrigcastle road towards the Cross, shouting and scuffling, and waving green boughs above their heads. In the midst of the crowd was a gig in which were seated two aged gentlemen, who every now and then lifted off their hats and bowed to those around them. The gig had two long ropes attached to it in front, and these were held by a line of men on either

side, who thus drew it along amid the cheering and hurrahing of the throng that accompanied them. The procession arrived at the
Cross, and then turned up the mountain road,
while the air rang with the shout of " The
Granvilles aboo!" "The Granvilles for ever!"
Having arrived at the entrance to Ash Grove
House, the throng entered the gates, and
advanced up the avenue; while cheers and
hurrahs and cries of " The Granvilles for
ever ! " rose into the air. The gig was drawn
up to the hall-door, and Uncle Ben and his
brother, Colonel Felix Brown, descended from
it and entered the house.

Colonel Brown had arrived at Cushport on
the day before, and was met there by his
brother Ben. As soon as it had become known
that they were on their way to Ash Grove the
country people flocked from every side to
meet them ; and they had been no sooner
met than the horse was taken from the gig,
and they were drawn triumphantly along in
the manner we have seen.

But what caused the arrival of Colonel
Brown at this particular time ? We have
seen that for some considerable time no letter
had been received from him by his brother or
any member of the Ash Grove family, and that

therefore Herbert Granville had made up his
mind to go to him without further delay.
The fact was that the Colonel had been for
some time in communication with Lord Milford in reference to the affairs of his late
brother, Herbert's father, and that his lordship had expressed a desire to see the colonel
in London as soon as possible, with the view
of making some arrangements relative to that
portion of his estates which had been formerly
held by the Ash Grove family. His lordship's
intention was to restore Gurtroo, now in the
possession of Bartley Croker, to the eldest
son of the late Mr. Granville, and to adopt
such other proceedings in connexion with
this matter as circumstances would warrant.

The colonel saw that there was no time to
be lost; and so, arranging his own personal
concerns in Canada, he hastened to London,
and there met Lord Milford. They soon
decided upon the matters which brought them
together. The colonel was in possession of
a quantity of correspondence and papers of
various kinds, which he had from time to time
received from his late brother, and which
threw such a flood of light upon the conduct
and proceedings of Bartley Croker as left no
doubt upon the mind of Lord Milford that

the grossest deception, wrong, and fraud had been committed by his agent in the management of his estates. The conclusion of their interview was that the colonel's nephew, Herbert Granville, was to take immediate possession of the property at Gurtroo, and that the colonel was to act as agent for the estates until his lordship had further time for consideration—the colonel having expressed himself as being unwilling to accept that position except for the time being.

In the meantime Bartley Croker received a communication from his lordship, desiring him to meet him in London, and to take with him the rent-rolls and other records connected with the estates. Bartley was necessarily thrown into a state of trepidation; but yet he relied much upon his dexterity and mental resources to extricate himself from the difficulties and dangers which he felt to be gathering around him. He hastened, however, to comply with the request of his lordship, and in due time arrived in London. Lord Milford, who had in the interim studied the documents which he had received from Colonel Brown, and made himself acquainted with all the circumstances connected with the transactions between the agent and the late

Mr. Granville, placed the whole matter before Bartley in such a clear and methodical manner that the latter was completely confounded and bewildered. His prepared defence became unavailable, as it had not contemplated the nature and force of the charges now brought against him, and he was therefore obliged to throw himself upon the resources of the moment, which consisted of quibbles, equivocations, and denials. But they availed nothing. His lordship informed him that his services as agent were dispensed with henceforward, and that further proceedings against him would be entrusted to the courts of law.

Thus Bartley Croker, who had hitherto been wafted along upon the tide of fortune, felt for the first time in his life that that tide had now receded from him and left him sprawling upon the strand. All the iniquities of his past life came crowding upon his mind, and he knew not whither he should turn to relieve himself from the overwhelming perplexity which was goading him to distraction. He had no business to detain him any longer in London, and therefore he returned to Gurtroo, with an uncertan resolution as to the course of conduct which it now behoved him to pursue.

Ash Grove became the scene of unusual festivity immediately after the colonel's arrival. On the night following that event bonfires blazed on every side; there was one at the Cross of Ballydine, and another on the road opposite the entrance to the lawn, and a dozen others at different points on the roads and elevated grounds round about the village. On the next day there was a long dance on the lawn, and the people came in crowds from all the villages around to participate in the enjoyments of the occasion. The Earl and Countess of Fairborough were there, as were also Sir Michael Carey and his wife and daughters, and the Rev. Dr. Markham; all the family of Brookfield Hall, and the Credans, and the Rev. Mr. Grigger, were also present. Tables, covered with refreshments, were ranged in lines along the hall, and the dancers as well as others went in from time to time to recruit themselves with the good things that were there prepared for them. In the afternoon a large party was entertained at dinner by the colonel; and it was not until near twelve o'clock that the gates at the entrance to Ash Grove closed upon the last retiring guest.

CHAPTER XXV.

CONCLUSION.

AFTER Bartley Croker had returned from London, he commenced an investigation into the best mode of arranging his future destiny. He knew now that it was all over with him, as far as land agencies were concerned. Lord Milford's discovery of his dishonest and treacherous proceedings would, of course, debar him from any employment of that kind for the future. As to returning to his profession of attorney, he felt that it was too late now to think of that. At the best of times and in his most energetic years he had not been very successful in that line—he had been generally regarded as a trickster and swindler; and no one cared to entrust his business to him, except those who had no means to employ a better and safer man; or who had nothing to lose, and went to law only on some wild speculation. To recover his lost position as agent to the Milford estates, he felt, was out of the question. Lord Milford was not a man to alter his decision when he had once determined to act in any particular direction. Bartley thus felt himself fenced in with difficulties ; and, notwithstanding his varied mental resources, on which he had hitherto prided himself, and which had always stood him in good stead in every pressing emergency, he was now forced to confess to himself that he was driven into a corner; and could see no way of escaping from his unfortunate position. The arrival of Colonel Brown, from Canada, was a most untoward event; but yet he would not have set very much value upon that—he thought he should have been able to get over that, if it had not been for the unfortunate failure of the attack on Ash Grove House. If that confounded fellow—so he designated Herbert Granville, as he thought of him in the course of his reveries—had been removed, all other difficulties would dissolve like snow before the meridian sun. Had he been removed, old Colonel Brown, and Uncle Ben, and all the rest of them would be no more than a cobweb in his way. His mind again began

to work in the direction of the destinies of
Herbert Granville. He would not despair;
something might be done yet. He cast back
his thoughts to the years gone by, and to
some of the events of those years; and he
saw there difficulties which he had sur-
mounted; and difficulties too of a dismal
complexion. He would not despair, no; a
man of genius should never despair. He
began to think that there remained in his
mind resources which had never been called
upon—which no extreme emergency had ever
called upon; let these be called into requi-
sition now—now was the time to prove his
great superiority over all men. He would
foil Lord Milford; he would take him on the
point of his lance, and spit him like a
sparrow. He began to wax triumphant in his
own imagination; and nothing now appeared
to him too difficult to be overcome. He still
fell back upon Joe Whitmore, as the most
convenient weapon for him to handle. Joe
was a jackass, to be sure, and a buffoon;
but jackasses and buffoons were intended for
use. Such animals could not have been made
in vain; they were intended for a purpose, and
that purpose was to subserve the plans and
designs of great and gifted men like himself.

But how was Joe progressing all this time? He had had some interviews with Mrs. Credan, Fanny's aunt; but they were of a very, very sombre nature. All encouragement in that quarter was withdrawn from him. Fanny had solemnly declared that she would not marry him if there was no other man in the world but himself—she had declared this, after every inducement, and persuasion, and argument had been exhausted in the endeavour to bring her around to favour his pretensions. Joe gave up the contest in despair; not that he cared much one way or the other. He hated Herbert Granville—that he knew at any rate; but he didn't know that he loved Fanny Moore; he liked to have her—that was all; pretty much as he'd like to have any other woman that came in his way, and for whom he conceived a present passion. If it hadn't been for Herbert Granville—for the deep hatred he bore that gentleman, his passion for Fanny Moore would have died out long ago. But now he had no hope. She would not marry him under any circumstances; and Herbert appeared to be getting too influential for him in every way. Yes, he was now restored to his father's property; and the agency of the

Milford estates was looming not far in the distance for him. Under all these circumstances, Joe Whitmore gave up the chase, and gave way to a new passion. He had a dairy-maid, an elderly woman, of gigantic stature, and with only one eye, and to her he now turned with the most devotional zeal. He called her his Diana, his Venus, his Cleopatra, and as she resisted his first advances, and sometimes used her great physical strength for that purpose, he was fain at last to lead her to the hymeneal altar, and make her an honest and a lawful wife, and mistress of Castle Whitmore. Joe's life, after this, was a caution to all romantic lovers. His Diana ruled her household, Joe included, with an iron rod, and, "as for ladies, and things of that sort," she declared her thorough contempt for them. The ladies, indeed, kept clear of her; and so did the gentlemen, with the exception of one or two penniless rowdies who found Joe's cellar, as well as his table, a convenient resort in times of scarcity. These rowdies were fortunate enough to fall into the good graces of the lady of the mansion, who always declared her high esteem for them, and her solemn belief that they were the only *real* gentlemen in that side of the country. But Bartley Croker had the *entrée*, too ; he was in particular favour with Mrs. Whitmore : she said, and " would always maintain it, that he was a gentleman to the backbone, and so she liked him in her heart —*she did so in troth.*"

It was about this time, or at least shortly after Joe's marriage, that Bartley Croker made a visit to Castle Whitmore. He was received by the mistress of the Castle with great good feeling ; and as for Joe he was delighted beyond expression to see his worthy and faithful friend once again under his roof. It must be remembered that Bartley's troubles had kept him away for some time from Castle Whitmore. What between his visit to London to answer the summons of his employer, Lord Milford, and his other occupations and distractions consequent upon that visit, he had had but very little time on his hands to devote to his friend Joe. Besides, Joe was not a man to whom he cared to confide his secrets, and from whom he would look for any consolation in his troubles. Indeed, as the reader must be well aware, he regarded Joe, and used him, as a mere tool for carrying out any low scheme or project he might have had in hand. But as to seeking advice

from him, or consulting him upon any important matter, there was nothing more remote
from Bartley's mind at any time than doing
such a foolish thing as that. So that his visit
at this time was altogether unconnected with
his private affairs, that is, as far as looking
for advice, or seeking the aid of Joe's judgment and discretion was concerned. Well, at
all events, he made his visit, and was, as we
have said, received with great cordiality by
the lord and lady of the Castle. It was late
in the evening when he drove up, and Joe
happened to be out, looking after some matters
connected with certain improvements which
he was making in a part of his demesne.
Bartley was met at the hall-door by Mrs.
Whitmore; and after having been seized by
the hand, and shaken with great vigour by
that lady, he was conducted into the back
sitting-room, and seated by the fire. Mrs.
Whitmore sat beside him in easy and familiar
conversation, placing her huge hand occasionally on his knee in confirmation of her
remarks, and sometimes giving him a punch
in the side with her clenched fist, with the
same object.

"And where the d——l were you, at all,
at all, this time back?" she went on to say.

"Shure Joe was axin' myself what happened you, that he didn't see you for ever so long."

"Well, Mrs. Whitmore, I have been rather busy this time back, and haven't had a moment to spare to call upon my friends."

"Busy! Whatever makes you so busy always? I never seen the like. You puts me in mind of the braccady cow that's ever and always busy doin' some harm or other. There, the other day she broke into the garden, and played the d——l wid everything in it. I don't know what to do with her at all, at all. Maybe, you'd want to buy her, Mr. Croker?"

"No, I don't require any increase of stock at present; in fact, I would rather dispose of some of my cattle."

"Now, tell me, how's the ould woman gettin' on? Why didn't you bring her wid you when you were comin' down? Shure you know I'd be very glad to see her. But I'm forgettin' myself—I never axed what would you take—there's the d——l of it. Will you take somethin' hot? You'll have it took before this fellow comes in."

"I thank you, Mrs. Whitmore; I shall take nothing at present."

"Do, now, afther your drive. And 'tis such

cowld weather besides; you'd want something to warm you. Faith, Joe takes a horn every hour in the day to warm his heart; and shure a man is nothin' widout a little drop now and then to put *misnagh* (spirit) in him. I'll go and bring you a warm drop."

"No, Mrs. Whitmore, I'd rathor not, thank you. By-and-by, when Mr. Whitmore comes in, I shall take a glass of wine with him. To tell you the truth, I have already taken some spirits. I had only just dined before I left the house; and I took a tumbler of whisky-punch after dinner, besides a few glasses of wine."

"Oh, drat the wine; what's the good of it for a man? There's *my* Joe, now; he wouldn't give a sthraw for all the wine in the world, without putting a *sthaul* (a dash) of whisky over it. You won't take it now. Well, when Joe 'll come in by-and-by, ye must have a hot tumbler together. Tell me, Mr. Croker,"—here she leant over, putting her hand upon his shoulder and her face close up to his,—"tell me; what the d——l is all this about the Granvilles? They tell me for cer- tain that the ould colonel is to be the agent of Lord Milford now; and that the young fellow is only waiting to get it himself the minute he'll be married to that *shkit* (silly creature) of a thing, Fanny Moore."

" I believe there is some truth in that report, though I cannot vouch for it."

" Ah, then, upon my sowl, if I was you, I'd put a bit o' lead in that fellow's gizzard. What call have he to be agent ? The like of him of a conceited whelp ? And Fanny Moore, too ! Och, the likes o' those sickens me. Ladies and gintlemen indeed ! By my sowl 'twould be fitther for some of 'em to earn their bread in honesty than to be pretindin' to be ladies and gintlemen when they haven't as much as 'ud jingle on a griddle. Isn't it thrue for me, Mr. Croker ? "

" Yes, I agree with you, that there is a great deal of vain pretension among some people that is not at all becoming. I know," —here he spoke in a low and confidential strain,—" I know that the Granville family are not friends of your husband, or of yourself. Indeed, that young fellow Herbert has spoken, as I have been told, in a most improper manner of you. But as I said, when I heard it, you are not obliged to bow to him any day ; you are as respectable as he is, or any of his family—I might say more so, indeed. You, at any rate, never demeaned yourself

by going about looking for favours, and
trying to keep up a consequence by mean
and beggarly ways."

"Spoke o' me, did they? To the d——l
I bob 'em all. I'm unbehouldin' to 'em, and
always was. What have they to say to me?
I am an honest father and mother's child;
and maybe, that's more than some o' themselves are. But what call have they to be
talkin' about me? Let 'em take care o' what
they're sayin'. I have people belongin' to
me that wouldn't be long about puttin' a
flay in their ear."

"Exactly; so I said at the time. It is
highly improper for an upstart fellow, like
Herbert Granville, to be maligning the
character of a respectable woman like you.
There are your brothers, and your cousins,
respectable men; and men too, who love
their country, and have the spirit to stand
up for her too. That's more than can be
said of that nincompoop, Herbert Granville.
And I tell you this,"—he placed his mouth at
her ear, and whispered softly,—"Herbert
Granville would hang every one of the
Whitefeet to-morrow, if he only had the
opportunity. What chance, then, I ask you,
have your brothers, or any one of those who

are trying to rightify their country—what chance have they of their lives as long as Herbert Granville has his eyes upon them?

Mrs. Whitmore's eyes flashed fire, and her bosom rose and fell like an agitated sea. But at this moment Joe Whitmore entered the room. She stood up, shuffled about the apartment for a few minutes, and then went out. Joe and his friend talked for awhile on indifferent subjects, and then retired to the library, where they would be more to themselves, and could indulge more comfortably in their libations. After talking for a time about the change that had taken place in the management of the Milford estates, and of the transfer of the Gurtroo property back to the Granvilles, Bartley assumed an appearance of perfect indifference as far as he himself was concerned, and only regretted what had taken place on the ground of the overbearing insolence of the Granville family, but most especially of that " young scoundrel, Herbert."

" The fellow triumphs," he observed, " over those who are his superiors in every sense, and loses no opportunity of turning them into ridicule. Besides, he is trying to curry favour with the Government by informing upon every man who is connected with that Whitefoot organization. I condemn the organization myself, as one not calculated to do any good; but then I should not take advantage of it in order to serve my own purposes. I put this matter to you, Whitmore, as an honest and independent man. Are you to be treated with contempt, ay, and with personal injury—I speak advisedly—by such a fellow as Herbert Granville? He scoffs at yourself; he scoffs at your wife, a lady whom I respect, and whom every gentleman should respect, for her virtuous and estimable qualities. And even here he is not satisfied to stop; he would bring disgrace upon her family by trying to implicate her brothers and cousins in this Whitefoot business, and getting them hanged, or transported at least. And through them he would desire to cast dishonour upon you. Look here, Whitmore," he lowered his voice, and spoke with a slow and measured emphasis, "your wife's brothers may, if they please, shut his mouth. Do you understand?"

Whitmore, who was gulping his wine very freely during this speech, looked dreamily at Bartley as he had concluded, and said, "What have you done with that hundred pounds I gave you on account of that Ash Grove affair? That was a botched job, cracko! I've never heard of such a thing. But the money, Croker? Where is the money?"

"My dear Whitmore, I expended it and a great deal more upon those fellows, those cowardly dogs whom Peter Mackey employed. They would not move an inch until they got ten pounds a man, that is, the common men; but their leader, Grinnex, had to be paid double that sum, I paid him ten pounds myself, and I gave Mackey ten pounds more to pay him on the day preceding the attack. Then Mackey would not move before I paid him thirty pounds. So you see, my dear sir, that your hundred pounds was nothing. I had to supplement it largely. But I shouldn't mind that if the business had been properly conducted. They were not the men, my dear Whitmore; they were not the men to be entrusted with important business of that sort. No, sir, not at all, sir. If your brothers-in-law would only undertake a thing of that sort, do you think a failure would take place? Do you think it could take place? Do you think it possible that it should take place? Herbert Granville triumphs over you. He does. He avails

himself of every occasion to do so ; especially
since your marriage. Do her brothers know
this ? Do her relatives know this ? I should
look to it if I were you. But yet it is no
business of mine. Perhaps I should not have
spoken of the matter at all. Nor should I,
but that I feel interested, as you must be
aware, in everything that affects your honour,
and the honour of your family."

" I must look to it," replied Joe, " I must
look to it. I am proud of my wife, I tell
you that, Croker, I am proud of my wife.
She may not be everything that a man might
desire ; but she is a woman whom I can
esteem ; and I do esteem her ; and I shall
permit no man to speak with disrespect of her.
Let Granville not meddle with my wife, or
my wife's family ; let him beware. Cracko !
I need but lift my finger, and the thing was
done. Her brothers—and her cousins !—why,
sir, I need but do that, and the thing was
accomplished."

He filliped with his thumb and forefinger
as he uttered the last sentence. Bartley at
once took up the idea: " Yes, Whitmore,
you are right," he said, "you need but do
that, just that, and the thing was accomplished."

It is remarkable to what lengths the spirit
of revenge may carry men of evil disposition.
Bartley Croker could have had no motive of
personal interest at this time in compassing
the destruction of Herbert Granville; at
least, there seemed to exist no ground for
such motive, for the relation that had existed
between himself and his late employer, Lord
Milford, had altogether ceased, and there did
not exist the slightest hope, on his part, of
its being ever restored.   And notwithstanding this, his hatred towards Herbert Granville
was such as to impel him to scheme and plot
for his destruction.   This was the object
which induced him to visit Joe Whitmore
this evening; and he felt now satisfied that
Joe would act upon the suggestion which he
had so insidiously thrown out for his adoption.
The old dairy-maid's brothers, that is the
brothers of Mrs. Whitmore, were daring,
reckless fellows, who would not hesitate to
take part in any design that invited their
passions of hatred and revenge.   They were
members of the Whitefoot organization, and
were regarded with terror by the moderate
men of their own party.   They were always
ready for any enterprise of a daring character,
they were full of courage, reckless of con-

sequences, and devoid of every principle of
morality and religion. They had been brought
up in the streets of Corrigcastle, a brood of
midnight scavengers, and were now leading
a life of semi-vagrancy, sometimes employed
about the bacon-yards and breweries of the
town, and sometimes scouring the country,
at night, in the capacity of Whitefeet.
Bartley Croker having now satisfied himself
that he had securely placed his train, had no
further object in wasting the hours with Joe
Whitmore, so he rose to depart. The night
had set in, and given indications of stormy
weather, so that he felt anxious to get to his
own house, which was seven or eight miles
distant, before the storm should break over
his head. He mounted his gig at the hall-
door, and his servant, taking the reins, drove
off at an easy pace down the lawn, and out
upon the public road. The night became
more and more threatening as they went
along; the clouds were heavy and dark; and
the wind came in fitful gusts, bearing a
sprinkling of thin rain upon its wings. They
were now driving along at a rapid pace upon
the road that crossed the hill within a couple
of miles of Gurtroo, when some animal, a dog
or fox, rushed from the hedge on the right

received intelligence of the sudden death of
his friend, he felt a sudden shock : but it was
a shock which had more relation to his own
individual and selfish interests than to anything that concerned the interests, temporal
or spiritual, of his dead friend. He felt
neither pity nor regret for him : but he felt
that he himself was deprived of a sort of
support, or resource, or refuge for his weak
and drivelling rogueries. Joe was a bad
man, without the ability necessary to nurse
and strengthen his roguish disposition : but
Bartley was a thorough knave, with all the
qualities and acquirements essential to the
execution of the most villainous designs.
They were a need to each other : and hence
Whitmore was shocked when he heard that
his support was suddenly taken from under
him. But we shall pass from the contem-
plation of these scenes and objects of human
depravity, and direct the reader's attention
to more kindly and agreeable subjects.

Colonel Brown, having established himself
with his brother and sister at Ash Grove
House, became soon acquainted with all the
circumstances relating to the different members of the family. He knew of the engagement between his nephew, Herbert Granville,

and Miss Moore; and also of that between
his niece Julia Granville and Henry Moore.
He approved of both; and expressed his
desire to have them carried out without
delay. He and his old friend, George Moore,
were constantly together; and they had
agreed upon the desirableness of the double
match. Mrs. Moore and her sister Mrs.
Credan were now of one accord as to the
excellence of the arrangement, and only
wondered at themselves for not having long
since seen how suitable and desirable it was
in every point of view. In fact, according to
their present view of the matter, nothing in
the world could be more fitting, or better
calculated to accomplish the happiness of all
parties. Mrs. Credan "was always sure,"
so she said, " that it was just the right
thing, for her niece idolized Herbert Granville, and Herbert Granville idolized her.
And where could you find a more accomplished, a more elegant, and a more noble-
minded man than Herbert Granville? He
was a match for a princess; and her niece
was the happiest of women to have won the
love of such a man. And as for Julia
Granville, she was a charming creature—so
amiable, so graceful, so accomplished, her

nephew was most fortunate in having obtained the affections of such a woman." In
short, all were delighted with the whole
arrangement, and we need not inform the
reader—for he, or she, already knows it as
well as ourselves—that the parties immediately concerned were the most delighted of
all, for to them the hour of their union was
the goal of their dearest wishes, and the
consummation of their earthly happiness.

A few weeks passed over, and the final
arrangements were made for the bridal ceremony. Both couples were to be married on
the same evening; and the ceremony was to
take place at Ash Grove House. This latter
part of the arrangement was adopted at the
instance of the colonel, notwithstanding the
efforts of the Moores and the Credans in
favour of Brookfield Hall. The Rev. Dr.
Markham was to bind the golden knot in
both cases; and the colonel was to give away
Julia. These formed the specific portions of
the colonel's arrangements ; to any other
parts of the general programme he was not
particularly wedded. A large party assembled at Ash Grove House on the evening of
the wedding. The Earl and Countess of
Fairborough, accompanied by Lord Milford,

were amongst the first arrivals. Sir Michael
Carey and his two daughters were present;
as were also the Rev. Mr. Grigger, Geoffrey
Credan, of Mooloch, his wife, son and
daughters, and several members of the
aristocratic families of the county.

The servants' hall was crowded with the
sons and daughters of the surrounding
peasantry; even the aged heads of families,
men and women, came "to have a look at
Miss Julia and Miss Fanny—the darlin' ladies
—in their lovely weddin' dresses. And shure,
they also wanted to look at their noble
Masther Herbert, and at Masther Moore.
May the blessin's of heaven rest upon their
hearts this night."

The captain was there, in a span-new
suit—a bottle-green frock-coat, and striped
trousers, with green vest, and neck-cloth of
the same colour—provided specially for the
occasion. He danced a hornpipe in the
drawing-room, in his very best style, to the
music of the piano; and received the plaudits
of all present. The colonel took wine with
him, and spoke of him in terms of affectionate
regard. The ladies chatted familiarly with
him; and Julia and Fanny, now Mrs. Moore
and Mrs. Granville, presented him each with

a bridal memento. Denny Mullins was there in the "height of good spirits," so he said. And, after having played for some time in the servants' hall, he was sent for to the drawing-room, where he played his best planxties and jigs, and received the warmest approbation of the ladies and gentlemen. He played "Haste to the Wedding" for Master Herbert and his lady, and then a quadrille, in which Lord and Lady Fairborough, Lord Milford, Sir Michael Carey, the Misses Carey, and some others took part. Denny was not forgotten by the brides— they each presented him with a gift, and he felt himself to be "one of the happiest men in all Ireland that minute." Soon after, Ned Doolin and Bill Cleary, with Peggy Cummins and Judy Casey, were performing a single reel in the hall to Denny's best music, while Paddy Larkin and Anty Dreelin were seated at a table at the upper end of the apartment, in company with Mr. Moore's fat butler, and with Nelly Corcoran and her granddaughter Minny Rice, enjoying themselves over a dish of roast beef and plum-pudding, with a garnish of turkey and wild fowl, enlivened with the sparkle of port wine and whisky in large decanters. There was merriment in the drawing-room, and there was merriment in the hall. The drawing-room guests retired about three o'clock the following morning, but the revellers in the hall kept it up for two hours longer. They then broke up, and as Nelly Corcoran was passing out through the hall, holding her granddaughter by the hand, she whispered into Denny's ear, "Didn't I tell you how 'twould be?"

THE END.

PRINTED BY GILBERT AND RIVINGTON, LIMITED, ST. JOHN'S SQUARE, E.C.

A Catalogue of American and Foreign Books Published or Imported by MESSRS. SAMPSON LOW & CO. *can be had on application.*

Crown Buildings, 188, *Fleet Street, London,*
September, 1883.

𝔄 𝔖election from tꞮje 𝔏ist of 𝔅ooks

PUBLISHED BY

SAMPSON LOW, MARSTON, SEARLE, & RIVINGTON.

ALPHABETICAL LIST.

ABOUT Some Fellows. By an ETON BOY, Author of " A Day of my Life." Cloth limp, square 16mo, 2s. 6d.

Adams (C. K.) Manual of Historical Literature. Crown 8vo, 12s. 6d.

Alcott (Louisa M.). Jack and Jill. 16mo, 5s.

—— *Proverb Stories.* 16mo, 3s. 6d.

—— *Old-Fashioned Thanksgiving Day.* 3s. 6d.

—— *Shawl Straps.* 2s. 6d.

—— See also "Low's Standard Novels" and "Rose Library."

Aldrich (T. B.) Friar Jerome's Beautiful Book, &c. Very choicely printed on hand-made paper, parchment cover, 3s. 6d.

—— *Poetical Works. Édition de Luxe.* Very handsomely bound and illustrated, 21s.

Allen (E. A.) Rock me to Sleep, Mother. With 18 full-page Illustrations, elegantly bound, fcap. 4to, 5s.

American Men of Letters. Lives of Thoreau, Irving, Webster. Small post 8vo, cloth, 2s. 6d. each.

Andersen (Hans Christian) Fairy Tales. With 10 full-page Illustrations in Colours by E. V. B. Cheap Edition, 5s.

Angler's Strange Experiences (An). By COTSWOLD ISYS. With numerous Illustrations, 4to, 5s.

Angling. See "British Fisheries Directory," "Cutcliffe," "Lambert," "Martin," and "Theakston."

Archer (William) English Dramatists of To-day. Crown 8vo, 8s. 6d.

Arnold (G. M.) Robert Pocock, the Gravesend Historian. Crown 8vo, cloth, 5s.

Art Education. See "Biographies of Great Artists," "Illustrated Text Books," "Mollett's Dictionary."

Audsley (G. A.) Ornamental Arts of Japan. 90 Plates, 74 in Colours and Gold, with General and Descriptive Text. 2 vols folio, £16 16s.

A

Audsley (*G. A.*) *The Art of Chromo-Lithography.* Coloured
Plates and Text. Folio, 63s.

Audsley (*W. and G. A.*) *Outlines of Ornament.* Small folio,
very numerous Illustrations, 31s. 6d.

Auerbach (*B.*) *Spinoza.* Translated. 2 vols., 18mo, 4s.

BALDWIN (*J.*) *Story of Siegfried.* Emblematical binding, 6s.

Bankruptcy : Inutility of the Laws. Lord Sherbrooke's Remedy.
Crown 8vo, 1s.

Bathgate (*Alexander*) *Waitaruna : A Story of New Zealand*
Life. Crown 8vo, cloth, 5s.

Batley (*A. W.*) *Etched Studies for Interior Decoration.* Imperial folio, 52s. 6d.

THE BAYARD SERIES.

Edited by the late J. HAIN FRISWELL.

Comprising Pleasure Books of Literature produced in the Choicest Style as
Companionable Volumes at Home and Abroad.

"We can hardly imagine better books for boys to read or for men to ponder
over."—*Times.*

*Price 2s. 6d. each Volume, complete in itself, flexible cloth extra, gilt edges,
with silk Headbands and Registers.*

The Story of the Chevalier Bayard.
By M. De Berville.

De Joinville's St. Louis, King of
France.

The Essays of Abraham Cowley, including all his Prose Works.

Abdallah ; or, The Four Leaves.
By Edouard Laboullaye.

Table-Talk and Opinions of Na-
poleon Buonaparte.

Vathek : An Oriental Romance.
By William Beckford.

Words of Wellington : Maxims and
Opinions of the Great Duke.

Dr. Johnson's Rasselas, Prince of
Abyssinia. With Notes.

Hazlitt's Round Table. With Biographical Introduction.

The Religio Medici, Hydriotaphia,
and the Letter to a Friend. By
Sir Thomas Browne, Knt.

Ballad Poetry of the Affections. By
Robert Buchanan.

Coleridge's Christabel, and other
Imaginative Poems. With Preface
by Algernon C. Swinburne.

Lord Chesterfield's Letters, Sentences, and Maxims. With Introduction by the Editor, and
Essay on Chesterfield by M. de
Ste.-Beuve, of the French Academy.

The King and the Commons. A
Selection of Cavalier and Puritan
Songs. Edited by Professor Morley.

Essays in Mosaic. By Thos. Ballan-
tyne.

My Uncle Toby ; his Story and his
Friends. Edited by P. Fitzgerald.

Reflections ; or, Moral Sentences and
Maxims of the Duke de la Roche-
foucauld.

Socrates : Memoirs for English
Readers from Xenophon's Memo-
rabilia. By Edw. Levien.

Prince Albert's Golden Precepts.

A Case containing 12 Volumes, price 31s. 6d. ; or the Case separately, price 3s. 6d.

Bell (Major) : Rambla—Spain. From Irun to Cerbere.
Crown 8vo, 8s. 6d.

Beumers' German Copybooks. In six gradations at 4d. each.

Biart (Lucien) Adventures of a Young Naturalist. Edited and
adapted by PARKER GILLMORE. With 117 Illustrations on Wood.
Post 8vo, cloth extra, gilt edges, New Edition, 7s. 6d.

Bickersteth's Hymnal Companion to Book of Common Prayer
may be had in various styles and bindings from 1d. to 21s. *Price
List and Prospectus will be forwarded on application.*

Bickersteth (Rev. E. H., M.A.) The Clergyman in his Home.
Small post 8vo, 1s.

—— *Evangelical Churchmanship and Evangelical Eclecticism.*
8vo, 1s.

—— *From Year to Year: a Collection of Original Poetical*
Pieces. Small post 8vo.

—— *The Master's Home-Call; or, Brief Memorials of Alice*
Frances Bickersteth. 20th Thousand. 32mo, cloth gilt, 1s.

—— *The Master's Will.* A Funeral Sermon preached on
the Death of Mrs. S. Gurney Buxton. Sewn, 6d. ; cloth gilt, 1s.

—— *The Shadow of the Rock.* A Selection of Religious
Poetry. 18mo, cloth extra, 2s. 6d.

—— *The Shadowed Home and the Light Beyond.* 7th
Edition, crown 8vo, cloth extra, 5s.

Bilbrough (E. J.) " Twixt France and Spain." [*In the press.*

Biographies of the Great Artists (Illustrated). Crown 8vo,
emblematical binding, 3s. 6d. per volume, except where the price is given.

Claude Lorrain.*	Mantegna and Fiancia.
Correggio, by M. E. Heaton, 2s. 6d.	Meissonier, by J. W. Mollett, 2s. 6d.
Della Robbia and Cellini, 2s. 6d.	Michelangelo Buonarotti, by Clément.
Albrecht Dürer, by R. F. Heath.	Murillo, by Ellen E. Minor, 2s. 6d.
Figure Painters of Holland.	Overbeck, by J. B. Atkinson.
Fra Angelico, Masaccio, and Botticelli.	Raphael, by N. D'Anvers.
Fra Bartolommeo, Albertinelli, and	Rembrandt, by J. W. Mollett.
Andrea del Sarto.	Reynolds, by F. S. Pulling.
Gainsborough and Constable.	Rubens, by C. W. Kett.
Ghiberti and Donatello, 2s. 6d.	Tintoretto, by W. R. Osler.
Giotto, by Harry Quilter.	Titian, by R. F. Heath.
Hans Holbein, by Joseph Cundall.	Turner, by Cosmo Monkhouse.
Hogarth, by Austin Dobson.	Vandyck and Hals, by P. R. Head.
Landseer, by F. G. Stevens.	Velasquez, by E. Stowe.
Lawrence and Romney, by Lord	Vernet and Delaroche, by J. R.
Ronald Gower, 2s. 6d.	Rees.
Leonardo da Vinci.	Watteau, by J. W. Mollett, 2s. 6d.
Little Masters of Germany, by W.	Wilkie, by J. W. Mollett.
B. Scott.	

* *Not yet published.*

Bird (*F. J.*) *American Practical Dyer's Companion.* 8vo, 42s.

Bird (*H. E.*) *Chess Practice.* 8vo, 2s. 6d.

Black (*Wm.*) *Novels.* See " Low's Standard Library."

Blackburn (*Henry*) *Breton Folk : An Artistic Tour in Brittany.*
With 171 Illustrations by RANDOLPH CALDECOTT. Imperial 8vo,
cloth extra, gilt edges, 21s.; plainer binding, 10s. 6d.

———— *Pyrenees* (*The*). With 100 Illustrations by GUSTAVE
DORÉ, corrected to 1881. Crown 8vo, 7s. 6d.

Blackmore (*R. D.*) *Lorna Doone. Édition de luxe.* Crown 4to,
very numerous Illustrations, cloth, gilt edges, 31s. 6d.; parchment,
uncut, top gilt, 35s. Cheap Edition, small post 8vo, 6s.

———— *Novels.* See " Low's Standard Library."

Blaikie (*William*) *How to get Strong and how to Stay so.*
A Manual of Rational, Physical, Gymnastic, and other Exercises.
With Illustrations, small post 8vo, 5s.

Boats of the World, Depicted and Described by one of the Craft.
With Coloured Plates, showing every kind of rig, 4to, 3s. 6d.

Bock (*Carl*). *The Head Hunters of Borneo: Up the Mahak-*
kam, and Down the Barita; also Journeyings in Sumatra. 1 vol.,
super-royal 8vo, 32 Coloured Plates, cloth extra, 36s.

———— *Temples and Elephants.* A Narrative of a Journey
through Upper Siam and Lao. With numerous Coloured and other
Illustrations, 8vo.

Bonwick (*James*) *First Twenty Years of Australia.* Crown
8vo, 5s.

———— *Port Philip Settlement.* 8vo, numerous Illustrations, 21s.

Borneo. See BOCK.

Bosanquet (*Rev. C.*) *Blossoms from the King's Garden : Sermons*
for Children. 2nd Edition, small post 8vo, cloth extra, 6s.

Boussenard (*L.*) *Crusoes of Guiana ; or, the White Tiger.*
Illustrated by J. FERAT. 7s. 6d.

Boy's Froissart. King Arthur. Mabinogion. Percy. See
LANIER.

Bradshaw (*J.*) *New Zealand as it is.* 8vo, 12s. 6d.

Brassey (*Lady*) *Tahiti.* With 31 Autotype Illustrations after
Photos. by Colonel STUART-WORTLEY. Fcap. 4to, very tastefully
bound, 21s.

Braune (*Wilhelm*) *Gothic Grammar.* Translated by G. H.
BULG. 3s. 6d.

Brisse (Baron) Ménus (366, *one for each day of the year*). Each Ménu is given in French and English, with the recipe for making every dish mentioned. Translated from the French of BARON BRISSE, by Mrs. MATTHEW CLARKE. 2nd Edition. Crown 8vo, 5*s*.

British Fisheries Directory, 1883-84. Small 8vo, 2*s*. 6*d*.

Brittany. See BLACKBURN.

Broglie (Duc de) Frederick II. and Maria Theresa. 2 vols., 8vo, 30*s*.

Browne (G. Lathom) Narratives of Nineteenth Century State Trials. First Period: From the Union with Ireland to the Death of George IV., 1801—1830. 2nd Edition, 2 vols., crown 8vo, cloth, 26*s*.

Browne (Lennox) and Behnke (Emil) Voice, Song, and Speech. Medium 8vo, cloth.

Bryant (W. C.) and Gay (S. H.) History of the United States. 4 vols., royal 8vo, profusely Illustrated, 60*s*.

Bryce (Rev. Professor) Manitoba: its History, Growth, and Present Position. Crown 8vo, with Illustrations and Maps, 7*s*. 6*d*.

Bunyan's Pilgrim's Progress. With 138 original Woodcuts. Small post 8vo, cloth gilt, 3*s*. 6*d*.

Burnaby (Capt.) On Horseback through Asia Minor. 2 vols., 8vo, 38*s*. Cheaper Edition, crown 8vo, 10*s*. 6*d*.

Burnaby (Mrs. F.) High Alps in Winter; or, Mountaineering in Search of Health. By Mrs. FRED BURNABY. With Portrait of the Authoress, Map, and other Illustrations. Handsomely bound in cloth, 14*s*.

Butler (W. F.) The Great Lone Land; an Account of the Red River Expedition, 1869-70. With Illustrations and Map. Fifth and Cheaper Edition, crown 8vo, cloth extra, 7*s*. 6*d*.

—— *Invasion of England, told twenty years after, by an Old* Soldier. Crown 8vo, 2*s*. 6*d*.

—— *Red Cloud; or, the Solitary Sioux.* Imperial 16mo, numerous illustrations, gilt edges, 7*s*. 6*d*.

—— *The Wild North Land; the Story of a Winter Journey* with Dogs across Northern North America. Demy 8vo, cloth, with numerous Woodcuts and a Map, 4th Edition, 18*s*. Cr. 8vo, 7*s*. 6*d*.

Buxton (H. J. W.) Painting, English and American. With numerous Illustrations. Crown 8vo, 5*s*.

CADOGAN (Lady A.) Illustrated Games of Patience. Twenty-four Diagrams in Colours, with Descriptive Text. Foolscap 4to, cloth extra, gilt edges, 3rd Edition, 12s. 6d.

California. See "Nordhoff."

Cambridge Staircase (A). By the Author of "A Day of my Life at Eton." Small crown 8vo, cloth, 2s. 6d.

Cambridge Trifles; or, Splutterings from an Undergraduate Pen. By the Author of "A Day of my Life at Eton," &c. 16mo, cloth extra, 2s. 6d.

Capello (H.) and Ivens (R.) From Benguella to the Territory of Yacca. Translated by ALFRED ELWES. With Maps and over 130 full-page and text Engravings. 2 vols., 8vo, 42s.

Carleton (W.). See "Rose Library."

Carlyle (T.) Reminiscences of my Irish Journey in 1849. Crown 8vo, 7s. 6d.

Carnegie (A.) American Four-in-Hand in Britain. Small 4to, Illustrated, 10s. 6d.

Chairman's Handbook (The). By R. F. D. PALGRAVE, Clerk of the Table of the House of Commons. 5th Edition, enlarged and re-written, 2s.

Challamel (M. A.) History of Fashion in France. With 21 Plates, coloured by hand, satin-wood binding, imperial 8vo, 28s.

Changed Cross (The), and other Religious Poems. 16mo, 2s. 6d.

Charities of London. See Low's.

Chattock (R. S.) Practical Notes on Etching. Second Edition, 8vo, 7s. 6d.

Chess. See BIRD (H. E.).

China. See COLQUHOUN.

Choice Editions of Choice Books. 2s. 6d. each. Illustrated by C. W. COPE, R.A., T. CRESWICK, R.A., E. DUNCAN, BIRKET FOSTER, J. C. HORSLEY, A.R.A., G. HICKS, R. REDGRAVE, R.A., C. STONEHOUSE, F. TAYLER, G. THOMAS, H. J. TOWNSHEND, E. H. WEHNERT, HARRISON WEIR, &c.

Bloomfield's Farmer's Boy.	Milton's L'Allegro.
Campbell's Pleasures of Hope.	Poetry of Nature. Harrison Weir.
Coleridge's Ancient Mariner.	Rogers' (Sam.) Pleasures of Memory.
Goldsmith's Deserted Village.	Shakespeare's Songs and Sonnets.
Goldsmith's Vicar of Wakefield.	Tennyson's May Queen.
Gray's Elegy in a Churchyard.	Elizabethan Poets.
Keat's Eve of St. Agnes.	Wordsworth's Pastoral Poems.

"Such works are a glorious beatification for a poet."—*Athenæum.*

Christ in Song. By Dr. PHILIP SCHAFF. A New Edition, revised, cloth, gilt edges, 6s. .

Chromo-Lithography. See "Audsley."

Cid (Ballads of the). By the Rev. GERRARD LEWIS. Fcap. 8vo, parchment, 2s. 6d.

Clay (Charles M.) Modern Hagar. 2 vols., crown 8vo, 21s. See also "Rose Library."

Colquhoun (A. R.) Across Chrysê ; From Canton to Mandalay. With Maps and very numerous Illustrations, 2 vols., 8vo, 42s.

Composers. See "Great Musicians."

Confessions of a Frivolous Girl (The) : A Novel of Fashionable Life. Edited by ROBERT GRANT. Crown 8vo, 6s. Paper boards, 1s.

Cook (Dutton) Book of the Play. New and Revised Edition. 1 vol., cloth extra, 3s. 6d.

—— *On the Stage : Studies of Theatrical History and the* Actor's Art. 2 vols., 8vo, cloth, 24s.

Coote (W.) Wanderings South by East. Illustrated, 8vo, 21s. New and Cheaper Edition, 10s. 6d.

—— *Western Pacific.* Illustrated, crown 8vo, 2s. 6d.

Costume. See SMITH (J. MOYR).

Cruise of the Walnut Shell (The). An instructive and amusing Story, told in Rhyme, for Children. With 32 Coloured Plates. Square fancy boards, 5s.

Curtis (C. B.) Velazquez and Murillo. With Etchings &c., Royal 8vo, 31s. 6d.; large paper, 63s.

Cutcliffe (H. C.) Trout Fishing in Rapid Streams. Cr. 8vo, 3s. 6d.

*D*ANVERS *(N.) An Elementary History of Art.* Crown 8vo, 10s. 6d.

—— *Elementary History of Music.* Crown 8vo, 2s. 6d.

—— *Handbooks of Elementary Art—Architecture; Sculp-* ture ; Old Masters ; Modern Painting. Crown 8vo, 3s. 6d. each.

Day of My Life (A) ; or, Every-Day Experiences at Eton. By an ETON BOY, Author of "About Some Fellows." 16mo, cloth extra, 2s. 6d. 6th Thousand.

Day's Collacon : an Encyclopædia of Prose Quotations. Imperial 8vo, cloth, 31s. 6d.

Decoration. Vol. II., folio, 6s. Vols. III, IV., V., and VI., New Series, folio, 7s. 6d. each.

—— See also BATLEY.

De Leon (E.) Egypt under its Khedives. With Map and
Illustrations. Crown 8vo, 4s.

Don Quixote, Wit and Wisdom of. By EMMA THOMPSON.
Square fcap. 8vo, 3s. 6d.

Donnelly (Ignatius) Atlantis ; or, the Antediluvian World.
Crown 8vo, 12s. 6d.

—— *Ragnarok : The Age of Fire and Gravel.* Illustrated,
Crown 8vo, 12s. 6d.

Dos Passos (J. R.) Law of Stockbrokers and Stock Exchanges.
8vo, 35s.

Dougall (James Dalziel, F.S.A., F.Z.A.) Shooting: its Ap-
pliances, Practice, and Purpose. New Edition, revised with additions.
Crown 8vo, cloth extra, 7s. 6d.
"The book is admirable in every way. . . . . We wish it every success."—*Globe.*
"A very complete treatise. . . . . Likely to take high rank as an authority on
shooting."—*Daily News.*

Drama. See ARCHER, COOK (DUTTON), WILLIAMS (M.).

Durnford (Col. A. W.) A Soldier's Life and Work in South
Africa, 1872-9. 8vo, 14s.

Dyeing. See BIRD (F. J.).

EDUCATIONAL Works published in Great Britain.
Classified Catalogue. Second Edition, revised and corrected, 8vo,
cloth extra, 5s.

Egypt. See "De Leon," "Foreign Countries," "Senior."

Eidlitz (Leopold) Nature and Functions of Art (The); and
especially of Architecture. Medium 8vo, cloth, 21s.

Electricity. See GORDON.

Emerson Birthday Book. Extracts from the Writings of R. W.
Emerson. Square 16mo, cloth extra, numerous Illustrations, very
choice binding, 3s. 6d.

Emerson (R. W.) Life. By G. W. COOKE. Crown 8vo, 8s. 6d.

English Catalogue of Books. Vol. III., 1872—1880. Royal
8vo, half-morocco, 42s.

English Philosophers. Edited by E. B. IVAN MÜLLER, M.A.
A series intended to give a concise view of the works and lives of English
thinkers. Crown 8vo volumes of 180 or 200 pp., price 3s. 6d. each.

Francis Bacon, by Thomas Fowler.	*John Stuart Mill, by Miss Helen
Hamilton, by W. H. S. Monck.	Taylor.
Hartley and James Mill, by G. S.	Shaftesbury and Hutcheson, by
Bower.	Professor Fowler.
	Adam Smith, by J. A. Farrer,

* *Not yet published.*

Episodes in the Life of an Indian Chaplain. Crown 8vo, cloth extra, 12s. 6d.

Episodes of French History. Edited, with Notes, Maps, and Illustrations, by GUSTAVE MASSON, B.A. Small 8vo, 2s. 6d. each.
  1. **Charlemagne and the Carlovingians.**
  2. **Louis XI. and the Crusades.**
  3. **Part I. Francis I. and Charles V.**
    ,, **II. Francis I. and the Renaissance.**
  4. **Henry IV. and the End of the Wars of Religion.**

Esmarch (Dr. Friedrich) Handbook on the Treatment of Wounded in War. Numerous Coloured Plates and Illustrations, 8vo, strongly bound, 1l. 8s.

Etcher (The). Containing 36 Examples of the Original Etched-work of Celebrated Artists, amongst others: BIRKET FOSTER, J. E. HODGSON, R.A., COLIN HUNTER, J. P. HESELTINE, ROBERT W. MACBETH, R. S. CHATTOCK, &c. Vols. for 1881 and 1882, imperial 4to, cloth extra, gilt edges, 2l. 12s. 6d. each.

Etching. See BATLEY, CHATTOCK.

Etchings (Modern) of Celebrated Paintings. 4to, 31s. 6d.

FARM Ballads, Festivals, and Legends. See "Rose Library."

Fashion (History of). See "Challamel."

Fawcett (Edgar) A Gentleman of Leisure. 1s.

Fechner (G. T.) On Life after Death. 12mo, vellum, 2s. 6d.

Felkin (R. W.) and Wilson (Rev. C. T.) Uganda and the Egyptian Soudan. With Map, numerous Illustrations, and Notes. By R. W. FELKIN, F.R.G.S., &c, &c.; and the Rev. C. T. WILSON, M.A. Oxon., F.R.G.S. 2 vols., crown 8vo, cloth, 28s.

Fenn (G. Manville) Off to the Wilds: A Story for Boys. Profusely Illustrated. Crown 8vo, 7s. 6d.

Ferguson (John) Ceylon in 1883. With numerous Illustrations. Crown 8vo.

Ferns. See HEATH.

Fields (J. T.) Yesterdays with Authors. New Ed., 8vo., 16s.

Florence. See "Yriarte."

Flowers of Shakespeare. 32 beautifully Coloured Plates, with the passages which refer to the flowers. Small 4to, 5s.

Foreign Countries and British Colonies. A series of Descriptive Handbooks. Each volume will be the work of a writer who has special acquaintance with the subject. Crown 8vo, 3s. 6d. each.

Australia, by J. F. Vesey Fitzgerald.
Austria, by D. Kay, F.R.G.S.
*Canada, by W. Fraser Rae.
Denmark and Iceland, by E. C. Otté.
Egypt, by S. Lane Poole, B.A.
France, by Miss M. Roberts.
Germany, by S. Baring-Gould.
Greece, by L. Sergeant, B.A.
*Holland, by R. L. Poole.
Japan, by S. Mossman.
*New Zealand.
*Persia, by Major-Gen. Sir F. Goldsmid.

Peru, by Clements R. Markham, C.B.
Russia, by W. R. Morfill, M.A.
Spain, by Rev. Wentworth Webster.
Sweden and Norway, by F. H. Woods.
*Switzerland, by W. A. P. Coolidge, M.A.
*Turkey-in-Asia, by J. C. McCoan, M.P.
West Indies, by C. H. Eden, F.R.G.S.

* *Not ready yet.*

Fortunes made in Business. 2 vols., demy 8vo, cloth, 32s.

Franc (Maud Jeanne). The following form one Series, small post 8vo, in uniform cloth bindings, with gilt edges:—

Emily's Choice. 5s.
Hall's Vineyard. 4s.
John's Wife: A Story of Life in South Australia. 4s.
Marian; or, The Light of Some One's Home. 5s.
Silken Cords and Iron Fetters. 4s.

Vermont Vale. 5s.
Minnie's Mission. 4s.
Little Mercy. 4s.
Beatrice Melton's Discipline. 4s.
No Longer a Child. 4s.
Golden Gifts. 4s.
Two Sides to Every Question. 4s.

Francis (F.) War, Waves, and Wanderings, including a Cruise in the "Lancashire Witch." 2 vols., crown 8vo, cloth extra, 24s.

Frederick the Great. See "Broglie."

French. See "Julien."

Froissart. See "Lanier."

GENTLE Life (Queen Edition). 2 vols. in 1, small 4to, 6s.

THE GENTLE LIFE SERIES.

Price 6s. each; or in calf extra, price 10s. 6d.; Smaller Edition, cloth extra, 2s. 6d., except where price is named.

The Gentle Life. Essays in aid of the Formation of Character of Gentlemen and Gentlewomen.

About in the World. Essays by Author of "The Gentle Life."

Like unto Christ. A New Translation of Thomas à Kempis' "De Imitatione Christi."

Familiar Words. An Index Verborum, or Quotation Handbook. 6*s.*

Essays by Montaigne. Edited and Annotated by the Author of "The Gentle Life."

The Gentle Life. 2nd Series.

The Silent Hour: Essays, Original and Selected. By the Author of "The Gentle Life."

Half-Length Portraits. Short Studies of Notable Persons. By J. HAIN FRISWELL.

Essays on English Writers, for the Self-improvement of Students in English Literature.

Other People's Windows. By J. HAIN FRISWELL. 6*s.*

A Man's Thoughts. By J. HAIN FRISWELL.

The Countess of Pembroke's Arcadia. By Sir PHILIP SIDNEY. New Edition, 6*s.*

George Eliot: a Critical Study of her Life. By G. W. COOKE. Crown 8vo, 10*s.* 6*d.*

German. See BEUMER.

Germany. By S. BARING-GOULD. Crown 8vo, 3*s.* 6*d.*

Gibbs (J. R.) British Honduras, Historical and Descriptive. Crown 8vo, 7*s.* 6*d.*

Gilder (W. H.) Ice-Pack and Tundra. An Account of the Search for the "Jeannette." 8vo, 18*s.*

—— *Schwatka's Search.* Sledging in quest of the Franklin Records. Illustrated, 8vo, 12*s.* 6*d.*

Gilpin's Forest Scenery. Edited by F. G. HEATH. Large post 8vo, with numerous Illustrations. Uniform with "The Fern World," re-issued, 7*s.* 6*d.*

Glas (John) The Lord's Supper. Crown 8vo, 5*s.*

Gordon (J. E. H., B.A. Cantab.) Four Lectures on Electric Induction. Delivered at the Royal Institution, 1878-9. With numerous Illustrations. Cloth limp, square 16mo, 3*s.*

—— *Electric Lighting.* [*In preparation.*

—— *Physical Treatise on Electricity and Magnetism.* New Edition, revised and enlarged, with coloured, full-page, and other Illustrations. 2 vols., 8vo, 42*s.*

Gouffé. The Royal Cookery Book. By JULES GOUFFÉ ; translated and adapted for English use by ALPHONSE GOUFFÉ, Head Pastrycook to Her Majesty the Queen. Illustrated with large plates printed in colours. 161 Woodcuts, 8vo, cloth extra, gilt edges, 42*s.*

—— *Domestic Edition, half-bound,* 10*s.* 6*d.*

12 · Sampson Low, Marston, & Co.'s

Great Artists. See "Biographies."

Great Historic Galleries of England (The). Edited by LORD RONALD GOWER, F.S.A., Trustee of the National Portrait Gallery. Illustrated by 24 large and carefully executed *permanent* Photographs of some of the most celebrated Pictures by the Great Masters. Vol. I., imperial 4to, cloth extra, gilt edges, 36s. Vol. II., with 36 large permanent photographs, 2l. 12s. 6d.

Great Musicians. Edited by F. HUEFFER. A Series of Biographies, crown 8vo, 3s. each :—

Bach.	Handel.	Purcell.
*Beethoven.	*Haydn.	Rossini.
*Berlioz.	*Marcello.	Schubert.
English Church Composers. By BARETT.	Mendelssohn.	*Schumann.
	Mozart.	Richard Wagner.
*Glück.	*Palestrina.	Weber.

* *In preparation.*

Grohmann (W. A. B.) Camps in the Rockies. 8vo, 12s. 6d.

Guizot's History of France. Translated by ROBERT BLACK. Super-royal 8vo, very numerous Full-page and other Illustrations. In 8 vols., cloth extra, gilt, each 24s. This work is re-issued in cheaper binding, 8 vols., at 10s. 6d. each.

"It supplies a want which has long been felt, and ought to be in the hands of all students of history."—*Times.*

————————— **Masson's School Edition.** The History of France from the Earliest Times to the Outbreak of the Revolution ; abridged from the Translation by Robert Black, M.A., with Chronological Index, Historical and Genealogical Tables, &c. By Professor GUSTAVE MASSON, B.A., Assistant Master at Harrow School. With 24 full-page Portraits, and many other Illustrations. 1 vol., demy 8vo, 600 pp., cloth extra, 10s. 6d.

Guizot's History of England. In 3 vols. of about 500 pp. each, containing 60 to 70 Full-page and other Illustrations, cloth extra, gilt, 24s. each ; re-issue in cheaper binding, 10s. 6d. each.

"For luxury of typography, plainness of print, and beauty of illustration, these volumes, of which but one has as yet appeared in English, will hold their own against any production of an age so luxurious as our own in everything, typography not excepted."—*Times.*

Guyon (Mde.) Life. By UPHAM. 6th Edition, crown 8vo, 6s.

HALL (W. W.) **How to Live Long; or,** 1408 Health Maxims, Physical, Mental, and Moral. By W. W. HALL, A.M., M.D. Small post 8vo, cloth, 2s. 2nd Edition.

Harper's Christmas No., 1882. Elephant folio, 2s. 6d.

Harper's Monthly Magazine. Published Monthly. 160 pages, fully Illustrated. 1s.
   Vol. I. December, 1880, to May, 1881.
   ,,   II. June to November, 1881.
   ,,   III. December, 1881, to May, 1882
   ,,   IV. June to November, 1882.
   ,,   V. December, 1882, to May, 1883.
Super-royal 8vo, 8s. 6d. each.

   "'Harper's Magazine' is so thickly sown with excellent illustrations that to count them would be a work of time; not that it is a picture magazine, for the engravings illustrate the text after the manner seen in some of our choicest *éditions de luxe.*"— *St. James's Gazette.*
   "It is so pretty, so big, and so cheap. . . . An extraordinary shillingsworth—160 large octavo pages, with over a score of articles, and more than three times as many illustrations."—*Edinburgh Daily Review.*
   "An amazing shillingsworth . . . combining choice literature of both nations."— *Nonconformist.*

Hatton (Joseph) Journalistic London : with Engravings and Portraits of Distinguished Writers of the Day. Fcap. 4to, 12s. 6d.

────── *Three Recruits, and the Girls they left behind them.* Small post 8vo, 6s.
   "It hurries us along in unflagging excitement."-- *Times.*

──── See also "Low's Standard Novels."

Heath (Francis George). Autumnal Leaves. New Edition, with Coloured Plates in Facsimile from Nature. Crown 8vo, 14s.

────── *Burnham Beeches.* Illustrated, small 8vo, 1s.

────── *Fern Paradise.* New Edition, with Plates and Photos., crown 8vo, 12s. 6d.

────── *Fern World.* With Nature-printed Coloured Plates. New Edition, crown 8vo, 12s. 6d.

────── *Gilpin's Forest Scenery.* Illustrated, 8vo, 12s. 6d.; New Edition, 7s. 6d.

────── *Our Woodland Trees.* With Coloured Plates and Engravings. Small 8vo, 12s. 6d.

──── *Peasant Life in the West of England.* Crown 8vo, 10s. 6d.

────── *Sylvan Spring.* With Coloured, &c., Illustrations. 12s. 6d.

────── *Trees and Ferns.* Illustrated, crown 8vo, 3s. 6d.

────── *Where to Find Ferns.* Crown 8vo, 2s.

Heber (Bishop) Hymns. Illustrated Edition. With upwards of 100 beautiful Engravings. Small 4to, handsomely bound, 7s. 6d. Morocco, 18s. 6d. and 21s. New and Cheaper Edition, cloth, 3s. 6d.

Heldmann (*Bernard*) *Mutiny on Board the Ship* "*Leander.*" Small post 8vo, gilt edges, numerous Illustrations, 7*s*. 6*d*.

Henty (*G. A.*) *Winning his Spurs*. Numerous Illustrations Crown 8vo, 5*s*.

—————— *Cornet of Horse : A Story for Boys*. Illustrated, crown 8vo, 5*s*.

—————— *Jack Archer : Tale of the Crimea*. Illust., crown 8vo, 5*s*.

Herrick (*Robert*) *Poetry*. Preface by AUSTIN DOBSON. With numerous Illustrations by E. A. ABBEY. 4to, gilt edges, 42*s*.

History and Principles of Weaving by Hand and by Power. With several hundred Illustrations. By ALFRED BARLOW. Royal 8vo, cloth extra, 1*l*. 5*s*. Second Edition.

Hitchman (*Francis*) *Public Life of the Right Hon. Benjamin Disraeli*, Earl of Beaconsfield. New Edition, with Portrait. Crown 8vo, 3*s*. 6*d*.

Hole (*Rev. Canon*) *Nice and Her Neighbours*. Small 4to, with numerous choice Illustrations, 16*s*.

Holmes (*O. W.*) *The Poetical Works of Oliver Wendell Holmes*. In 2 vols., 18mo, exquisitely printed, and chastely bound in limp cloth, gilt tops, 10*s*. 6*d*.

Hoppus (*J. D.*) *Riverside Papers*. 2 vols., 12*s*.

Hovgaard (*A.*) See "Nordenskiöld's Voyage." 8vo, 21*s*.

Hugo (*Victor*) "*Ninety-Three.*" Illustrated. Crown 8vo, 6*s*.

—————— *Toilers of the Sea*. Crown 8vo, fancy boards, 2*s*.

—————— *and his Times*. Translated from the French of A. BARBOU by ELLEN E. FREWER. 120 Illustrations, many of them from designs by Victor Hugo himself. Super-royal 8vo, cloth extra, 24*s*.

—————— *History of a Crime* (*The*) ; *Deposition of an Eye-witness*. The Story of the Coup d'État. Crown 8vo, 6*s*.

Hundred Greatest Men (*The*). 8 portfolios, 21*s*. each, or 4 vols., half-morocco, gilt edges, 10 guineas.

Hutchinson (*Thos.*) *Diary and Letters*. Demy 8vo, cloth, 16*s*.

Hutchisson (*W. H.*) *Pen and Pencil Sketches : Eighteen Years in Bengal*. 8vo, 18*s*.

Hygiene and Public Health (*A Treatise on*). Edited by A. H. BUCK, M.D. Illustrated by numerous Wood Engravings. In 2 royal 8vo vols., cloth, 42*s*.

Hymnal Companion of Common Prayer. See BICKERSTETH.

ILLUSTRATED Text-Books of Art-Education. Edited by
EDWARD J. POYNTER, R.A. Each Volume contains numerous Illus-
trations, and is strongly bound for the use of Students, price 5*s*. The
Volumes now ready are :—

PAINTING.

Classic and Italian. By PERCY R. HEAD.
German, Flemish, and Dutch.

French and Spanish.
English and American.

ARCHITECTURE.

Classic and Early Christian.
Gothic and Renaissance. By T. ROGER SMITH.

SCULPTURE.

Antique: Egyptian and Greek. | Renaissance and Modern.
Italian Sculptors of the 14th and 15th Centuries.

ORNAMENT.

Decoration in Colour. | Architectural Ornament.

Irving (Washington). Complete Library Edition of his Works
in 27 Vols., Copyright, Unabridged, and with the Author's Latest
Revisions, called the " Geoffrey Crayon " Edition, handsomely printed
in large square 8vo, on superfine laid paper. Each volume, of about
500 pages, fully Illustrated. 12*s*. 6*a*. per vol. *See also* "Little Britain."

————————————— ("American Men of Letters.") 2*s*. 6*d*.

JAMES (C.) Curiosities of Law and Lawyers. 8vo, 7*s*. 6*d*.

Japan. See AUDSLEY.

Jarves (J. J.) Italian Rambles. Square 16mo, 5*s*.

Johnson (O.) W. Lloyd Garrison and his Times. Crown 8vo,
12*s*. 6*d*.

Jones (Major) The Emigrants' Friend. A Complete Guide to
the United States. New Edition. 2*s*. 6*d*.

Jones (Mrs. Herbert) Sandringham : Past and Present. Illustrated, crown 8vo, 8*s*. 6*d*.

Julien (F.) English Student's French Examiner. 16mo. 2*s*.

—————— *First Lessons in Conversational French Grammar.*
Crown 8vo, 1*s*.

—————— *Conversational French Reader.* 16mo, cloth, 2*s*. 6*d*.

—————— *Petites Leçons de Conversation et de Grammaire.* New
Edition, 3*s*. 6*d*.; without Phrases, 2*s*. 6*d*.

—————— *Phrases of Daily Use.* Limp cloth, 6*d*.

Jung (Sir Salar) Life of. [*In the press*

*K*EMPIS (*Thomas à*) *Daily Text-Book.* Square 16mo, 2s. 6d.; interleaved as a Birthday Book, 3s. 6d.

Kingston (*W. H. G.*) *Dick Cheveley.* Illustrated, 16mo, gilt edges, 7s. 6d.; plainer binding, plain edges, 5s.

—— — *Fresh and Salt Water Tutors: A Story.* 3s. 6d.

—— — *Heir of Kilfinnan.* Uniform, 7s. 6d.; also 5s.

—— *Snow-Shoes and Canoes.* Uniform, 7s. 6d.; also 5s.

—— *Two Supercargoes.* Uniform, 7s. 6d.; also 5s.

—— *With Axe and Rifle.* Uniform, 7s. 6d.; also 5s.

Knight (*E. F.*) *Albania and Montenegro.* Illust. 8vo. 12s. 6d.

Knight (*E. J.*) *The Cruise of the "Falcon."* A Voyage round the World in a 30-Ton Yacht. Numerous Illust. 2 vols., crown 8vo.

*L*AMBERT (*O.*) *Angling Literature in England; and* Descriptions of Fishing by the Ancients. With a Notice of some Books on other Piscatorial Subjects. Fcap. 8vo, vellum, top gilt, 3s. 6d.

Lanier (*Sidney*) *The Boy's Froissart, selected from the Chroni-*cles of England, France, and Spain. Illustrated, extra binding, gilt edges, crown 8vo, 7s. 6d.

—— *Boy's King Arthur.* Uniform, 7s. 6d.

—— • *Boy's Mabinogion; Original Welsh Legends of King* Arthur. Uniform, 7s. 6d.

—— *Boy's Percy: Ballads of Love and Adventure, selected* from the "Reliques." Uniform, 7s. 6d.

Lansdell (*H.*) *Through Siberia.* 2 vols., demy 8vo, 30s.; New Edition, very numerous illustrations, 8vo, 10s. 6d.

Larden (*W.*) *School Course on Heat.* Second Edition, Illus-trated, crown 8vo, 5s.

Lathrop (*G. P.*) *In the Distance.* 2 vols., crown 8vo, 21s.

Legal Profession : Romantic Stories. 7s. 6d.

Lennard (*T. B.*) *To Married Women and Women about to be* Married, &c. 6d.

Lenormant (*F.*) *Beginnings of History.* Crown 8vo, 12s. 6d.

Leonardo da Vinci's Literary Works. Edited by Dr. JEAN PAUL RICHTER. Containing his Writings on Painting, Sculpture, and Architecture, his Philosophical Maxims, Humorous Writings, and Miscellaneous Notes on Personal Events, on his Contemporaries, on Literature, &c. ; for the first time published from Autograph Manu-scripts. By J. P. RICHTER, Ph.Dr., Hon. Member of the Royal and Imperial Academy of Rome, &c. 2 vols., imperial 8vo, containing about 200 Drawings in Autotype Reproductions, and numerous other Illustrations. Twelve Guineas.

Leyland (R. W.) Holiday in South Africa. Crown 8vo, 12s. 6d.

Library of Religious Poetry. A Collection of the Best Poems of all Ages and Tongues. Edited by PHILIP SCHAFF, D.D., LL.D., and ARTHUR GILMAN, M.A. Royal 8vo, 1036 pp., cloth extra, gilt edges, 21s.; re-issue in cheaper binding, 10s. 6d.

Lindsay (W. S.) History of Merchant Shipping and Ancient Commerce. Over 150 Illustrations, Maps, and Charts. In 4 vols., demy 8vo, cloth extra. Vols. 1 and 2, 11s. each; vols. 3 and 4, 14s. each. 4 vols. complete, 50s.

Lillie (Lucy E.) Prudence: a Story of Æsthetic London. Small 8vo, 5s.

Little Britain; together with *The Spectre Bridegroom,* and *A Legend of Sleepy Hollow.* By WASHINGTON IRVING. An entirely New *Edition de luxe,* specially suitable for Presentation. Illustrated by 120 very fine Engravings on Wood, by Mr. J. D. COOPER. Designed by Mr. CHARLES O. MURRAY. Re-issue, square crown 8vo, cloth, 6s.

Logan (Sir William E.) Life. By BERNARD J. HARRINGTON. 8vo, 12s. 6d.

Long (Mrs. W. H. C.) Peace and War in the Transvaal. 12mo, 3s. 6d.

Low's Standard Library of Travel and Adventure. Crown 8vo, bound uniformly in cloth extra, price 7s. 6d., except where price is given.

1. The Great Lone Land. By Major W. F. BUTLER, C.B.
2. The Wild North Land. By Major W. F. BUTLER, C.B.'
3. How I found Livingstone. By H. M. STANLEY.
4. Through the Dark Continent. By H. M. STANLEY. 12s. 6d.
5. The Threshold of the Unknown Region. By C. R. MARK-HAM. (4th Edition, with Additional Chapters, 10s. 6d.)
6. Cruise of the Challenger. By W. J. J. SPRY, R.N.
7. Burnaby's On Horseback through Asia Minor. 10s. 6d.
8. Schweinfurth's Heart of Africa. 2 vols., 15s.
9. Marshall's Through America.
10. Lansdell's Through Siberia. Illustrated and unabridged, 10s. 6d.

Low's Standard Novels. Small post 8vo, cloth extra, 6s. each, unless otherwise stated.

Work. A Story of Experience. By LOUISA M. ALCOTT.

A Daughter of Heth. By W. BLACK.

In Silk Attire. By W. BLACK.

Kilmeny. A Novel. By W. BLACK.

Low's Standard Novels—continued.

Lady Silverdale's Sweetheart. By W. BLACK.

Sunrise. By W. BLACK.

Three Feathers. By WILLIAM BLACK.

Alice Lorraine. By R. D. BLACKMORE.

Christowell, a Dartmoor Tale. By R. D. BLACKMORE.

Clara Vaughan. By R. D. BLACKMORE.

Cradock Nowell. By R. D. BLACKMORE.

Cripps the Carrier. By R. D. BLACKMORE.

Erema; or, My Father's Sin. By R. D. BLACKMORE.

Lorna Doone. By R. D. BLACKMORE.

Mary Anerley. By R. D. BLACKMORE.

An English Squire. By Miss COLERIDGE.

Mistress Judith. A Cambridgeshire Story. By C. C. FRASER-TYTLER.

A Story of the Dragonnades; or, Asylum Christi. By the Rev. E. GILLIAT, M.A.

A Laodicean. By THOMAS HARDY.

Far from the Madding Crowd. By THOMAS HARDY.

The Hand of Ethelberta. By THOMAS HARDY.

The Trumpet Major. By THOMAS HARDY.

Two on a Tower. By THOMAS HARDY.

Three Recruits. By JOSEPH HATTON.

A Golden Sorrow. By Mrs. CASHEL HOEY. New Edition.

Out of Court. By Mrs. CASHEL HOEY.

History of a Crime: The Story of the Coup d'État. VICTOR HUGO.

Ninety-Three. By VICTOR HUGO. Illustrated.

Adela Cathcart. By GEORGE MAC DONALD.

Guild Court. By GEORGE MAC DONALD.

Mary Marston. By GEORGE MAC DONALD.

Stephen Archer. New Edition of "Gifts." By GEORGE MAC DONALD.

The Vicar's Daughter. By GEORGE MAC DONALD.

Weighed and Wanting. By GEORGE MAC DONALD.

Diane. By Mrs. MACQUOID.

Elinor Dryden. By Mrs. MACQUOID.

My Lady Greensleeves. By HELEN MATHERS.

John Holdsworth. By W. CLARK RUSSELL.

A Sailor's Sweetheart. By W. CLARK RUSSELL.

Wreck of the Grosvenor. By W. CLARK RUSSELL.
The Lady Maud. By W. CLARK RUSSELL.
Little Loo. By W. CLARK RUSSELL.
My Wife and I. By Mrs. BEECHER STOWE.
Poganuc People, Their Loves and Lives. By Mrs. B. STOWE.
Ben Hur: a Tale of the Christ. By LEW. WALLACE.
Anne. By CONSTANCE FENIMORE WOOLSON.
For the Major. By CONSTANCE FENIMORE WOOLSON. 5s.

Low's Handbook to the Charities of London (Annual). Edited and revised to date by C. MACKESON, F.S.S., Editor of "A Guide to the Churches of London and its Suburbs," &c. Paper, 1s.; cloth, 1s. 6d.

McCORMICK (R., R.N.). Voyages of Discovery in the Arctic and Antarctic Seas in the "Erebus" and "Terror," in Search of Sir John Franklin, &c., with Autobiographical Notice by R. McCORMICK, R.N., who was Medical Officer to each Expedition. With Maps and very numerous Lithographic and other Illustrations. 2 vols., royal 8vo, 52s. 6d.

Macdonald (A.) "Our Sceptred Isle" and its World-wide Empire. Small post 8vo, cloth, 4s.

MacDonald (G.) Orts. Small post 8vo, 6s.

—— See also "Low's Standard Novels."

Macgregor (John) "Rob Roy" on the Baltic. 3rd Edition, small post 8vo, 2s. 6d.; cloth, gilt edges, 3s. 6d.

—— *A Thousand Miles in the "Rob Roy" Canoe.* 11th Edition, small post 8vo, 2s. 6d.; cloth, gilt edges, 3s. 6d.

—— *Description of the "Rob Roy" Canoe.* Plans, &c., 1s.

—— *Voyage Alone in the Yawl "Rob Roy."* New Edition, thoroughly revised, with additions, small post 8vo, 5s.; boards, 2s. 6d.

Macquoid (Mrs.). See LOW'S STANDARD NOVELS.

Magazine. See DECORATION, ETCHER, HARPER, UNION JACK.

*Magyarland. A Narrative of Travels through the Snowy Car-*pathians, and Great Alföld of the Magyar. By a Fellow of the Carpathian Society (Diploma of 1881), and Author of "The Indian Alps." 2 vols., 8vo, cloth extra, with about 120 Woodcuts from the Author's own sketches and drawings, 38s.

Manitoba. See RAE.

Maria Theresa. See BROGLIE.

Marked "In Haste." A Story of To-day. Crown 8vo, 8s. 6d.

Markham (Admiral) A Naval Career during the Old War.
Svo, cloth, 14s.

Markham (C. R.) The Threshold of the Unknown Region.
Crown 8vo, with Four Maps, 4th Edition.　Cloth extra, 10s. 6d.

——— *War between Peru and Chili,* 1879-1881.　Crown
8vo, with four Maps, &c.　Third Edition.　10s. 6d.　See also " Foreign
Countries."

Marshall (W. G.) Through America.　New Edition, crown
8vo, with about 100 Illustrations, 7s. 6d.

Martin (F. W.) Float Fishing and Spinning in the Nottingham
Style.　Crown 8vo, 2s. 6d.

Marvin (Charles) Russian Advance towards India.　8vo, 16s.

Maury (Commander) Physical Geography of the Sea, and its
Meteorology.　Being a Reconstruction and Enlargement of his former
Work, with Charts and Diagrams.　New Edition, crown 8vo, 6s.

Men of Mark : a Gallery of Contemporary Portraits of the most
Eminent Men of the Day taken from Life, especially for this publica-
tion　Complete in Seven Vols., handsomely bound, cloth, gilt edges,
25s. each.

Mendelssohn Family (The), 1729—1847.　From Letters and
Journals.　Translated from the German of SEBASTIAN HENSEL.
3rd Edition, 2 vols., 8vo, 30s.

Mendelssohn.　See also " Great Musicians."

Mitford (Mary Russell) Our Village.　Illustrated with Frontispiece Steel Engraving, and 12 full-page and 157 smaller Cuts.　Crown
4to, cloth, gilt edges, 21s.; cheaper binding, 10s. 6d.

Mollett (J. W.) Illustrated Dictionary of Words used in Art
and Archæology.　Explaining Terms frequently used in Works on
Architecture, Arms, Bronzes, Christian Art, Colour, Costume, Decoration, Devices, Emblems, Heraldry, Lace, Personal Ornaments,
Pottery, Painting, Sculpture, &c., with their Derivations.　Illustrated
with 600 Wood Engravings.　Small 4to, strongly bound in cloth, 15s.

Morley (H.) English Literature in the Reign of Victoria.　The
2000th volume of the Tauchnitz Collection of Authors.　18mo,
2s. 6d.

Muller (E.) Noble Words and Noble Deeds.　Containing many
Full-page Illustrations by PHILIPPOTEAUX.　Square imperial 16mo,
cloth extra, 7s. 6d.; plainer binding, plain edges, 5s.

Music.　See " Great Musicians."

NEWBIGGIN'S Sketches and Tales. 18mo, 4s.

New Child's Play (A). Sixteen Drawings by E. V. B. Beautifully printed in colours, 4to, cloth extra, 12s. 6d.

New Zealand. See BRADSHAW.

Newfoundland. See RAE.

Norbury (Henry F.) Naval Brigade in South Africa. Crown
8vo, cloth extra, 10s. 6d.

Nordenskiöld's Voyage around Asia and Europe. A Popular
Account of the North-East Passage of the "Vega." By Lieut. A.
HOVGAARD, of the Royal Danish Navy, and member of the "Vega"
Expedition. 8vo, with about 50 Illustrations and 3 Maps, 21s.

Nordhoff (C.) California, for Health, Pleasure, and Residence.
New Edition, 8vo, with Maps and Illustrations, 12s. 6d.

Northern Fairy Tales. Translated by H. L. BRAEKSTAD. 5s.

Nothing to Wear; and Two Millions. By W. A. BUTLER
New Edition. Small post 8vo, in stiff coloured wrapper, 1s.

Nursery Playmates (Prince of). 217 Coloured Pictures for
Children by eminent Artists. Folio, in coloured boards, 6s.

O'BRIEN (P. B.) Fifty Years of Concessions to Ireland.
8vo.

―――― *Irish Land Question, and English Question.* New
Edition, fcap. 8vo, 2s.

Our Little Ones in Heaven. Edited by the Rev. H. ROBBINS.
With Frontispiece after Sir JOSHUA REYNOLDS. Fcap., cloth extra,
New Edition—the 3rd, with Illustrations, 5s.

Outlines of Ornament in all Styles. A Work of Reference for
the Architect, Art Manufacturer, Decorative Artist, and Practical
Painter. By W. and G. A. AUDSLEY, Fellows of the Royal Institute
of British Architects. Only a limited number have been printed and
the stones destroyed. Small folio, 60 plates, with introductory text,
cloth gilt, 31s. 6d.

Owen (Douglas) Marine Insurance Notes and Clauses. 10s. 6d.

*P*ALGRAVE (*R. F. D.*).   See "Chairman's Handbook."

Palliser (*Mrs.*) *A History of Lace, from the Earliest Period.*
A New and Revised Edition, with additional cuts and text, upwards of
100 Illustrations and coloured Designs.   1 vol., 8vo, 1*l.* 1*s.*

—— *Historic Devices, Badges, and War Cries.*   8vo, 1*l.* 1*s.*

—— *The China Collector's Pocket Companion.*   With upwards of 1000 Illustrations of Marks and Monograms.   2nd Edition,
with Additions.   Small post 8vo, limp cloth, 5*s.*

Perseus, the Gorgon Slayer.   Numerous coloured Plates, square
8vo, 5*s.*

Pharmacopœia of the United States of America.   8vo, 21*s.*

Photography (*History and Handbook of*).   See TISSANDIER.

Pinto (*Major Serpa*) *How I Crossed Africa: from the Atlantic*
to the Indian Ocean, Through Unknown Countries; Discovery of the
Great Zambesi Affluents, &c.—Vol. I., The King's Rifle.   Vol. II.,
The Coillard Family.   With 24 full-page and 118 half-page and
smaller Illustrations, 13 small Maps, and 1 large one.   2 vols., demy
8vo, cloth extra, 42*s.*

Pocock.   See ARNOLD (G. M.).

Poe (*E. A.*) *The Raven.*   Illustrated by GUSTAVE DORÉ.
Imperial folio, cloth, 63*s.*

Poems of the Inner Life.   Chiefly from Modern Authors.
Small 8vo, 5*s.*

Polar Expeditions.   See KOLDEWEY, MARKHAM, MACGAHAN,
NARES, NORDENSKIÖLD, GILDER, MCCORMICK.

Politics and Life in Mars.   12mo, 2*s.* 6*d.*

Powell (*W.*) *Wanderings in a Wild Country; or, Three Years*
among the Cannibals of New Britain.   Demy 8vo, Map and numerous
Illustrations, 18*s.*

Prisons, Her Majesty's, their Effects and Defects.   New and
cheaper Edition, 6*s.*

Poynter (*Edward J., R.A.*).   See "Illustrated Text-books."

Publishers' Circular (*The*), *and General Record of British and*
Foreign Literature.   Published on the 1st and 15th of every Month, 3*d.*

RAE (W. Fraser) From Newfoundland to Manitoba ; a Guide through Canada's Maritime, Mining, and Prairie Provinces. With Maps. Crown 8vo, 6s.

Rambaud (A.) History of Russia. 2 vols., 8vo, 36s.

Reber (F.) History of Ancient Art. 8vo, 18s.

Redford (G.) Ancient Sculpture. Crown 8vo, 5s.

Reid (T. W.) Land of the Bey. Post 8vo, 10s. 6d.

Rémusat (Madame de), Memoirs of, 1802—1808. By her Grandson, M. PAUL DE RÉMUSAT, Senator. Translated by Mrs. CASHEL HOEY and Mr. JOHN LILLIE. 4th Edition, cloth extra. 2 vols., 8vo, 32s.

—— *Selection from the Letters of Madame de Rémusat to her* Husband and Son, from 1804 to 1813. From the French, by Mrs. CASHEL HOEY and Mr. JOHN LILLIE. In 1 vol., demy 8vo (uniform with the "Memoirs of Madame de Rémusat," 2 vols.), cloth extra, 16s.

Richter (Dr. Jean Paul) Italian Art in the National Gallery. 4to. Illustrated. Cloth gilt, 2l. 2s.; half-morocco, uncut, 2l. 12s. 6d.

—— See also LEONARDO DA VINCI.

Robin Hood; Merry Adventures of. Written and illustrated by HOWARD PYLE. Imperial 8vo, cloth. [*In the press.*

Robinson (Phil) In my Indian Garden. With a Preface by EDWIN ARNOLD, M.A., C.S.I., &c. Crown 8vo, limp cloth, 4th Edition, 3s. 6d.

—— *Noah's Ark. A Contribution to the Study of Unnatural* History. Small post 8vo, 12s. 6d.

—— *Sinners and Saints : a Tour across the United States of* America, and Round them. Crown 8vo, 10s. 6d.

—— *Under the Punkah.* Crown 8vo, limp cloth, 5s.

Robinson (Sergeant) Wealth and its Sources. Stray Thoughts. 5s.

Roland; the Story of. Crown 8vo, illustrated, 6s.

Romantic Stories of the Legal Profession. Crown 8vo, cloth, 7s. 6d.

Rose (J.) Complete Practical Machinist. New Edition, 12mo, 12s. 6d.

Rose Library (*The*).   Popular Literature of all Countries.   Each
volume, 1*s.*; cloth, 2*s. 6d.*   Many of the Volumes are Illustrated —

Little Women. By LOUISA M. ALCOTT.   Dble. vol., 2*s.*

Little Women Wedded. Forming a Sequel to "Little Women."

Little Women and Little Women Wedded. 1 vol., cloth gilt, 3*s. 6d.*

Little Men. By L. M. ALCOTT.   2*s.*; cloth gilt, 3*s. 6d.*

An Old-Fashioned Girl. By LOUISA M. ALCOTT.   2*s.*; cloth,
3*s. 6d.*

Work. A Story of Experience. By L. M. ALCOTT. 2 vols., 1*s.* each.

Stowe (Mrs. H. B.) The Pearl of Orr's Island.

———— **The Minister's Wooing.**

——— **We and our Neighbours.**   2*s.*; cloth, 3*s. 6d.*

——— **My Wife and I.**   2*s.*; cloth gilt, 3*s. 6d.*

Hans Brinker; or, the Silver Skates. By Mrs. DODGE.

My Study Windows. By J. R. LOWELL.

The Guardian Angel. By OLIVER WENDELL HOLMES.

My Summer in a Garden. By C. D. WARNER.

Dred. Mrs. BEECHER STOWE.   2*s.*; cloth gilt, 3*s. 6d.*

Farm Ballads. By WILL CARLETON.

Farm Festivals. By WILL CARLETON.

Farm Legends. By WILL CARLETON.

The Clients of Dr. Bernagius. 2 parts, 1*s.* each.

The Undiscovered Country. By W. D. HOWELLS.

Baby Rue. By C. M. CLAY.

The Rose in Bloom. By L. M. ALCOTT.   2*s.*; cloth gilt, 3*s. 6d.*

Eight Cousins. By L. M. ALCOTT.   2*s.*; cloth gilt, 3*s. 6d.*

Under the Lilacs. By L. M. ALCOTT.   2*s.*; also 3*s. 6d.*

Silver Pitchers. By LOUISA M. ALCOTT.

Jimmy's Cruise in the "Pinafore," and other Tales.   By
LOUISA M. ALCOTT.   2*s.*; cloth gilt, 3*s. 6d.*

Jack and Jill. By LOUISA M. ALCOTT.   2*s.*

Hitherto. By the Author of the "Gayworthys."   2 vols., 1*s.* each;
1 vol., cloth gilt, 3*s. 6d.*

Friends : a Duet. By E. STUART PHELPS.

A Gentleman of Leisure. A Novel. By EDGAR FAWCETT.

The Story of Helen Troy.

Round the Yule Log : Norwegian Folk and Fairy Tales.
Translated from the Norwegian of P. CHR. ASBJÖRNSEN.   With 100
Illustrations after drawings by Norwegian Artists, and an Introduction
by E. W. Gosse.   Imperial 16mo, cloth extra, gilt edges, 7*s. 6d.*

Rousselet (Louis) Son of the Constable of France. Small post 8vo, numerous Illustrations, 5*s.*

—— *The Drummer Boy: a Story of the Days of Washington.* Small post 8vo, numerous Illustrations, 5*s.*

Russell (W. Clark) The Lady Maud. 3 vols., crown 8vo, 31*s.* 6*d.* New Edition, small post 8vo, 6*s.*

—— *Little Loo.* 6*s.*

—— *My Watch Below; or, Yarns Spun when off Duty.* 2nd Edition, crown 8vo, 2*s.* 6*d.*

—— *Sailor's Language.* Illustrated. Crown 8vo, 3*s.* 6*d.*

—— *Sea Queen.* 3 vols., crown 8vo, 31*s.* 6*d.*

—— *Wreck of the Grosvenor.* 4to, sewed, 6*d.*

—— See also LOW'S STANDARD NOVELS.

Russell (W. H., LL.D.) Hesperothen: Notes from the Western World. A Record of a Ramble through part of the United States, Canada, and the Far West, in the Spring and Summer of 1881. By W. H. RUSSELL, LL.D. 2 vols., crown 8vo, cloth, 24*s.*

—— *The Tour of the Prince of Wales in India.* By W. H. RUSSELL, LL.D. Fully Illustrated by SYDNEY P. HALL, M.A. Super-royal 8vo, cloth extra, gilt edges, 52*s.* 6*d.*; Large Paper Edition, 84*s.*

SAINTS and their Symbols: A Companion in the Churches and Picture Galleries of Europe. With Illustrations. Royal 16mo, cloth extra, 3*s.* 6*d.*

Scherr (Prof. J.) History of English Literature. Translated from the German. Crown 8vo, 8*s.* 6*d.*

Schuyler (Eugène). The Life of Peter the Great. By EUGÈNE SCHUYLER, Author of "Turkestan." 2 vols., 8vo.

Schweinfurth (Georg) Heart of Africa. Three Years' Travels and Adventures in the Unexplored Regions of Central Africa, from 1868 to 1871. With Illustrations and large Map. 2 vols., crown 8vo, 15*s.*

Scott (Leader) Renaissance of Art in Italy. 4to, 31*s.* 6*d.*

Sedgwick (Major IV.) Light the Dominant Force of the Universe. 7s. 6d.

Senior (Nassau IV.) Conversations and Journals in Egypt and Malta. 2 vols., 8vo, 24s.

Shadbolt (S. H.) South African Campaign, 1879. Compiled by J. P. MACKINNON (formerly 72nd Highlanders) and S. H. SHADBOLT; and dedicated, by permission, to Field-Marshal H.R.H. the Duke of Cambridge. Containing a portrait and biography of every officer killed in the campaign. 4to, handsomely bound in cloth extra, 2l. 10s.

────── *The Afghan Campaigns of* 1878—1880. By SYDNEY SHADBOLT, Joint Author of "The South African Campaign of 1879." 2 vols., royal quarto, cloth extra, 3l.

Shakespeare. Edited by R. GRANT WHITE. 3 vols., crown 8vo, gilt top, 36s.; *édition de luxe*, 6 vols., 8vo, cloth extra, 63s.

────── See also " Flowers of Shakespeare."

Sidney (Sir P.) Arcadia. New Edition, 6s.

Siegfried : The Story of. Crown 8vo, illustrated, cloth, 6s.

Sikes (Wirt). Rambles and Studies in Old South Wales. With numerous Illustrations. Demy 8vo, 18s.

────── *British Goblins, Welsh Folk Lore.* New Edition, 8vo, 18s.

────── *Studies of Assassination.* 16mo, 3s. 6d.

Sir Roger de Coverley. Re-imprinted from the " Spectator." With 125 Woodcuts, and steel Frontispiece specially designed and engraved for the Work. Small fcap. 4to, 6s.

Smith (G.) Assyrian Explorations and Discoveries. By the late GEORGE SMITH. Illustrated by Photographs and Woodcuts. Demy 8vo, 6th Edition, 18s.

────── *The Chaldean Account of Genesis.* By the late G. SMITH, of the Department of Oriental Antiquities, British Museum. With many Illustrations. Demy 8vo, cloth extra, 6th Edition, 16s. An entirely New Edition, completely revised and re-written by the Rev. PROFESSOR SAYCE, Queen's College, Oxford. Demy 8vo, 18s.

Smith (J. Moyr) Ancient Greek Female Costume. 112 full-page Plates and other Illustrations. Crown 8vo, 7s. 6d.

────── *Hades of Ardenne : a Visit to the Caves of Han.* Crown 8vo, Illustrated, 5s.

Smith (*T. Roger*) *Architecture, Gothic and Renaissance.* Illustrated, crown 8vo, 5*s.*

——————————————— *Classic and Early Christian.*
Illustrated. Crown 8vo, 5*s.*

South Kensington Museum. Vol. II., 21*s.*

Spanish and French Artists. By GERARD SMITH. (Poynter's
Art Text-books.) 5*s.* [*In the press.*

Spry (*W. J. J., R.N.*) *The Cruise of H.M.S. "Challenger."*
With Route Map and many Illustrations. 6th Edition, demy 8vo, cloth,
18*s.* Cheap Edition, crown 8vo, with some of the Illustrations, 7*s. 6d.*

Stack (*E.*) *Six Months in Persia.* 2 vols., crown 8vo, 24*s.*

Stanley (*H. M.*) *How I Found Livingstone.* Crown 8vo, cloth
extra, 7*s. 6d.* ; large Paper Edition, 10*s. 6d.*

—————— *"My Kalulu," Prince, King, and Slave.* A Story
from Central Africa. Crown 8vo, about 430 pp., with numerous graphic
Illustrations after Original Designs by the Author. Cloth, 7*s. 6d.*

———— *Coomassie and Magdala.* A Story of Two British
Campaigns in Africa. Demy 8vo, with Maps and Illustrations, 16*s.*

—— — *Through the Dark Continent.* Cheaper Edition,
crown 8vo, 12*s. 6d.*

Stenhouse (*Mrs.*) *An Englishwoman in Utah.* Crown 8vo, 2*s. 6d.*

Stoker (*Bram*) *Under the Sunset.* Crown 8vo, 6*s.*

Story without an End. From the German of Carové, by the late
Mrs. SARAH T. AUSTIN. Crown 4to, with 15 Exquisite Drawings
by E. V. B., printed in Colours in Fac-simile of the original Water
Colours ; and numerous other Illustrations. New Edition, 7*s. 6d.*

———— square 4to, with Illustrations by HARVEY. 2*s. 6d.*

Stowe (*Mrs. Beecher*) *Dred.* Cheap Edition, boards, 2*s.* Cloth,
gilt edges, 3*s. 6d.*

—— — *Footsteps of the Master.* With Illustrations and red
borders. Small post 8vo, cloth extra, 6*s.*

—— — *Geography.* With 60 Illustrations. Square cloth,
4*s. 6d.*

—— — *Little Foxes.* Cheap Edition, 1*s.;* Library Edition
4*s. 6d.*

—— — *Betty's Bright Idea.* 1*s.*

Stowe (Mrs. Beecher) My Wife and I; or, Harry Henderson's History. Small post 8vo, cloth extra, 6s.*

—— *Minister's Wooing.* 5s.; Copyright Series, 1s. 6d.; cl., 2s.*

—— *Old Town Folk.* 6s.; Cheap Edition, 2s. 6d.

—— *Old Town Fireside Stories.* Cloth extra, 3s. 6d.

—— *Our Folks at Poganuc.* 6s.

—— *We and our Neighbours.* 1 vol., small post 8vo, 6s. Sequel to "My Wife and I."*

—— *Pink and White Tyranny.* Small post 8vo, 3s. 6d. Cheap Edition, 1s. 6d. and 2s.

—— *Poganuc People: their Loves and Lives.* Crown 8vo, cloth, 6s.

—— *Queer Little People.* 1s.; cloth, 2s.

—— *Chimney Corner.* 1s.; cloth, 1s. 6d.

—— *The Pearl of Orr's Island.* Crown 8vo, 5s.*

—— *Woman in Sacred History.* Illustrated with 15 Chromo-lithographs and about 200 pages of Letterpress. Demy 4to, cloth extra, gilt edges, 25s.

Sullivan (A. M., late M.P.) Nutshell History of Ireland. From the Earliest Ages to the Present Time. Paper boards, 6d.

TACCHI (A.) Madagascar and the Malagasy Embassy. Demy 8vo, cloth.

Taine (H. A.) "Les Origines de la France Contemporaine" Translated by JOHN DURAND.
Vol. 1. **The Ancient Regime.** Demy 8vo, cloth, 16s.
Vol. 2. **The French Revolution.** Vol. 1. do.
Vol. 3. **Do.** do. Vol. 2. do.

Talbot (Hon. E.) A Letter on Emigration. 1s.

Tauchnitz's English Editions of German Authors. Each volume, cloth flexible, 2s.; or sewed, 1s. 6d. (Catalogues post free on application.)

Tauchnitz (B.) German and English Dictionary. Paper, 1s. 6d.; cloth, 2s.; roan, 2s. 6d.

* *See also* Rose Library.

Tauchnitz (B.) French and English Dictionary. Paper, 1s. 6d.; cloth, 2s.; roan, 2s. 6d.

—— *Italian and English Dictionary.* Paper, 1s. 6d.; cloth, 2s.; roan, 2s. 6d.

—— *Spanish and English.* Paper, 1s. 6d.; cloth, 2s.; roan, 2s. 6d.

Taylor (W. M.) Paul the Missionary. Crown 8vo, 7s. 6d.

Thausing (Prof.) Preparation of Malt and the Fabrication of Beer. 8vo, 45s.

Theakston (Michael) British Angling Flies. Illustrated. Cr. 8vo, 5s.

Thoreau. By SANBORN. (American Men of Letters.) Crown 8vo, 2s. 6d.

Thousand Years Hence (A). By NUNSOWE GREENE. Crown 8vo, 6s.

Tolhausen (Alexandre) Grand Supplément du Dictionnaire Technologique. 3s. 6d.

Tolmer (Alexander) Reminiscences of an Adventurous and Chequered Career. 2 vols., 21s.

Trials. See BROWNE.

Tristram (Rev. Canon) Pathways of Palestine : A Descriptive Tour through the Holy Land. First Series. Illustrated by 44 Permanent Photographs. 2 vols., folio, cloth extra, gilt edges, 31s. 6d. each.

Tuckerman (Bayard) History of English Prose and Fiction. 8s. 6d.

Tunis. See REID.

Turner (Edward) Studies in Russian Literature. Crown 8vo, 8s. 6d.

UNION Jack (The). Every Boy's Paper. Edited by G. A. HENTY. Profusely Illustrated with Coloured and other Plates. Vol. I., 6s. Vols. II., III., IV., 7s. 6d. each.

Up Stream : A Journey from the Present to the Past. Pictures and Words by R. ANDRÉ. Coloured Plates, 4to, 5s.

BOOKS BY JULES VERNE.

CELEBRATED TRAVELS and TRAVELLERS. 3 Vols., Demy 8vo, 600 pp., upwards of 100 full-page Illustrations, 12*s.* 6*d.*; gilt edges, 14*s.* each :—

I. The Exploration of the World.
II. The Great Navigators of the Eighteenth Century.
III. The Great Explorers of the Nineteenth Century.

☞ The letters appended to each book refer to the various Editions and Prices given at the foot of the page.

a e TWENTY THOUSAND LEAGUES UNDER THE SEA.
a e HECTOR SERVADAC.
a e THE FUR COUNTRY.
a f FROM THE EARTH TO THE MOON, AND A TRIP ROUND IT.
a e MICHAEL STROGOFF, THE COURIER OF THE CZAR.
a e DICK SANDS, THE BOY CAPTAIN.
b c d FIVE WEEKS IN A BALLOON.
b c d ADVENTURES OF THREE ENGLISHMEN AND THREE RUSSIANS.
b c d AROUND THE WORLD IN EIGHTY DAYS.
b c { *d* A FLOATING CITY.
       { *d* THE BLOCKADE RUNNERS.
b c { *d* { DR. OX'S EXPERIMENT.
            { MASTER ZACHARIUS.
        { *d* { A DRAMA IN THE AIR.
            { A WINTER AMID THE ICE.
b c { *d* THE SURVIVORS OF THE " CHANCELLOR."
       { *d* MARTIN PAZ.
b c d THE CHILD OF THE CAVERN.
        THE MYSTERIOUS ISLAND, 3 Vols.:—
b c d I. DROPPED FROM THE CLOUDS.
b c d II. ABANDONED.
b c d III. SECRET OF THE ISLAND.
b c { *d* THE BEGUM'S FORTUNE.
       {   THE MUTINEERS OF THE "BOUNTY."
b c d THE TRIBULATIONS OF A CHINAMAN.
        THE STEAM HOUSE, 2 Vols.:—
b c I. DEMON OF CAWNPORE.
b c II. TIGERS AND TRAITORS.
        THE GIANT RAFT, 2 Vols.:—
b I. EIGHT HUNDRED LEAGUES ON THE AMAZON.
b II. THE CRYPTOGRAM.
b GODFREY MORGAN.
    THE GREEN RAY. Cloth, gilt edges, 6*s.*; plain edges, 5*s.*

a Small 8vo, very numerous Illustrations, handsomely bound in cloth, with gilt edges, 10*s.* 6*d.* ; ditto, plainer binding, 5*s.*
b Large imperial 16mo, very numerous Illustrations, handsomely bound in cloth, with gilt edges, 7*s.* 6*d.*
c Ditto, plainer binding, 3*s.* 6*d.*
d Cheaper Edition, 1 Vol., paper boards, with some of the Illustrations, 1*s.* ; bound in cloth, gilt edges, 2*s.*
e Cheaper Edition as (*d*), in 2 Vols., 1*s.* each ; bound in cloth, gilt edges, 1 Vol., 3*s.* 6*d.*
f Same as (*e*), except in cloth, 2 Vols., gilt edges, 2*s.* each.

VELAZQUEZ and Murillo. By C. B. CURTIS. With Original Etchings. Royal 8vo, 31s. 6d.; large paper, 63s.

Victoria (Queen) Life of. By GRACE GREENWOOD. With numerous Illustrations. Small post 8vo, 6s.

Vincent (F.) Norsk, Lapp, and Finn. By FRANK VINCENT, Jun., Author of "The Land of the White Elephant," "Through and Through the Tropics," &c. 8vo, cloth, with Frontispiece and Map, 12s.

Viollet-le-Duc (E.) Lectures on Architecture. Translated by BENJAMIN BUCKNALL, Architect. With 33 Steel Plates and 200 Wood Engravings. Super-royal 8vo, leather back, gilt top, with complete Index, 2 vols., 3l. 3s.

Vivian (A. P.) Wanderings in the Western Land. 3rd Edition, 10s. 6d.

Voyages. See McCORMICK.

WALLACE (L.) Ben Hur: A Tale of the Christ. Crown 8vo, 6s.

Waller (Rev. C. H.) The Names on the Gates of Pearl, and other Studies. By the Rev. C. H. WALLER, M.A. New Edition. Crown 8vo, cloth extra, 3s. 6d.

—— *A Grammar and Analytical Vocabulary of the Words in* the Greek Testament. Compiled from Brüder's Concordance. For the use of Divinity Students and Greek Testament Classes. By the Rev. C. H. WALLER, M.A. Part I. The Grammar. Small post 8vo, cloth, 2s. 6d. Part II. The Vocabulary, 2s. 6d.

—— *Adoption and the Covenant.* Some Thoughts on Confirmation. Super-royal 16mo, cloth limp, 2s. 6d.

—·—— *Silver Sockets; and other Shadows of Redemption.* Eighteen Sermons preached in Christ Church, Hampstead. Small post 8vo, cloth, 6s.

Warner (C. D.) Back-log Studies. Boards, 1s. 6d.; cloth, 2s.

Washington Irving's Little Britain. Square crown 8vo, 6s.

Webster. (American Men of Letters.) 18mo, 2s. 6d.

Weismann (A.) Studies in the Theory of Descent. One of the most complete of recent contributions to the Theory of Evolution. With a Preface by the late CHARLES DARWIN, F.R.S., and numerous Coloured Plates. 2 vols., 8vo, 40s.

Wheatley (H. B.) and Delamotte (P. H.) Art Work in Porce- lain. Large 8vo, 2s. 6d.

—— *Art Work in Gold and Silver.* Modern. Large 8vo, 2s. 6d.

White (Rhoda E.) From Infancy to Womanhood. A Book of Instruction for Young Mothers. Crown 8vo, cloth, 10s. 6d.

White (*R. G.*) *England Without and Within.* New Edition, crown 8vo, 10s. 6d.

Whittier (*J. G.*) *The King's Missive, and later Poems.* 18mo, choice parchment cover, 3s. 6d.

—— *The Whittier Birthday Book.* Extracts from the Author's writings, with Portrait and numerous Illustrations. Uniform with the "Emerson Birthday Book." Square 16mo, very choice binding, 3s. 6d.

—— *Life of.* By R. A. UNDERWOOD. Cr. 8vo, cloth, 10s. 6d.

Wild Flowers of Switzerland. With Coloured Plates, life-size, from living Plants, and Botanical Descriptions of each Example. Imperial 4to, 52s. 6d.

Williams (*C. F.*) *The Tariff Laws of the United States.* 8vo, cloth, 10s. 6d.

Williams (*H. W.*) *Diseases of the Eye.* 8vo, 21s.

Williams (*M.*) *Some London Theatres: Past and Present.* Crown 8vo, 7s. 6d.

Wills, A Few Hints on Proving, without Professional Assistance. By a PROBATE COURT OFFICIAL. 5th Edition, revised, with Forms of Wills, Residuary Accounts, &c. Fcap. 8vo, cloth limp, 1s.

Winckelmann (*John*) *History of Ancient Art.* Translated by JOHN LODGE, M.D. With very numerous Plates and Illustrations. 2 vols., 8vo, 36s.

Winks (*W. E.*) *Lives of Illustrious Shoemakers.* With eight Portraits. Crown 8vo, 7s. 6d.

Woodbury (*Geo. E.*) *History of Wood Engraving.* Illustrated, 8vo, 18s.

Woolsey (*C. D., LL.D.*) *Introduction to the Study of International Law*; designed as an Aid in Teaching and in Historical Studies. 5th Edition, demy 8vo, 18s.

Woolson (*Constance F.*) See "Low's Standard Novels."

Wright (*the late Rev. Henry*) *The Friendship of God.* With Biographical Preface by the Rev. E. H. BICKERSTETH, Portrait, &c. Crown 8vo, 6s.

Y RIARTE (*Charles*) *Florence: its History.* Translated by C. B. PITMAN. Illustrated with 500 Engravings. Large imperial 4to, extra binding, gilt edges, 63s.
 History; the Medici; the Humanists; letters; arts; the Renaissance; illustrious Florentines; Etruscan art; monuments; sculpture; painting.

London:
SAMPSON LOW, MARSTON, SEARLE, & RIVINGTON,
CROWN BUILDINGS, 188, FLEET STREET, E.C.

www.ingramcontent.com/pod-product-compliance
Lightning Source LLC
Chambersburg PA
CBHW021040030726
47496CB00006B/1625